THE FRACTURED EYE

PART 2 OF THE BLOOD MOON CHRONICLE

MICHAEL BRITTON

SWEETSPIRE LITERATURE
MANAGEMENT

CONTENTS

Chapter 1

THE STRENGTH TO SURVIVE

The moon's grace shone down upon the dark calm water, providing the companions with enough light to see the boat slowly draw near as they stood knee deep in the cold sea. The only thing going their way tonight.

The moons grace dimed behind light cloud cover as two pairs of tired, wet hands took hold of the timber sides. Thankfully, as all the two pirates in the boat could see was people being lifted up and in, one after another. Between the alcohol on their breaths and the boat bobbing with the waves, wounded and healthy all floundered in just the same to their eyes.

One friend had already been lost tonight, one friend to many. They refused to lose another. Regardless of how trying, how vexing he may be. So, Flynn's unconscious form slouched forward on the timber bench. Helpless form supported by the twins seated either side.

Ropes creaked, straining against the burden they bore as the boat was slowly raised onto the deck of the Rose. Dread growing with each inch, fearing what would happen when the crew realised Flynn was incapacitated.

By some miracle or feat of determination Flynn dragged himself over the side onto the deck. Crawling on all fours, Vashti helped him to his feet before the crew noticed. Ailish joined her and leaning on them both for support they made a beeline for the cabin.

"I guess the celebrations began early" Griff said stopping in front of them. 'I don't believe it. Standing here shivering, frozen to the bone because they tried to hide Flynn's condition and they just think he's drunk.'

Wordlessly Flynn dropped both bags of gems into Griff's hand. One bag tumbling free of his grasp scattering a sparkling blend of colours across the deck as gems spilled free.

When Griff stood after scooping up the gems Flynn and the girls had locked themselves in the cabin. "The nearest port and we will leave from there" Vaike told Griff. "Disembark" corrected Griff, before answering after a moment's ponder.

"Iodem. A small village near Koyake." "Perfect" Vaike answered. "Oh, and take your time. I don't think Twin Blade wants to be disturbed because we've hit a storm or broken a mast."

"No, I would imagine not. Especially considering the quality of those two girls. Great firm tits on one and an arse that wars would be waged over on the other." Baird had to admit Vaike showed great control not striking down Griff right there, rather responding with laughter and agreeing boisterously.

❧

Vashti had barely locked the door when he collapsed on the wooden floor of the cabin. To make it worse he was shivering and cold to the touch. "Vashti quick. What do we do?" Ailish asked truly concerned for Flynn. While the two regularly butted heads she still counted him as a friend. Well usually.

"We need to quickly heat up his core" she answered grabbing hold of his trousers and pulling them off boots and all. "Wh. What are you doing" stammered Ailish. "Don't talk just help. Grab his coat and shirt." Lying there completely naked she found herself starring at Flynn. Not with desire or sexual thoughts just curiosity, having never seen someone's manhood before.

The filthy woollen blanket from the bed was thrown over his prostrated form. Looking up, Vashti stood also completely naked. Long toned legs reaching to a white pubic bush and firm arse developed by years of running. Bust smaller than her own making archery easier for the elven princess and flawless skin, unmarred by scar or blemish.

She had seen Vashti naked before but each time it portrayed the differences between their species. At nineteen she was also fully developed, but unlike Vashti her body showed scars and won't hold its youthfulness.

"Smell that?" Vashti asked. Both girls now naked, lying under the same dirty blanket as their bodies pressed hard up against Flynn's. "It's the poison. He's sweating it out." "So, he's not going to die?" "Still too soon to say. A small dosage can be treated in humans but we have none of the herbs available. But he is no longer shivering so that is a good sign."

They stayed like that all night until someone knocked on the door with breakfast. Wrapping the blanket around herself, she opened the door enough to fit the heavily laden tray through. The sailor stood frozen as the tray was yanked free from his grip. Gaze remaining fixated on her chest until the wooden door slammed shut in his face.

Having eaten, she now laid with Flynn again while Vashti ate. Vashti felt confident his body was warm enough to only require one person at most and Vashti was happy to do it after eating. Ailish can't say she wasn't glad to hear that. Never had she lain with a naked man before now, meaning in a way Flynn was her first. Something he could never know.

Vashti laid with him through lunch and until the evening when Flynn was warm enough by himself. Rousing enough to drink some water was the extent of his improvements.

It was a further two days until they reached the nearest port. Unsure of where or which port that was, they took faith in Vaike and continued to watch Flynn. He'd regained consciousness briefly on the second day, eating and talking briefly before sleeping again. Confident that he was through the worst and now requiring rest, Vashti relaxed resting likewise.

⚓

"Should we go get them?" Baird asked of the others. It had been a difficult time for the three of them. Waiting around, unsure if they'd lost a second companion or not was taking its toll. Having arrived in Iodem, they would now learn the fate of the pirate Flynn.

"No, it's best we wait until we're ready to depart." Vaike answered. "We don't know what state Flynn is in and I would rather avoid any trouble" whispering the second part so only Garett and Baird could hear.

Their packs retrieved, bundled beside seven horses standing on the wharf and three waited on the cabin door to open.

Baird clenched his jaw as the door swung inwards, breath held in anticipation. Out strode Flynn, looking sickly grey, 'but at least he is walking' Baird thought. Vashti and Ailish both walked beside him, hands gripping his arms. Any comments made about Flynn's appearance were in the area of him being exhausted because of his bedwarmers.

All eyes were on the girls once they joined Flynn. Vashti now wore Ailish's furs. While her own coat was draped across Ailish's shoulders. The real distraction was the corset with the top few knots loose. Without the furs it was fully exposed along with her cleavage. Feeling his own manhood rise, Baird had to look away.

Walking down the gangway first, he marched straight to Sterben climbing up onto the saddle. The other five joined him and Vaike led them out of the town. Sterben followed the other horses while Flynn slept in the saddle, Vashti riding beside keeping him upright.

An hour out of town they climbed a hill not far off the road. The hill offered views off the road and surrounding area while hiding them from anyone on the road.

They spent three days resting here while Flynn recovered. Flynn wasn't the only one recovering either. Seeing the light brown horse grazing nearby now riderless, brought emotional pain felt by the others.

The second day Vaike and Garrett headed back into town for supplies. Having given Griff and his men a day to become incoherently drunk.

They woke the third day to find Foden's horse had disappeared during the night. No one had the heart to look for it and decided it was for the best, unsure what else they were to do with him.

With Flynn strong enough to travel they left as the fourth day ashore dawned. It would take them a week to reach Koyake, their next destination. They were in need of supplies since Iodem didn't have much available other than fish.

Vaike started Baird on a new training regime that night. Everyone having repeated the tale of their encounters on the island with the exception of Flynn who slept. Vaike decided Baird should learn to fight shoulder to shoulder, as a pair.

Vaike stood on his left, pairing of against Ailish and Garrett. Fighting in pairs was filled with advantages but came with a new set of challenges. While Vaike's strength made up for his flaws, those same flaws brought Vaike down. Then if your timing was off you ended up hindering your partner more than help. Garett and Ailish weren't perfect at fighting in unison but their coordination was better, allowing them to claim overall victory for that session.

❧

Vashti watched on as her brother fought three people at once. Baird once again reeling from Ailish, bashing him with her shield, only for him to crash into his own partner. Sighing she looked down at Flynn's arm removing the bandage. The wound was small but not healing resulting in her applying the same tincture that he'd caused Baird to require so much of.

"Why the sigh?" he asked looking at the fight with a bored expression. "Just thinking. This training is good for Baird but he could never fight side by side with my brother. It would have to be you fighting by his side. Well only if you two could actually get along."

"Yeah. Can't see that happening anytime soon. Mutual respect is one thing, friendship quite another" agreed Flynn. "So, is it healing?" "Slowly. I don't think it will scar either." "Hmm, little difference that will make" he responded dryly.

"Seventy four." "What?" "You have seventy four scars on your body, oddly enough only two on your back. Not to mention the brand on your backside" Vashti answered, annoyed by Flynn's indifference. "Don't you think you're being way to reckless, several of the wounds could've killed you, especially the one you cover on your back"

"I cover it because scars on the back are a swordsman's shame. But" Flynn continued breathing out. "That scar is responsible for the way I am." Vashti looked Flynn in the eye as he told her how he got the wound, being more honest than she'd ever thought possible.

While the others trained, she whittled away the evening listening to Flynn tell the real story of his life. He was a bastard child who never knew his father. His mother was a whore working in a brothel in Voldengird.

He spent his childhood sitting in a room out the back with the other bastard kids. A former whore who was friends with the madam watched over them during this time, even teaching them letters and numbers. They weren't very proficient but he could at least read.

He was eight and left on the streets when his mother grew sick and died. Falling in with the other street urchins they became his new family. A family where everyone looked out for each other. Six months of living on the street and he was inseparable from another boy, Klein. The two were best friends doing everything together.

Four years were spent living on the streets as the forgotten kids. By this time, he was one of the older kids and responsible for the youngsters. Most kids didn't survive to be much older with those few who did joining the army or becoming whores themselves. Following in the footsteps of their misplaced parents.

One day the body of Jenna, an eight year old girl was found washed up in the warrens. She was caught stealing an apple from a merchant. Her younger sister escaped but she was caught. The town guards didn't care. Taking the word of the rich and influential over the poor.

She was beaten, sliced up and raped. We were kids but we unfortunately knew what rape was. I didn't even know how or when she died. If it was the wounds or if she drowned when tied up and tossed in the harbour. Eight years old and violently cut short by some sick pervert.

After seeing the body, I saw red. I grabbed the blade we had squirreled away, the same rusted one I still have in fact. Klein and myself tracked down the merchant with the intention of scaring him, try and get him to confess. He had no remorse, no value on our lives. He said the same would happen to any of us caught stealing and the girls will feel all his guards next time not just himself.

I snapped, plunging the blade into his gut. I don't know how many times I stabbed him or how long it took. Next thing I remember is Klein dragging me off his body. My clothes were stained red, my arms slick with his blood. Now the guards cared. Chasing us all over town. We didn't know what to do so we ran. Through shortcuts and boltholes known only to us we fled, nowhere in particular.

Our aimless running led to the landing outside a dingy tavern near the port. We crashed into a group of pirates as they were leaving. As bad as pirates are, they were always willing to pay the street kids well for small errands.

Probably because many were urchins themselves. But here we stood. Two twelve year old kids scared out of our minds. I was covered in blood, dirt and grime and still held the knife.

This turned out to be Bloodfist's crew, who asked us if we wanted an escape. Freedom to do whatever we wanted, to never again wonder when our next meal was coming. Somewhere we could sleep safe. We both jumped at the offer, only ever looking back once to think about the others.

Bloodfist was quickly impressed with me and I soon found myself being privately tutored by the legendary captain. Not just in seamanship and fighting but he would get me to read books from world history to foreign culture and language. I was slow at first not having looked at letters in four years but it quickly returned.

Three years of raiding, plundering and drinking went by fast when the position of quarter master became available. His current quartermaster set out on his own so the position was vacant. Bloodfist put my name forward as his replacement which didn't sit to well with the crew. Klein who had developed quite the talent with words and was well liked by the hands, was also nominated with the required votes.

Resolving it like pirates, we fought. I was trained personally by Bloodfist while Klein developed his skills amongst the other sailors. I still only used one sword at this stage but it was still no contest. Klein couldn't match my speed or technical ability. I won but for our friendship and old time's sake I didn't kill him.

This proved a mistake with him valuing position over our friendship. Stabbing me in the back with his knife when I turned around. I no longer felt very generous at this point. As I felt the blade pulled free, I spun around separating his arm from his body. Blacking out after nailing his foot to the deck with my sword.

I woke up five days later in the officer's cabin as the crew's new quartermaster. Klein was flayed alive then strung up as the ships' new figurehead for a month. This betrayal taught me to shut others out. Think of myself first and last. To live only for myself, to love only myself.

Sometimes I wonder if the silence of my own heart has sent me mad.

Tears rolling down her face fell unhindered onto her lap Vashti was moved by the story. The story that explained so much.

Flynn said he had never told anyone that before. Nor would she share it with the others, it is his story, his life, his pain.

Taking Flynn's face in her hands she looked him in the eyes telling him. His heart might be silent but it wakens louder and louder each day and for him to not give up on humanity just yet.

Chapter 2

THE WALL

Koyake was a city built within view of the Blue mountains. Sitting on a rising hill with the keep built on its highest point. A wooden palisade surrounded the city, watchtowers periodically placed offered no blind spots of approach.

Leaving Iodem they passed through a pass at the southern end of the ranges, little more than hills. Further north the mountains rose significantly in height until they towered over Koyake.

These ranges when combined with the ranges in the southern part of Dal, are what cause the extreme weather in the eye. Flynn had explained how the wind gets trapped by the impassable mass of the mountains. With nowhere to go it feeds of itself, spinning faster and in different directions.

A pair of bored guards leaning against their pikes welcomed them into the city. Finding a cheap inn with only one available room they stabled their horses before visiting the market. Koyake was bubbling with people going about their daily lives, completely oblivious to the threat looming over them. Women purchasing food for that evening's dinner, children playing in the streets and dogs barking, snapping at their heels.

"Looks peaceful" Ailish mentioned as several kids ran past her. "Yeah, nothing like Crows perch" Baird agreed. "They're not rich but everyone's happy here" Garrett said. "I grew up around here. Most people are farmers with Koyake being the trade hub for the west."

"So why did you leave?" Baird asked. "I grew up in the mountain fortress. Son of a guardsmen so my options were limited. I wanted to see the world and seek my fortune. So, I joined a passing caravan as a guard and intended never to return. Now four years later, I'm back."

That night sitting in the inns common room enjoying freshly roasted beef and reasonable ale everyone felt relaxed. Except for Flynn who seemed out of place, with no drunken idiots around he excused himself early and was the first asleep.

So, Flynn wasn't there to hear Garrett talk about the fortress he grew up in. It was a hard day's ride from the city. Housing the garrison for Koyake and was a refuge for the city. The fortress was built in the fork of the mountain with a stone wall encircling it. The fortress predates the city, already built when humans arrived. It was assumed to be dwarven built but was abandoned when they found it. With no known name it simply became referred to as the rock.

Flynn was sound asleep on the floor underneath the window when everyone entered finally calling it a night. The girls shared the bed leaving the boys to find a spot on the floor. The wooden planks felt comfortable to Baird after all the time spent sleeping on hard ground using rocks as pillows.

<hr>

A cool breeze seeping through the cracked window disturbed his sleep. 'He never opened it, one of the others must've opened it before going to bed. But why didn't he wake then?' Flynn thought as he heard the wooden frame of the window slowly scrape as it slid open wider.

'No creaking or weight shifting across the floor boards so it's not one of the others trying to do it quietly so they don't wake me.' Flynn pondered eyes still shut maintaining a steady rhythm of breathing. 'It's being opened from the outside. Impressive, considering they were on the second floor in a room with no ledge. Is it a thief or something more sinister?'

Whoever it was they were experienced. Taking ten long minutes to fully open the window so they could climb in. Ten minutes of maintaining slow steady breathing for the waiting host. The intruder saw Flynn as he placed feet either side of his own. Weight coming down so light and gently the floor boards never creaked.

A hand clasped over his mouth to muffle any sound. Eyes snapping open, Flynn looked his attacker in the eye. His own hands already clasped around his wrist, knife stopped short from its target. A large broad bladed knife with a sharp point designed to punch through rib cage and pierce the heart. An assassin's weapon. If he was asleep, he would be dead right now.

He wasn't asleep however and assassins are only effective with the element of surprise. Even unarmed he was the fighter and had the advantage. The assassin pressed down on the knife with two hands drawing the same conclusion. Freeing up his own mouth to shout for help, not that he ever would. Smiling he rolled away from the window onto his right side planting the knife in the floor.

Shifting his weight more Flynn ended up on top, his opponent trapped on his back. Left foot pressed firmly onto his right wrist hand still gripping the knife his sole life line. Tongueless mouth open in a silent cry for help. The others sleeping soundly through the scuffle. 'This will wake them' Flynn thought grabbing his assailant by the face.

Lifting the head up he smashed it against the floor. Once, twice, three times. Stopping as blood flowed freely from a crushed skull, red puddle pooling on the floor. Looking at the puzzled and horrified expressions of his companions only one thought sprang to mind. "Morning."

•

Rudely awoken to Flynn caving in someone's skull against the floor of their room. Baird like the others was surprised, confused and furious.

"Why did you kill him. Now we can't ask who sent him." Vaike quietly screamed at Flynn after he explained what happened. "Check his mouth." "What?" "Just do it" Flynn answered in a tired voice.

Garrett who was closer opened the dead man's mouth. "No tongue." "Exactly. So even if I left him alive, he wouldn't answer anything so I saw no reason not to kill him." "His pockets are empty also" Garrett stated after digging through them. "Great so we've nothing to go on" Vaike sighed. 'Is it Maroxis and his servants or Olaf' Vaike thought.

"Is that your blood?" Vashti asked sitting down beside Flynn. "Don't think so" Flynn answered looking at the blood covering his hands. "Yes, it is. Your bleeding." Lifting up the right sleeve of Flynn's shirt she tended to a fresh wound.

"I guess I'm not completely healed yet if he cut me." "Well your lucky its neither deep or long, it's just bleeding profusely." "I'm lucky I wasn't drunk or he would've gotten us all."

"Done" Vashti said lowering Flynn's sleeve over a fresh bandage. "Thanks. It's better treatment than I deserve."

❦

They left the inn at first light, tired and yawning with only Flynn unperturbed by the dead body getting any more sleep. The inn keeper was surprised to learn the source of the noise last night and was angry to learn about the remaining body. No longer apologetic he hurried them out the door telling them to never return. Not a huge loss in anyone's opinion happy to put the place behind them.

Vaike didn't think the attacker was a local but they still put as much distance between them and Koyake as possible. Seeing the pass that lead to the rock around noon. Garrett longingly stared in the direction of the fort. "Are you wondering about your father?" Ailish asked of him. "Yeah I'm wondering how he is." "We do have time to visit. A day or two won't hurt" Vaike informed from the front without slowing.

"No, its fine" Garrett answered through clenched teeth. "We didn't part on the best of terms. He said he doesn't want to see me again until I've come to my senses and am ready to join the guard."

"I don't know. If you visit him with Ailish on your arm you'll be fine. She is enough to make any dad love their son again" Flynn offered. "Idiot" Vashti muttered hitting the back of Flynn's head. "What. What did I say?" They continued wordlessly on till evening.

"So, what Is the plan exactly because I have no idea?" Flynn asked sitting around the fire that evening. "That's because you slept through the discussions" mocked Garrett. Flynn stared daggers at Garrett with Vaike answering before a fight erupted.

"We are going to Maroxis stronghold and kill him. He is vulnerable now and it is our best chance. We are travelling to the Red cliffs and passing through the wall at the end." "and into the western lands of Dal" Flynn finished.

"Yes, and from there its north, away from the cities of men towards the wastelands of the north. Home to the goblins." "Awesome" grinned Flynn. "I'm surprised, I thought you would've left because of the foolishness of the plan." "Oh, it's definitely doomed to fail but it is my best chance to get revenge on that fucking Vampire."

Three days of journeying north left the Blue mountains behind them as their surroundings became rolling grasslands and hills in all directions. "The grass sea" Baird exclaimed in excitement realising where they were. "Yes, we're in the south-western end of it. Gism was opposite on the north-eastern outskirts" Vaike answered.

"Yeah one of three outskirt towns. Even living so close I've never crossed or entered it" Baird continued. "Probably a good idea" Garrett spoke joining the conversation. "I've crossed a few times and even with guides it's difficult. Just as desolate and devoid of life as the desert. Many travellers enter unprepared or become lost and die."

"Don't worry from here we cut due west heading for the cliffs. Two days at most we'll spend in the sea before we reach the coastal road from the north. It takes over a week to reach Gism from here to give you some perspective" Vaike finished ruffling Baird's hair.

Eagles circled overhead, keen eyes searching the endless plains for small game. Baird saw nothing. Climbing the top of a hill just to see more hills, more grass behind. The next hill offering more of the same. Two days without seeing a tree, a river and only the birds to keep them company. They remained at the southern end of the sea. Twice Baird saw peaks over his left shoulder before they were swallowed up behind hills.

Late on the second day the top of a hill presented Baird with a new view. Mountains on two sides merging together to form a narrow pass. In that pass stood an immense stone wall spanning the width of one mountain to the other. Even at this distance with the sun in his eyes he could see that it was an imposing defensive structure.

Chapter 3

THE BLOOD BONDS

Standing naked from the waist up, right hand grasped the familiar hilt of his sword, a ring of steel surrounded him. The morning breeze was cool against the thin layer of sweat forming on his chest. It felt good. It had been too long since he last did this, grinning as the first man took a swing at his exposed back.

Hands on hips breathing deeply, he stood trying to catch his breath. 'Definitely out of shape' he thought surveying the outcome. A dozen soldiers all on the ground. Some rolling or groaning in pain, others unconscious and a few dead. 'No matter he has plenty of soldiers to spare.'

"My liege." An out of breath messenger knelt outside the ring of carnage. Without speaking Olaf stared down the man who continued, understanding the silent message. "Duke Ivan requires your presence. At your earliest convenience." The second part coming late like the messenger realised it sounded like he was ordering the king.

Kneeling terrified, waiting for some sort of reprisal. Olaf backhanded the man for his insolence as he passed. It probably felt like being struck with a cast iron pan but it was hardly the man's fault either. Duke Ivan, the only man who gets away with summoning him without requesting. More than one messenger has died relaying the Dukes exacts words.

Olaf stepped into his war room. An enclosed circular room situated near the centre of his keep. No windows, they are a structural weakness. The only light came from candles lining the walls and a fire smouldering in the hearth.

No furniture other than a large round table in the centre and a few shelves stacked full with old worn books on strategy and battles rested against the walls. A large-scale model of eastern Thaldesa sat atop the table, showing his realms and military positions.

"Ah my king." "What is it Ivan?" "I just received word that our assassin was found dead in Koyake, no other bodies were found." "Hmm, Koyake" Olaf pondered. "Well they can't travel west, so they must be heading to the Nibban forest to hide with Queen Yisolde." "Yes, that was my assumption as well."

❦

Baird sat atop Jorra staring up at a great stone wall. What he mistook for a wall turned out to actually be a fort, its vast outer wall stretched across the ravine. Spiked wooden palisade surrounded the fort in a semi-circle enclosing a stone well and stable housing a few dishevelled horses. Wooden training dummies and straw targets stood unused in the yards as soldiers filled barrels with arrows.

"This doesn't look good" Garrett announced. "No, they're stockpiling and fletching arrows. Something must be happening" confirmed Vaike riding through the un-guarded gap in the palisade fence.

Soldiers watched the six companions ride past as they went about their duties. The fort was massive. A hundred strides across reaching five floors high Baird guessed, hard to know for certain with no windows on this side. The fort door was flanked by two tired soldiers resting against the wall. Showing an impressive amount of speed, they snapped to attention as Vaike approached, presenting Olaf's golden wolves head sigil. The sentries seemed unusually excited to see the symbol, immediately grabbing a squire to escort them to the commander.

❦

"This is getting stranger by the minute." "You read my mind" Flynn said from the shadows in the corner. Vaike couldn't help but agree with both of them. Flynn and Garrett following him up several flights while the others where lead away to the kitchens.

The door behind them opened and a greying man in his fifties entered. "Sorry to keep you waiting, I'm Commander Black and you must be the vanguard for our reinforcements. So, tell me how many are coming and how far behind are they."

"Reinforcements, so that's it" Flynn snorted as the commander sat behind a large oak desk. "And who might you be? I was of the idea I was seeing the one who carried Olaf's authority."

"You are" Vaike answered. "These two are trusted advisors and companions." "Very well, so about the reinforcements?" "We aren't them and we know nothing about them" answered Vaike. "We are on a mission from the king and require passage through to Dal." "That's impossible. In fact, if it wasn't for the fact you carried the Kings sigil, I would arrest you here."

"Why is it impossible?" Flynn asked unperturbed by the threat. "Because of the army at the door. It's why we sent a request for reinforcements to the capitol a month ago and Koyake last week. "We left Voldengird several months ago and haven't been in contact since."

"Well that explains part of it" Black continued looking at Vaike. "But what about the fact there isn't a gate in the wall." "What" Vaike exclaimed in surprise. "Since when?" "Over twenty years now. I would've thought being on a mission from Olaf himself you would know about that, key detail."

Shaking of the surprise and confusion Vaike played along. "Come now Black we're both commanders, you know how it is. Officers intentionally overlook details so they don't need to provide solutions. That way they get to blame failures on subordinates." "Forced delegation. I suppose you are right" Black concurred.

"I suppose I should fill you in on everything so you can plan your solution" Black said opening the door and talking to the guards outside. "I've just sent for some food to be brought up. Now, can I know who I'm speaking to." "That's much appreciated. I'm Vaike, that's Garrett and the surly one skulking in the shadows is Flynn. We have three more with us."

"Just six. Well that's not much help if you stay, well no matter. Two moons ago the Dalthenian army showed up at the wall. They do this every year with not much happening other than a few exchanges of arrows. This year they kept coming in numbers four times greater than ever before. Fearing an actual attempt to breach the wall I sent for reinforcements. A week ago, they still hadn't made a move when goblins arrived. The goblins didn't attack the Dalthenian's, instead swelling their ranks with countless more. That's when I sent a runner to Koyake asking for aid."

"Two days ago, they made their first attempt on the wall. Only fifty or so goblins that were quickly driven off. Three more waves happened that night with more small attempts last night. A large-scale attack is imminent they're just probing our defences for now." A small lad returned carrying a tray of cold meats, cheese and fruit.

"So, what happened to the gate" Vaike asked picking up a shiny red apple. "The gate was rusted and in a poor state of repair. Rather than spend the money needed to replace something that hadn't been opened in a century it was decided to fill it in with stones." A cry echoed in from outside and the door was thrown open. "I'm sorry but it sounds like the raids have begun. I'll leave my office open for you should you need it. Now if you'll excuse me."

"What now?" Garrett asked as the door closed on Black. "The gate isn't the pressing issue. The army at the door is what bothers me." "Me too" Garrett agreed with Vaike. "We could always kill them." "What the six of us" Garrett scoffed at Flynn. "Well I can't see us affording another ship so unless you have the ability to shit gold we have to cross here."

"He's right" interjected Vaike, putting a stop to the bickering. Sighing, he rubbed his temples, eyes shut in thought. 'Why did they continue to squabble like such children, it must be a human thing.'

"Our only way ahead is through the pass. We do however have time so we don't have to go through the army. However," continuing loudly seeing both men open mouths to retort. "If the army takes the fort, we will be significantly worse off. So, do we stay and help or leave and hope they hold?"

"I suggest we discuss it with the others and wait until we can see the army tomorrow before we decide. "Makes no difference to me, you already know my vote." "Sadly, Flynn I do.

❧

The sun cast its light over countless tents and banners stretching beyond the horizon. Green banners with prancing horses, yellow and black banners with rearing boars and blue banners with sea monsters swimming. Several regions of Dalthenian soldiers gathered together forming a countless sea of humanity. Surrounded by the red cliffs on both sides. Named for the high copper content turning the stone an earthy red.

Torn and tattered scraps of cloth marked the goblins legions. Bloody hand prints, dragons and skulls swarmed around the mass of humanity, dwarfing it by comparison. "How many. How many are there?" It was Ailish asking, more out loud than to anyone. "How many blades of grass grow in the field" Vaike answered either showing elven humour or wisdom Baird wasn't sure which.

The wall was strong at least. Being the only thing keeping the tide of destruction at bay. They walked it at first light past the soldiers dumping goblin corpses onto waiting wagons to be carted away.

Thirty feet high and a hundred long crossing the ravine at its narrowest point bringing attackers into a choke point. A ditch on the outer side filled with sharpened stakes congested attackers further, forcing them to climb single file up ladders.

Loophole windows on the forts outer wall provided a height advantage for archers to reign death outside the invaders effective range and battlements on the wall for defenders to seek cover from any arrows that are fired upon them. The only weak spot that Baird could see was a patch of stone in the centre of the wall that didn't match the surrounds. Stones haphazardly fitted filling the arched hole from the gate.

Vaike said a hundred could hold of ten thousand here and Baird believed him. It was unfortunate however, that more than ten thousand were knocking at the door.

"I vote we stay and help" Vaike said. Black was sleeping, so they were eating breakfast in his office discussing their next move. "Seconded" Flynn said between swigs from his wine skin. 'No alcohol in the fort, yet that doesn't stop him getting drunk. Typical' Baird thought before agreeing with Vaike.

Vaike left with Flynn to talk with Black. Everyone having agreed to help stop the horde reaching their homes. Baird now sat in the mess talking with some of the soldiers. They were grateful for any help they could get, having lost ten comrades this past month leaving the fort at a hundred and twelve souls.

Baird was surprised to learn not everyone here was a soldier. Some were convicted criminals given the choice to serve a life sentence. The officers and most sergeants were all soldiers posted here as punishment of some kind. It's a life sentence for most. Dying to sword or age very few ever leave once they arrive.

❦

Baird shivered, the cool late afternoon breeze brushing against his clammy skin. Nerves racking his body as he stood atop the wall staring at an endless horde of enemies seeking the destruction of the east. He's fought in many battles but this was on a whole other scale.

"Just relax" Vaike reassured him placing a fatherly hand on his shoulder for comfort. "Look at their formations. Most of them are not preparing for anything it's just another skirmish to wear us down. The real attack will come later." Removing his hand Vaike took position on the wall.

Vaike and Black came up with a good defensive strategy. They split the wall into quarters with both of them commanding the middle two sections. Garrett and Anders, Blacks second in command took control of the outer two. The girls have taken up residency in the fort joining the undermanned archers leaving Baird to join Vaike.

"Why isn't Flynn with Garrett?" Baird questioned seeing him sitting in the courtyard behind the wall. "Flynn's role is to be the anchor. He sits in reserve with a few elite fighters to give aid if any section starts to collapse. Or worst case and the wall is lost they cover the retreat. Well that and I don't trust him to not be a problem on the wall. It is cramped up here."

Four times the goblins climbed the wall that day and four times they were repelled. The last tendrils of light disappearing with the final attack. As the last goblin fell a lone solitary figure approached the wall stopping just outside bow range. Hands raised he slowly approached close enough to be heard. The first non-goblin near the wall all day.

"If you want to live leave tonight. We know your weaknesses. We have the numbers. Tomorrow we attack with everything. Tomorrow we take the fort and kill anyone still inside. Tomorrow we open the door to the east." A quivering arrow struck the ground by his feet, his only reply before leaving arms still raised.

Most of the corpses were thrown down to the courtyard but even so the ditch was slowly being filled in with bloody corpses. Baird even managed to kill a few. A cut above his left eye the only wound sustained when he was accidently elbowed by the soldier beside him.

Flynn was found sitting cross legged resting against the fort outer wall. Half empty wineskin in his hand like he was bored by the afternoon's events. "Five more depart us" Black announced walking up to the group now joining Flynn in relaxing.

"Do you think tomorrow they will attack?" Vaike asked the only one still standing. "Probably, if not the next day for sure. The trench is nearing full in places and we are worn down. You had best get some rest, it might be our last chance" Black said leaving. "Will do. And sorry for your loss" consoled Vaike. "Don't be, they won't be the last."

"Right get some food then try to sleep." "If you can't, do something constructive like checking your weapons or borrowed chainmail. Anything to take your mind of tomorrow" Garrett added nodding to Vaike.

❦

"Can't sleep huh" Flynn asked Baird as he joined him on the wall staring into oblivion. "You worried about tomorrow?" Yes, I've been in battles before but never anything of this magnitude." "I wouldn't worry about it" Flynn said patting him on the back, offering some reassurance. "You have as much chance of surviving this as me, actually more chance since I'm the anchor."

"I doubt that" Baird said disheartened. "I've watched you fight incredible odd's, survive against vampires and tie with Vaike. How can my chances be better than yours?"

"Because its war kid. Skill means nothing in a battle this large, luck deciding peoples fates more often than not." "You mean like wrong place, wrong time?" "Exactly. Don't get me wrong however, once the arrows stop and it becomes an uncontrolled brawl skill is needed then but an unlucky sword from behind can still end it."

"If it's mostly luck why wear that red cape, isn't that just putting a giant target on yourself?" Baird asked with a confused expression. "Yeah pretty much. But if I am to die, I wish to look smashing for the occasion" Flynn smirked. "Besides it draws the best warriors to me."

Sitting in silence watching the moon light up the mass of warriors spread out before them, Baird prayed he was lucky tomorrow. "So, tell me" Baird asked breaking the silence. "What is it like to be with a woman?"

"That's right I forgot you we're a virgin. That will have to be amended, if you survive that is. There is no way however, to answer that question as its different for everyone."

"How so?" "Well" Flynn began trying to find the words to explain. "Some women lie there and don't move, while others suck on your balls while you slap them in the face with your cock. Some like to be choked or scream your ear off, while others enjoy it up their arse. I've seen a woman fuck a horse, and another who liked to be pissed on, even women who enjoy multiple guys at once.

Then there is the woman themselves" Flynn continued. "Some have tight little vaginas that always snap back or some that lose you could shove your leg up there. Others have so much skin it's like peeling an onion. Then the breasts. Big fat and hanging past their waist with nipples the size of your hand. Small plump breasts with little gold coin nipples or weird pointy ones."

"It sounds like it's over rated then." "Oh, it is and for some reason men spend their whole lives chasing it because she's out there. The perfect girl, we just have to shift through the shit first to find her." "So then do you have favourite girl?"

"Catherine" Flynn whispered his eyes lighting up. "She was this gorgeous red head I met. Sixteen and had just started working in this high-end establishment. Small petite girl, nice tight round arse and firm breasts. A pair of lungs on her that could wake the dead and she would squirt. Sort of like pissing" Flynn answered seeing Baird's puzzled expression.

"That sounds awful." "It is but in a very good way" chuckled Flynn. "Anyway. I ended up purchasing her contract and took her with me when we sailed. There wasn't much she wouldn't try. She even licked my cock clean once after I fucked her arse.

But after three months I found out she was stealing from me. I tied her up to the main mast naked for three days while the crew went through her one after another. She was whipped, dehydrated and beaten before we threw her overboard."

"That's awful" Baird said mortified. "Pirates remember" Flynn laughed. "You had best return to bed. Even if you can't sleep resting with your eyes closed will help." "What about you?" "Me. I'm fine. I'll finish this then head inside."

'More wine. Where does he possible find it.' "Your right I'm going to sleep. Don't drink too much we need your sword tomorrow." "You need more than just that kid" Flynn whispered to the empty space Baird left.

❧

Baird struggled to sleep that night. What sleep he did find was plagued with dreams, with horrors.

Dreams of battle, of war. Harbinger cut and sliced. Blood raining as bodies from both sides fell around him.

Beasts with hardened scales and razor sharp talons slashed at soldiers. Naught but the sturdiest of armour halting those deadly nails. Long heavy tails struck like a hammer, men and dwarves slumped dead from the impact.

Long jaws full of serrated teeth bit cleanly through armour. Men fell screaming, clutching at bloodied stumps.

Arrows rained from the sky bouncing of armour and hides. Searching for eyes, the weak points. Monsters displaying their physical advantages over man.

Harbinger fed its purpose from a hand that wasn't Baird's. From a battle that wasn't here, wasn't now. Baird watched monsters fight harbinger. Watched them fight Ithiel.

❧

"Where's your armour?" "I'm not wearing any." "I can see that. Why?" Baird groaned, too tired to deal with the arguing. The sun hadn't risen, yet the fort was alive with activity. People gathering weapons, buckling up armour, stuffing food into mouths. Everybody moving with purpose shifting into a battle mindset.

Now Vashti was screaming at Flynn for being stupid and not wearing the chainmail shirts Black lent them. Baird had just finished wrestling into his own and even the twins each wore a set."Wearing armour is accepting the possibility that you might need it. Besides it slows you down" Flynn added as an afterthought. "Your covered in scars. I think you need it" Vashti roared going red in the face. "Aye. I'm covered but not dead."

"And why the red coat it'll only make you a target." "Exactly. Bring the strongest enemies to me." "You know one of these days you're going to get yourself killed" Vashti sighed deciding it wasn't worth arguing about. "Perks of being mortal, we all die. I intend to at least deserve it."

The cooks brought up a dozen clay jars handing some to the girls. A few other soldiers grabbed some with the cooks and carried their loads joining the other archers at their posts. "What was in those jars?" Baird asked Vaike. "Oil. There is a stockpile on the forts roof with a single catapult." "What good is, oh." Baird went quiet, answering his own question when Flynn put a candle flame out with his fingers.

"Just wait kid. Nothing smells quite like burning flesh. It's a smell you never forget and the screaming. No one screams loader then a man when he's on fire." "Flynn's right." Vaike continued. "Although people don't normally sound excited to revisit it. I suggest you eat as much as you can. You're about to lose your appetite."

❧

The tide of warriors broke upon the wall like the sea does against the surrounding cliffs. The wall held firm as goblins and men scaled ladders to fight the defenders at the top. The defenders used spears to push the ladders off but for every three they pushed off, a fourth one was scaled.

Baird once again stood shoulder to shoulder with Vaike in the centre of the wall where most of the enemies' fury was targeted. Dawn was several hours ago, with the rising sun bringing the attack. No emissary was sent, seeing the defenders on the wall they answered with a charge.

The oil jars still rained down blanketing men in flames. The scent of seared flesh and burning meat thick in the air. Acrid black smoke drifted towards the southern end of the wall. Dying men on the walls, missing limbs or guts spilled out didn't scream as loud as those that burnt.

Still the tide swelled, crashing against the break wall. Stepping over the arrow riddled bodies of allies, driving burning soldiers away with weapons trying not to burn themselves.

Slowly the defenders gave ground on the wall. First one step then two as more and more ladders managed to be secured against the ramparts. Ladders continued to be raised, with the bodies littering the wall making It difficult to shove them off before snarling goblins leapt onto the wall.

⚔

'This doesn't look good' Flynn thought watching the wall slowly be overrun. He sat in the courtyard with four soldiers behind him. He already sent eight of his men to assist Blacks section in the centre but they still struggled to hold ground. Vaike's side fairing little better, the elven prince's skill with a blade the only difference.

The two sections had become completely cut off from each other as more enemies swelled between them slowly taking the wall. "It's time we get busy." No comment from the others as they stood following his lead.

A single bucket of arrows was all he managed to get with the four still with him being the better archers in the group. The arrows went quick with Flynn planting the last one between the eyes of a Dalthenian soldier who looked no older than Baird. The middle was still separated but the pressure was greatly reduced on the two groups.

⚔

Cut off from Blacks group they were fighting on two fronts. Flynn performing his role as anchor splendidly, launching arrows from forty feet granting them a small respite. One arrow whistling past, inches from his head to stick out of a goblins throat who was leaping over the parapet. Ears twitching from the arrows path Vaike briefly glanced behind him to see a smirking pirate wearing a red coat. 'A war of these odds and he still manages to be annoying. Does he think this is a game? Probably' Vaike thought turning his attention to the matter at hand.

❦

Leaning against the parapet for support, legs shaking struggling to hold himself up. The sun sunk below the horizon as the moon climbed replacing it in the sky. Corpses littered the wall and surrounding ground but it seems the enemy has called it a day. They held the wall.

"That's a shame." Baird saw it was Flynn who spoke standing with Blacks remaining men, swords bloody from a busy day's work. "When did you join us?" "Three or four hours ago I guess. This section was close to being overrun."

"Well whatever I feel like I could sleep for a week." "Sleep is still a long way off" Black said after thanking Flynn for the support. "We have bodies to clear and wounded that need tending to. We'll be lucky to get more than a couple of hours sleep if any." "How are we meant to fight tomorrow?" "We're not that's how a siege works" Vaike answered. "You did well today also."

They worked late into the night and into the next day. Stacking all the bodies high on the southern section of the wall. After securing them in place with excess swords and spears protruding out. Effectively doubling the height of that section of wall preventing ladders and enemies from climbing it.

With thirty seven dead or unable to fight they can barely hold three sections of the wall let alone four. The trade-off for less to hold? Exhaustion. Only time will tell if it was worth it Baird though rubbing tired eyes as he climbed into his cot.

Chapter 4

THE SORROW OF WAR

They lined the walls, standing shoulder to shoulder as orange crept across the sky. Exhaustion racking their sleep deprived bodies as tired and stiff muscles screamed in protest. Even the smallest movements were a battle in their own rights.

Seasoned veterans, hardened from experience or new recruits little older than fifteen. It made no difference they all lined up with the same looks of hopelessness and despair and who could blame them. Heavily outnumbered and fighting well rested foes, it was hopeless.

'We have no choice but to succeed. If Vaike thinks we can win, then there is hope. No matter how slim.' Baird thought looking at Vaike standing beside him, right at the moment when the sun broke over the horizon surrounding him with radiant light, looking almost godlike.

Divine intervention or not it worked. Baird finding strength and resolve in himself as cheers roared around him. Cries of encouragement and reassurance. "It seems they think I'm the Elven god Elisa." Vaike whispered quietly enough so only Baird could hear. "Well whatever helps" he shrugged.

Horns sounded the advance. Three blast's echoing of the mountain faces long after the march began. No foreplay, no feeling pushes. The attackers picking up right where they left of yesterday with the same vigour and intensity. The besieged defenders fighting with their all but giving ground from the first wave.

He grinned in excitement as a breeze tore at the red cloak draped over his shoulders. The defenders are about to crumble and surrender the wall. Hands resting on the hilts of his swords, the only reassurance he ever needs, Flynn waited. He waited for the courtyard to become the battlefield so he could get to work.

⚬

It was slow at first with one soldier backing down the stairs behind the wall, then a second. Before long they were in full retreat as defenders where shoved of the walls as they rushed for the stairs. Baird remained fighting as one of the few covering the retreat, unable to save them all as goblins swarmed around them killing the stragglers.

"Time to go" Vaike shouted over the din of battle. Adrenaline coursing through his veins, Baird heard but didn't understand the order. Grabbed by the scruff of his neck, Vaike dragged him to the edge of the wall and jumped. The shock of this action snapping Baird's full attention to the situation at hand. It was chaos and disarray.

Men ran in all directions or fought in small groups. The huge reinforced doors into the fort stood open. Soldiers ran through the opening in full retreat as Flynn's group covered the courtyard. Running flat out for the door only looking back as he was passing through, Vaike no longer at his side. "Go, get inside, I'll get him" Vaike said motioning to Flynn.

"Fuck he's gone battle drunk" Garrett said joining Baird in the threshold. "Aye it's not good" agreed Black as the doors started to slowly swing shut. "I'll leave it open as long as I can, but I won't let them take the fort for the sake of a few men." "We understand" Garrett said silencing Baird with a firm hand on his shoulder. "But we had best hope they make it. Without those two the fort is lost."

⚬

Fighting on the stairs as the first few men turn tailed and fled throwing away their weapons. Finally, it's time. The first two cowards that ran past him received his swords in their backs. "Die to them or die to me, there is no retreat yet." Even screaming he's not sure how many heard his words but the intention was clear as swords were retrieved, deserters returning to the fight.

It was clear when the wall was lost. No need to sound the retreat as men were shoved of the edge. His numbers swelling slightly as the more determined took up arms covering the courtyard. Others formed a human wall around the fort's doors guarding the last portal to the west. 'Well it must be almost that time' Flynn thought as he spotted Vaike drag a body over the wall.

Try as hard as he might they were still being pushed back, as more and more bodies swarmed over the wall to fight them. The arrows that continued to rain death down the only thing stalling the death that came. Killing a Dalthenian officer wearing steel armour laced with veins of gold he prepared for the withdrawal.

Before the words left his head ordering his remaining men back, a black shadow flitted over the wall landing in the yard. Rage, bloodlust, revenge all reached bursting point as Flynn went crazy with rage. Letting roar a myriad of curses, threats and cries Flynn cut down all in his path trying to reach the far side of the courtyard. Strong arms wrapped around his waist dragging him back behind a wall of shields before he'd managed more than a few steps.

❧

Kicking and screaming with promises of a painful death to everyone it took five men to drag Flynn inside. Only once the echoing boom of the doors slamming shut had disappeared did they let him go.

Vaike was in discussion with Black and the other commanders. Flynn was absent as he continued to pace back and forth inside the door, muttering about how he was going to kill him. Vashti spoke to him successfully putting a stop to the frantic pacing. It seemed her presence ended his blood lust as Vaike returned to the group.

"Black wants to dig in. Block the door and wait for reinforcements" Vaike informed the group, Flynn in particular. "Bloody coward" sneered Flynn. "They can't hold longer than a day or two at most. They might as well die as warriors with courage." "A last-ditch effort you mean?" Baird asked not thrilled by the idea.

"Oddly enough, I find myself agreeing with Flynn" Vaike said receiving mixed expressions he continued. "As we are the fort will fall. With the fort the west will fall before this horde.

There are too many for us to cut our way through but if we can fell the commander, maybe, just maybe they will abandon the campaign.

Black still thinks we're on a mission from Olaf so he's willing to let us make a suicide charge, his words not mine" he added as shock appeared on Baird's face. "He won't order anyone to join us but he will allow any volunteers to."

"Excellent" grinned Flynn, smiling ear to ear. "The vampire is mine however. "And sister, I want you and Ailish to remain behind. If the worst should happen, I want you to carry word to mother and take up your responsibilities." Even with all the shouting and activity happening around them, everyone still heard the crack of Vashti's hand as she slapped her brothers face.

"I won't speak for Ailish but I'm riding out with you and to hell with mother and my duties." "Sis' I'm sorry." "Shhh, it's alright" Vashti said pressing her forehead to Vaike's. "Through the good and the bad, till the bitter end we'll be together."

"I'm glad you're coming" Flynn said softly as Vashti stood tall and proud beside him. "But promise me one thing. No matter what happens stick with Vaike, he has the best chance of pushing through them."

"I promise, but what about you, aren't you following us?" "Don't know. If the blood lust overcomes me again then I can't promise anything. Best chance is to hope I can kill the vampire quick enough." "Then let us help." "No. If I'm worried about others I can't fight to my full potential and that spells doom for us all."

❧

Staring at the wooden doors as they shook under the impact from the other side. Each echoing boom and creak of timber caused others to shake and tremble with fear but not him. Flynn stood feeling a steady calm wash over him.

Death loomed over them all as Grimmlocke the god of death prepares to collect what is owed him. Finally, some emotions and situations that he was familiar with. Comfortable with.

Killing, killing comes easy. Saying what he means to Vashti, that was hard. 'It might not matter soon' Flynn thought. Grinning as two soldiers readied to lift the heavy bar sealing the door.

It seems twenty men found the courage to join them. All exhausted, in various states of distress and injuries, yet willing to do what needs to be done. "I've missed this."

"Missed what?" Vaike asked standing on his left. "Don't tell me it's the looming shadow of Grimmlocke's collectors." 'Hmm, I must have said that louder than I meant to' thought Flynn before answering. "No this" he said indicating those with them.

"The comradery. A band of brothers willing to lay down it all for each other." Vaike looked at Flynn opening his mouth to respond. Whatever Vaike had to say was never heard for at that moment Black bellowed an order and the doors were thrown open. 'It's probably for the best he didn't know what Vaike was thinking' Flynn thought stabbing a shocked soldier through the chest as he stood holding a battering ram staring at the now open door.

The momentum didn't last long as everyone swiftly overcame the shock of the doors opening and being attacked. By the time the doors slammed shut behind them, somehow heard over the noise of battle the enemies had regrouped and begun to mount resistance. With no option of retreat only to fight to the death the defenders found new strength.

The courtyard was packed with enemies both men and goblins. With the wall now completely breached having torn down the stones filling in the gate. Atop the rubble in a flowing black cloak stood the vampire. 'It's funny how things work out' he thought pointing his sword and charging.

❦

Cutting a path through the wall of flesh before him Flynn raced ahead. The tide flowed into the path behind him, cutting of all reinforcements and preventing them from following. "Stick to the plan we push" Vaike screamed. Not sure if he was heard he pushed forward.

Their group getting smaller and smaller with each meter gained and unable to close the gap with Flynn who now crossed swords with his target. More enemies swelled in replacing those killed yet they ignored Flynn. Forming a circle around the two foes as they circled each other before springing forward.

'It's the same vampire he fought in the tower' Vaike thought. Remembering how that vampire was more interested in fighting Flynn alone then stopping their advance. 'Come to think of it, they probably crossed blades in the clearing not long after Flynn joined them.

Ten of their volunteers had fallen before they stalled. Now completely surrounded they fought on all sides unable to advance. If Flynn was here, they might have been able to push on but it took everything to stay alive.

Stuck close enough to see the sweat on his brow and unable to reach any closer. Grinning from ear to ear Flynn danced and spun parrying blows while delivering his own. No point wasting his breath calling out to him. In the maddening chaos that swarms around them. They remain two lone figures trapped in their own world, completely oblivious to the storm that rages around them.

—

It was a choreographed dance with each movement exact and purposeful. With death being the prize for any wrong or faltering movements. Surrounded by an obedient audience as the swarming mass of enemies respected the duel giving them a wide berth.

They're as evenly matched as they were the last time they fought. Both trying new tricks or tactics anything to gain the advantage. All it took was the gargled wailing of a dying goblin to unbalance the scales. Hands clamped around a shaft protruding from its neck the goblin fell at Flynn's feet causing him to slightly stumble.

This distraction was all it took for him to earn a scratch over his left eye. It wasn't deep but still bled enough to obscure his vision, causing his pulse to rise as panic spread. The vampires keen hearing can probably hear his quickening heartbeat as he attacked Flynn's left side. One, two, three slashes with the last one opening up a deep cut on his left shoulder.

Creating space, it takes all the remaining strength in his left arm to grip the hilt of his sword now slick with his own blood. Focusing his attention on the worn grip of his swords. On their familiar weight. Flynn knew every detail about those swords, every scratch and blemish or the exact wave pattern on the blade. Every groove carved into the scabbards. He knew them better and more intimately then any lover. They have brought him riches and glory as he's fed their purpose.

A steely calm flowed through him as he once again gripped those hilts ready to fulfil their purpose. To feast on the blood of their enemies.

Standing across from a deadly foe, grinning ear from ear and completely calm he sheathed one sword his left arm now near useless.

It was like time stood still for Flynn as he circled around his opponent. He could feel the faintest breeze tickle against the beads of sweat rolling down his neck. Hear the pebbles shift as their feet moved and smell the scent of pine leaves making up Vashti's perfume. Grinning at the thought of her being nearby he gripped one sword in both hands and leapt into battle.

Bearing down with its full strength, sword against sword. Flynn was no match in the contest with his left arm going numb and hand sliding off the hilt. With a flick of the wrist Flynn's sword was twisted free from his hand and sent spinning away.

Exhausted, wounded and defeated, Flynn stared absently ahead. Falling to his knees as the vampire raised his sword high above his head, preparing for the final blow before letting the proverbial hammer fall.

Not defeated, merely a ploy. Rolling clear as the sword whistled a past. Missing by a hair's breadth Flynn stood behind drawing his remaining sword. As the tip cleared the sheath it was cutting into the vampire in the same motion.

A surprised look painted on its face as the sword stopped wedged against its ribs, almost cut cleanly in half. The motion of following Flynn's roll left his entire left side exposed. It seems the assassin beetle could strike twice, grinned Flynn.

Holding on long enough to hear the sound of a sword clatter on the stones of the courtyard and see the life drain out of his face. Flynn collapsed knowing his task was complete. He was finished but he was victorious.

There was no shockwave, no dying shriek signalling the vampires defeat. Vashti's cry of dismay when they both collapsed, the only person who seemed to notice the evil leave the world.

Efforts were redoubled to reach Flynn as the circle around them collapsed on top of the incapacitated warriors.

Resistance died off as the speed they rushed to Flynn's side increased. With complete bedlam erupting in their ranks by the time Vashti hugged a barely conscious Flynn to her bosom.

Goblins fought other goblins. Goblins fought humans. Humans not yet through the breach dropped weapons and fled. Soldiers charged past the heavy doors again open as Black led the clean-up.

Harbinger scraped along the cobblestoned courtyard leaving a trail through the blood. No strength left in his arms to lift the sword yet Baird couldn't unclench his fist.

With no soldiers left to give chase, a few scouts were sent to make sure the fleeing army didn't return the mop-up began. Despair and grief threatened to drown survivors as they found the bodies of comrades, of brethren. While others dug through pockets of the fallen or collected new weapons.

Baird was lost. Still dragging Harbinger around until Garrett pried the sword free from his white knuckled grip and pointed him to a group of soldiers who needed help piling bodies onto carts.

He lost count of the number of bodies they carted away. Everyone working themselves beyond exhaustion, helping them to ignore their losses.

Chapter 5

THE FALLING OUT

Five days later the scouts returned to find a now clear archway, armed soldiers standing guard in place of a gate. Black acrid smoke drifted in the wind from fires still burning corpses as people scrubbed blood out of the courtyard's stone.

Messengers were dispatched three days prior, informing Olaf of what transpired here along with a request for more soldiers and stone masons.

The forts recent acquisition of thousands of weapons and armour was expected to take the sting out of the news, as Olaf was having issues arming his new recruits.

The scouts reported that as of three days ago the enemy was still in full retreat with no semblance of order. Several officers lay dead by the roadside. Killed trying to regain control, ordering the troops to return. Whatever goblins escaped the slaughter fled down bolt holes into the cliffs and disappeared.

Black took Vaike into his confidence calling him into his office after the scouts left for a meal and rest. They found Anders body after the battle, confirming his death and until Black replaced him Vaike was acting as his council. Garrett had joined in a few of these discussions whenever a third perspective was required.

Flynn was awake and pleasantly surprised to find himself still alive. He expected Hearthenfoil root to have coated the blade that cut him. Instead It was blood loss and exhaustion that brought him to his knees. "It seems he is human after all," was all Vaike said when Vashti informed them that he'll be okay the first night.

Flynn slept for two whole days. Two peaceful days. The peace shattered like glass once Flynn's eyes cracked open. Now he was awake it has taken all of the girl's time and energy just to keep him confined to his bed, to give his body the time to heal.

He received several more injuries when the retreating enemies trampled over his limp form. Broken ribs, bruised and swollen legs, bandaged head and left arm in a sling yet all Flynn wanted to do was loot some corpses. The pirate in him Baird supposed.

A week after the scouts arrived the six gathered at the breach in the wall astride their mounts. Flynn had recovered enough to travel and the clean-up was all complete. Aside from the gaping hole in the wall needing repairs.

Black handed Flynn a bag of coins as they left saying it was his share of the bounty. Baird suspected Vaike had a hand in this and if so, it certainly had the desired effect in making Flynn slightly more tolerable.

Even Garrett was happy having lost his spear during the chaos, he managed to scrounge up a replacement from the fallen Dalthenian soldiers. There was nothing special about the spear. It had a long blade, an acute point with a rounded tail end for easy extraction.

Plain design and a sturdy wooden shaft. But for the humble caravan guard he had never held or owned a spear to rival it. Griff's sword that Flynn gave him was the only weapon he'd ever owned that was of better quality.

"How its changed in two weeks" Ailish said. Baird couldn't agree more. No more clamour of soldiers bustling around masking the shouted orders. No enemies camped outside the wall, which now has a large hole in it and the scent of rotting and burning flesh no longer filled the air clogging the lungs.

"It's like a storm passed through clearing everything in its path washing away the destruction." The first words Flynn had spoken in days that wasn't shouted or screamed. "A storm did pass through here" Vaike replied. "You were just in the eye of it."

Everyone laughed at this comment even Flynn managing a few chuckles. Light hearted they set off on the next stage of their journey, Baird wiping away tears of joy. After what happened here it felt good to leave in high spirits.

The journey through the pass separating eastern from western Thaldesa was slow going. No one in the party had ever crossed it. Flynn having always sailed around and none of Vaike's people had left the west since he was born. Their expectations were completely wrong however. The hardships and challenges faced were on par with those faced when Foden led them through the desert.

The ground was rocky, hard soil where nothing grew save the hardiest of weeds. No game was to be found. The only signs of life were from the gulls cawing out over the ocean.

The waves forced themselves through the cliffs, shooting up into the air in spouts at irregular intervals. Not only drenching the companions but flooding the ground causing them to trudge knee deep through cold water across slippery stones.

The horses were of little help, the ground proving too treacherous to ride. The only break they received was that fresh water was readily available and what little grass grew was enough for their mounts.

Evidence of the fleeing army was evident everywhere. Broken boots and discarded tools littered the ground. The occasional corpse marred the path, providing food for the scavengers. Usually stabbed in the back and wearing a badge of command.

After a week of walking the southern mountain range ended opening up to a rocky beach leading out to the ocean. From what he knew from charts Flynn stated they were halfway across.

The torments on the second half of the crossing changed. They were no longer sprayed with water or crossing pools. Instead, replaced with a chilly sea breeze causing coats to be pulled tight around shoulders and making it impossible to start fires at night. The salty tang of the ocean was carried along with it causing Flynn and Vashti to stare longingly towards the horizon.

The ground became softer with cart tracks spread out across the grass. Able to ride again they made good time with signs of game and wild fruits seen but never able to find the source. Vaike guessed the retreating army picked the place clean.

Five more days of riding and cold grey stones of fortress walls came into view. The fortress of Ararait, the stronghold watching the eastern end of the pass. Built centuries ago but manned to keep Olaf's influence out.

Unlike the stronghold at the Blood Cliffs, Ararait was built more traditionally. With the cliffs having ended the land bridge was just a narrow strip wide enough to allow fifty abreast at its western end.

Located just outside range of siege weapons sat a walled fortress. The keep built on a slight hill allowing for greater sight lines and range. Boxed in by square, guarded by towers in each corner. According to Flynn it houses a skeleton crew of four hundred and can hold up to five thousand.

Resting behind a rise they waited out the afternoon. Baird was lectured by Garrett and Vaike on how the Dalthenian's use numbers and the terrain to hold the Western end.

It was achieved with the flat expanse of land surrounding the stronghold. No other hills or high ground existed so you were always disadvantaged by the defender's range. Then whatever soldiers made it beyond the raining arrows came face to face with charging cavalry.

Horses and mounts would crash against attackers driving them towards the stone walls. Either arrow or blade the defenders would fell the attackers. Wedged in with no escape.

Circumventing the fortress was hard. With unobstructed views an army was impossible to hide from rested horses ready to give chase.

Well after sunset they stole out like thieves, creeping towards the fort. "We're lucky it's a cloudy night with a waning moon" observed Vaike as they neared the stone walls. "Otherwise this might have been impossible. Without killing anyone or dying ourselves" Vaike added, answering Flynn's scoff.

It took all night to creep around the walls. With no cover they had to dash from shadow to shadow, avoiding the flickering light of the torches along the walls whilst not being seen by the patrolling sentries.

The sun rose behind the fortress walls with the group well out of sight. Without killing the horses or themselves they rode till sunset.

"We are truly behind enemy lines now" Vaike said over dinner that night. "Vashti and myself will be attacked on sight and the rest of you are only safe in a port town."

"Safe is a strong word" Flynn countered "but I get your point." "We are running low on supplies so we will have to make do with what we can scavenge. We will head north to the coast and follow it north west to the Dead forest."

"Oh, don't look like that" Flynn said slapping Baird's back. "It's only called that cause the northern end is a swamp that has killed off half the forest." Vashti remarked comforting the boy. "We'll that and the reanimated dead are said to inhabit the tree's" joked Flynn.

"Relax" Vaike said confirming Flynn was being half serious. "While some of the necromancer's failures still lurk in the forest, they are mere shells and easy to avoid or defeat. That's why he needs the transformation. Then he could have countless corpses roam freely throughout those dark shadows."

The western lands were as barren and empty as the grass sea. The difference being the flat landscape stretching to the horizon in all directions. Roads crossed through the expanse allowing travellers to keep a true course.

The unobstructed views allowed the companions to flee from the road whenever the twin's keen eyes spotted dust rising from hooves in the distance.

A week passed during this time with the companions hiding away from the roads each evening. Small villages appeared every day or so and caused the group to take long detours in order to remain hidden.

Wells were placed along the road at strategic points, keeping their water skins full and horses satisfied. That was where their luck ran out. Nothing grew or lived in the wastes. Birds of prey circled overhead in the distance, yet not even Vaike's tracking skills could turn up a single mouse.

If not for the horses Baird doubted, they would have even had the strength to travel the distance themselves.

Vaike and Flynn returned from scouting as the others finished eating the first meal they'd had in five days. It wasn't much. A stew made from a small squirrel like creature they found hiding in the trees, and a few wild vegetables.

There was nothing around other than a large walled town and a farmstead. Still more than a week travel from the coast made it impossible for even Flynn to enter the town without unwanted attention.

The debate lasted late into the night until the fire was nothing more than glowing embers. Weighing up the risk of buying supplies and the potential for discovery against the risk of not finding anything to forage and starving.

The discussion was made moot the next morning when they woke to find enough food to fill their saddle bags and aching stomachs.

Flynn was stirring a pot of porridge over the fire when Vaike accusingly demanded to know where the food came from. Thinking Flynn sneaked away during the night and stole it from the town, without the group reaching a consensus.

"I snuck out while the boy was on watch and stole it from the farmstead." "I can't believe you did that, what if you were seen?" Vaike exclaimed in disgust.

"Would've made no difference" shrugged Flynn. "Meaning?" asked Garrett. "Meaning, dead men tell no tales." "There are women, and children there" Vaike raged. "Were" Flynn corrected.

Flynn's admission ended in shock, horror and disgust from the group. Vaike leapt three strides tackling Flynn mid stir, pinning him to the ground at knife point.

"They were innocent, we don't hurt the innocent. The only reason you are still breathing is because you are a valuable asset with a blade. But that value is quickly withering so convince me as to why I shouldn't kill you."

"Firstly no one is innocent. They either have done something that makes them deserve to die or they eventually will. I would've thought someone as old as you would know that." Baird begrudgingly admitted Flynn had a point here.

"Secondly it was the lesser of two evils. We can't enter a town. We can't scavenge enough. We are too weak to fight if we are discovered. The chances of reaching a port town are slim enough without worrying about food. If you're determined to kill the necromancer this was the best chance of reaching him."

Flynn was still pinned but Vaike had lowered the knife. "I understand your motives but did you have to kill them?"

"You and I both know I had no choice. They would've noticed the missing supplies and reported it to the guards by now. This way we hopefully buy a week before they are discovered, and when they finally do, they'll think it was a large group of bandits. I took all the food, valuables and freed the horses. That way the place is empty except for corpses."

"If it makes you feel any better" Flynn continued, sitting up now that Vaike had released him. "They all died quickly in their sleeps before I brutalized them to make it look convincing." "You mean you raped a corpse" Garrett cried in disgust.

"I thought we established this already" Flynn replied exasperated. "I don't rape because it is too much effort. But yes, I made it look like they had been ravaged. Now who's hungry?"

Baird shook his head in amazement. Flynn hadn't let go of the spoon during the whole incident. Even at knife point he remained perfectly calm. He should be used to it by now but Flynn's fearlessness and indifference to death still amazed him.

By mid-morning they reached the farmstead. Tendrils of white smoke drifted skyward from the smouldering remnants of the barn. Three corpses hung from ropes draped around the branch of a large oak tree out front. With a fourth, the father Baird assumed. Tied in a kneeling position metres away, decapitated head on the ground beside him with open eyes staring blankly skywards.

The scene caused several to feel remorse and guilt about the gratitude they felt towards Flynn as they filled their empty bellies that morning.

Despite everyone acting civil to each other, Baird could see rifts forming between members of the group. Primarily between Vaike and Flynn.

Chapter 6

THE WESTERN LANDS

The pliers clanged against the steel bench, missing the leather pouch unrolled beside it. One of his nameless scooped it up placing it in the pouch containing the rest of the tools as Olaf wiped the grime off his hands.

Blacks fortitude surprised him. Now a dishevelled wreck slouched in a chair. Teeth missing, gums now a bloody mess. An ear cut off, broken fingers, burnt feet even branded by a hot iron. Yet nothing. If it wasn't for his lieutenants squealing like pigs, he would've thought Black truly knew nothing.

Not that he expected Black to give him anything Olaf thought as two more masked nameless entered the room and dragged the broken figure of a man from the cold cell.

"Should we resume questioning later my lord?" Wearing black robes and identical masks there was no way to distinguish between them. Hence nameless. Still if he is the one remaining behind, he is in charge. "No point. If a man is going to speak, he does it after the first tooth is pulled" Olaf answered holding an incisor up to the flickering light of a torch.

"You should know this first hand." "I do sire. I was just hoping to start on his finger nails." A wicked grin tugged at the corners of Olaf's face. This is just what he wants out his torturers, a love of what they do. "He's all yours. Kill him if you want, I don't need him anymore."

"Thank you, my lord. We might cut of his dick and force feed it to him." Joking or not Olaf couldn't care as he left the dark dungeon of the fortress.

Leaving Voldengird, they arrived at the fortress three days ago. Signs of a large-scale battle evident everywhere. Mostly in how few men stood guard atop the now destroyed wall.

He didn't learn much. The twins were here with the boy and Twin blade. They helped save the fortress, something he should be grateful for he supposes. They then set out heading west using his Wolves Sigil to gain passage.

Not much he can do now except hope they survive and wait for them to return back this way. When they do, he'll be ready.

❧

They journeyed north, heading for the coast. Avoiding the road as often as able they journeyed through what little woodlands there were. More than once they found themselves cutting through fields and farms.

Vaike had to shoot a dog that chased them across one property. Flynn scratched Sterben behind the ears smiling as Vaike retrieved his arrow and slashed up the dog, making it look like a wild animal.

"The worlds not so black and white, now is it." "It was just a dog." Vaike directed at Flynn. "And mine was five peasants." Baird thought better of asking after the missing body.

"You make it sound like there is no difference." "Is there? They were both lesser beasts" "How can you think so little of humans when you yourself are one?" "How can you think so highly of them. You've lived long enough to know better."

Flynn and Vaike stared each other down as Flynn continued. "We're mortal. Lack the hardiness of dwarves or the wisdom of elves. We wage war against each other over petty differences. We kill each other over gold. We breed like rabbits, spreading out destroying everything in our path. We are a complete write off as a species yet somehow we continue to thrive."

Even Baird had to admit he raised some valid points. "So, is that why you kill so senselessly then?" Vaike asked sarcastically. "No. Like you said I'm human. I'll kill for gold. For survival. For women. For slights. For gain or even for boredom. I'm no different from any other human except I have no delusions about what I am."

"What about the greater good?" Vashti asked. The most words she'd spoken since seeing the farm three days ago. "Since you joined us all those months ago everybody you've killed. Human or goblin. Innocent or not has been for the greater good."

"I joined you to seek wealth in the mines. I stayed for self-preservation, in preventing Maroxis taking over Thaldesa."

"You can lie to yourself but we can all see the truth. You forfeited your wealth to Griff. Maroxis is defanged. He can't take over until long after you're dead. Yet here you are why? The greater good."

"Shit. Your right." Everyone laughed at this, even Vaike. It seemed it hadn't occurred to Flynn that he was working for others benefit. "It's not funny you guys. I'm going to have to massacre a whole village now just to get my reputation back." Well that killed the mood with the chuckles dying down. Fearing that it wasn't a complete joke.

❧

Flynn breathed deeply, enjoying the salty tang of the sea breeze. They had been travelling more openly on the roads the last few days. This close to the ocean they can pass off as sailors and merchants. Provided the twins cover their ears.

Now that everyone was well fed, they resumed Baird's training. Miraculously having improved greatly, both with sword and fists. A full-scale battle seemed to be the motivation or experience he required.

The wooden buildings of Dernst came into view, the dark blue ocean stretching past the horizon behind. A port town. A pirate town. Breathing deeply again, Flynn savoured the smells. "Feels like home."

❧

'Anyplace that Flynn feels at home is no where they should linger' Baird thought. Walking down the main road, street full of puddles and smelling strongly of piss. Duraa was a civilised trading port in comparison to this dive.

Barely noon and fights spilled from taverns into the street. Whores applied their trade in the open and more than one body lay in the dirt. Whether dead or passed out made no difference, as passer-by's stepped over their limp forms. Coins adorned the hair of the town's worst offenders.

A drunken occupant staggered from a tavern, mug in hand and bumped into Flynn as he walked beside Sterben. An incoherent muttered apology or curse, Baird wasn't sure which passed his lips. It came as no surprise when Flynn flattened him. One punch left him sprawled on the ground. Impressively Flynn now held the mug of grog that he downed in a single swig.

"We'd be better off sleeping outside the city at this rate" Vaike said, nose turned up to the stench. "Hardly. It's safer to play the game. Intimidate them into respect" Flynn said waving to a pair of particularly vocal whores.

"All newcomers need to pay the toll." A smaller man, Flynn's height stood before them. Tanned forearms and calloused hands showed outside the dirty fraying cloak he wore. "It's ten coppers per person. Five for a horse." "Ninety coppers that's ridiculous." Baird shouted after a brief delay as he worked it out in his head. Flynn shot him a look, warning him to be quiet.

"It is what it is boy" he continued as four large muscular enforcers stood behind him. "I'm feeling generous so I'll tell you what. If you can't afford it the girls can work it off. One night with the both of them sounds reasonable doesn't it." He stood grinning as his muscle-bound goons cracked their knuckles or flashed well-worn knives.

It was no surprise that Flynn was the one to respond. 'In fact, it was probably the cheeky grin that enraged him' Baird thought as Flynn handed him Sterben's reigns, looking the offender in the eyes.

"How about a new offer. Ninety gold coins." "What. That's even more." "Perhaps I wasn't clear enough" Flynn continued approaching the leader as he spoke. "Ninety gold coins and you can leave with your teeth in your head."

"You're not serious" he laughed. "Three men, two women and a boy against the five off us. Not to mention my lads are all bigger than the lot off you." It was true Baird had to admit. The closer Flynn walked the more he seemed to pale in stature next to those hulking brutes.

"Man, you must suck at counting even worse than the runt." Flynn said insulting the leader as he stood mere feet from them. "You're bluffing" he replied after a moment's hesitation.

"One." "One what" he asked Flynn now confused and agitated. "One on five." The five Clutched their sides and laughed uproariously. "I like you. After my boys rough you up a bit, I might have some work for you."

"Can't say I didn't warn you."

"Four, three, two, one and zero." Flynn counted down as he dispatched each assailant with ease. Saving the leader for last whom he stomped on repeatedly, knocking out all but a few teeth.

"What happened to respect?" Garrett sarcastically asked. "Fear works too." Flynn replied in his usual emotionless flat tone, somehow making the simple statement sound much worse.

They visited four inns' before Vaike finally agreed to spend the night. The first three were full of drunken patrons, broken tables and scantily dressed women. No surprise Flynn favoured them.

The foreshore inn it was called and the keeper gave them the attic room. Five beds stood along the back wall with an extra cot brought up for Baird. The side wall had a large window overlooking the ocean, which Vashti slid open. The sound of waves crashing against the rocky shore and the salty tang of the ocean filled the room.

"Make sure to take care of our horses" Flynn said tossing a bag of coins to the young boy who showed them the room. "No worries mister ill feed them meself."

"And boy, that includes the tac and saddles." Removing the cloth from his head, Flynn let the concealed coins fall free from their bonds. The boy nodded understandingly and backed out the room.

"What was that about?" asked Baird. "My guess. To keep our horses and gear from getting stolen" Vaike answered. "What I'm unsure on was why you showed him your hair?" "Same reason. That boy would've probably left them alone after he was paid but now, he'll get the word out. No one will touch the horses for fear of me."

❧

Baird strolled through the tavern's front door, old timber creaking closed on rusted hinges. Eyes adjusting to the dimly lit room he noticed Garrett joined by Ailish and the twins sitting at the table furthest from the door. Several empty mugs lay scattered across the worn table.

"How was hanging out with Flynn" Garrett smirked guessing how well it went. "About as well as expected." "Well drink up" Vaike said pushing a full mug towards him. "The beers are on Flynn tonight."

❦

'You try to do something nice for people and this is how they thank you.' After handing over most of the coins he looted from those thugs he grabbed Baird and took him out for a night of fun. The first stop was the nearest brothel where he immediately got the man maker for the runt. Flynn then chose the two girls with the biggest tits and followed Baird to the room next door.

Not five minutes later she stood in his room saying the boy had left, running away from the act. It wasn't like she was the worst man maker he'd seen or taken virgin boys too. Middle aged with dark hair and lightly tanned skin that was starting to wrinkle. Tits that sagged probably from three or four kids sucking them dry. But still he had already paid so she joined in.

He was disappointed in Baird. Not that he was too scared to have sex plenty of young kids ran away from their first time. No. He was disappointed because the real fun hasn't even started yet. There are a few pubs frequented by pirates to visit. Boxing matches, gambling and public indecency still to experience.

❦

They woke late the next morning. All experiencing upset stomachs and ringing heads from last night. An empty unslept in bed stood closest to the door. Flynn it seems never came back last night.

Garrett and Baird visited the docks after eating what little breakfast they could stomach. Relying on ships to survive all trade was done at the port and they needed more supplies.

With Dernst being a port town Baird expected fish to be the main export much like Crows perch. While the heavy scent of fish was prevalent the source was lacking. Fisherman seem to avoid the port, either by choice or mandated by pirate's Baird was unsure. Merchants from near and far pushed their wares in place of the fisherman, risking the dangers in favour of profits.

Spices, silks, perfumes, passed from pirate to merchant. Traded for barrels of wine and coin. Alcohol seemed to be the preferred commodity for pirates. 'No surprise there' thought Baird.

After weaving their way amongst stands haphazardly placed in an attempt to screw over the other merchants they found what they sought. A smaller vendor probably from a nearby town seeking profit and supplies for their own needs.

When they returned to the inn, they found the others nursing a drink at the same table from last night. "Flynn's right it does help" Vaike said while the girls just nodded a silent agreement. "How'd you go?"

"Well the picking was slim so we got mostly oats and dried fish" Baird answered while Garrett got two more mugs. "Well it beats starving." "We heard something interesting while we were at the docks" Garrett said returning with the cheap ale.

"The sailors were talking about a newcomer who beat all the top fighters in town. Apparently, a huge fight is planned for tonight between the current champion and the new guy."

"And we think this new guy is Flynn?" asked Vaike. "Well if the stories are to be believed he took down three fighters at once. So yeah it's a safe bet."

"So, what do we do then?" "Nothing. Flynn knows we leave first thing tomorrow. He will be back by then." Baird wasn't so sure.

❧

A dry mouth, evidence of heavy drinking the previous night. Hard timber floor beneath his back, the scent of damp spots in the room and the sound of lapping water. 'Oh fuck' he thought opening his eyes.

Flynn's suspicions were correct. He was aboard a ship. Finding his feet, he took in his surroundings. He was in the ships hold and they weren't underway. 'Well that's a start' he thought opening the nearest barrel and grabbing some dried fruit from inside.

The upper decks revealed the ship was still tied up alongside. Bumping into the first mate on the gangway he learnt they were sailing today but decided to wait until after his fight tonight. 'What fight?'

His confusion passed when the first mate filled him in on last night's details. After he stopped laughing anyway.

He did more than watch last night, beating most of the city's fighters in a single night. He is apparently scheduled to fight the champion tonight. The champion who happens to be the blacksmith in the next town inland hence why he wasn't there last night. The captain, who won big betting on Flynn last night invited him over to celebrate.

The captain himself was still passed out, but considering he'd blacked out forgetting the entire previous night Flynn was still impressed with his tolerance.

He disembarked the ship saying he had best prepare for the fight. Walking down the docks Flynn saw Garrett and Baird talking with traders and merchants. Still disappointed in the kid he walked past them into the nearest brothel. He does need to prepare after all.

Chapter 7

THE DARK TOWER

Flynn didn't return at all yesterday. Absent through dinner and even missing out on the group of sailors who entered singing drunken songs. Vaike didn't like the glares he received during breakfast that morning. Like it's his fault, Flynn is capable of making his own decisions.

"So, what do we do?" Garett asked as they gathered up their belongings getting ready to leave. "Do we wait or look for him?"

Walking down stairs in a sullen silence Vaike thought it over. 'Flynn could be passed out in any brothel in the city. He could be on a ship in harbour or out at sea. Waiting at the main gates or lying dead in the dirt somewhere. Being honest that last one was really unlikely.'

"Well" Garrett demanded as they reached the inn's front door.

"The morning sun shone directly into their faces. Blinking as their eyes adjusted to the harsh light. Six horses stood before them, all saddled and ready to depart with Sterben at the rear.

"About time. I was beginning to think I had the wrong day." Flynn said sounding irritated as he slumped against the wall of the inn. Arms folded across his chest, fresh cuts on his knuckles. Dark rings forming under his eyes suggesting he hadn't slept the last few days and the scent of grog and sweat wafting off him.

Stepping of the wall he placed a foot on Sterben's stirrup. "We'll are we heading.." Baird flinched at the sound Vashti's hand made as it struck Flynn flush on the face. He could've stopped it or dodged it. But he just stood still as her hand struck his left cheek.

"You're not a pirate anymore. Your behaviour was completely unacceptable. Baird isn't anything like you." "You're right" Flynn said blood dripping from a freshly cut lip as a red hand print already bloomed across his face. "For better or worse the runt is nothing like any of us. But I am forever a child of the sea. So, my drinking, my fighting and killing. Its forever a part of who I am."

Vaike was saved from having to answer Garrett and the often unpleasant task of reprimanding Flynn. But taking on the leadership role once again he mounted and set off, the others in tow.

Hands rested on hilts as they rode out of the town. Heads turned and eyes followed them as they passed weather worn thresholds of buildings and not in a good way. It felt like they were seconds away from being run out of town.

Tension was thick in the air making it difficult to even breathe. Only Flynn, carefree as usual seemed unperturbed by the local's mood or the displeased looks of his companions. In fact, he was already swigging from a wineskin.

Only once the town disappeared from view did they relax. Baird releasing a deep breath, he breathed freely once more.

"Well that was a fun stop. We should do that again." Baird groaned. 'How could Flynn even begin to think that was fun.'

"How could you possible think that was fun. I'm surprised they didn't attack us on the way out?" Garrett asked tired of Flynn's shit it seemed.

"What wasn't fun about it. There was women and booze in plenty. People died and I won a ton of money. As for the warm farewells. They were just upset because they lost a lot of money betting against me last night." Flynn answered before taking another long drink.

They continued training again that night. Baird had improved by leaps and bounds these last few weeks. While he still couldn't beat Vaike or Flynn he loses less and manages to score a few hits against the others.

Sitting around the fire Vaike recapped on the sparring session. He always found something for him to improve on. Shift his foot less before striking, follow through more on some attacks and less on others. But considering he and Flynn continually pick out flaws and openings in each other's own efforts Baird doubted you ever stopped improving.

Afterwards Baird asked Flynn if he could beat three guys at once, why would people bet against him. So began his nights lecture on gambling and odds.

While the champion was undefeated, Flynn was the favourite to win making his payout less. As such some bet against him chasing the bigger prize. Most people lost money betting on the duration or how it would finish. Once again greater risk for greater reward.

The fight lasting more than five minutes or ending in a submission was the most common choice. Killing the champion with a single kick to the head crushed everyone's hopes. Only the captain who won big the first night bet on Flynn coming out on top.

"What was the champion like?" Baird asked trying to not sound interested. "Big, broad shoulders and wide chest. Rough calloused fingers, thick like sausages and a thick bushy beard. Which was odd seeing as most people shave their beards before entering the ring. It gives opponents something to grab hold of. Not a wise move in a brawl. Either way he was your typical blacksmith" Flynn shrugged indifferently.

"Do you perhaps think the townsfolk were more pissed at you for killing the town's blacksmith rather than costing them money? Garrett sarcastically asked.

"Maybe." Flynn answered. "But sailors don't care for blacksmiths, only carpenters and shipwrights so I doubt it.

So, ask yourself. Do you think they care more about a useless trade or money that can purchase what they need?" Flynn asked rhetorically.

Vaike didn't allow any hunting or scavenging of food as they journeyed north. The dead forest was two weeks travel away with Maroxis fortress situated on the far side. The corruption of those lands was likely to have spread so they will eat whatever rations they bought in town. They have six weeks' worth with them, the trouble will he fresh water.

After a week of sleeping on the ground outside and Baird was back to finding himself on the ground repeatedly of an evening. Nose throbbing from another of Flynn's punches Baird gingerly felt the bone. 'Not broken. Well that's a relief' he sighed standing up and dusting off his trousers. It had been months since he suffered worse than a cut lip or eyebrow but try as he might he can't stay on his feet after three punches.

"There is nothing left to gain from training with me runt. I'll still spar with the sword when mister stick up his arse needs it." Flynn informed him, jerking his head towards Vaike with the last part. "But as for bare knuckle. You now need real world experience and different opponents."

"But I've been stuck on three punches for months. I haven't improved" Baird stammered. "Is that what you think?" Flynn laughed uproariously, like it was the funniest joke he'd ever heard. "I lied to you kid, that very first session. I have been holding back, gradually increasing my strength so as to not kill you."

'Thinking back on the last few weeks and it actually made sense. No matter how much muscle he put on swinging around Harbinger he always seemed weak against Flynn. Every week stronger than the previous yet he was no closer to overpowering the pirate in a grapple.'

"But if it's your full power shouldn't we train until I'm taking five, ten or even twenty blows?" It was a fair question thought Baird, Flynn however was now in hysterics.

"Now you can take the hits means I would get serious. Increasing the risk of a significant injury." Flynn answered catching his breath. "More importantly you know my fighting style. I don't want you to start developing bad habits from anticipating my moves, leaving yourself open to attacks from other styles."

"You did good kid" Flynn continued now standing beside him and placing a hand on his head. "When I stopped getting trained by Bloodfist I was on two punches and still unconscious not just flat on my arse. It takes something inside you to persevere and survive this training. You should be proud."

He was proud. Even when Flynn returned to his usual gruff self and called him runt, he held his head high and took it not as an insult but a term of endearment.

❧

'Well he finally told him' Vashti mused as she sat oiling her bow. It was obvious to her while tending to Baird's wounds that Flynn had been slowly hitting harder. Her brother the genius he is, probably noticed subtle changes in Flynn's stance or muscle tension to figure it out. But still it's good to see Flynn's heart wasn't totally hardened.

Sweat glistened of his bare chest as he pat Baird's head before walking towards where she sat. Blushing she averted her gaze downward realising she was staring at his exposed mid rift. When she dared a glance up, she could have sworn she saw him grinning as he pulled the stopper out of his wine skin. Winking as their eyes locked, he then drunk deeply from his skin while walking away.

'Was that being friendly or did he notice her staring?' She was starting to get hot under the collar now.

❧

A week after completing Flynn's training they reached the dead forest. An obvious yet apt name considering that is what it was, a dead forest. The grey husks of ancient tree's stood guard, their skeletal fingers interlaced overhead forming a web over the whole forest.

They camped a hundred yards back, Vaike preferring to enter the forest in the morning. Baird couldn't agree more, the sight of those grey trees sent shivers down his back.

❧

He could hear the footsteps as they approached, the scent telling him it was Vashti. "Your early" he said not even turning his head.

She wasn't surprised Flynn new it was her. His senses heightened through years of fighting for his life, plus she wasn't exactly being silent. But here he sat, or slouched more accurately against Sterben's saddle. On watch and completely relaxed like they were miles from danger. It was hours before she had to relieve him for her own watch, she should be sleeping.

"Can't sleep?" he asked as she sat down beside him. "No. The forest gives me the creeps. I feel like it's alive and watching us."

"Here, take this" Flynn said handing over a half full wineskin. "It helps trust me." He said answering her puzzled expression.

She had to cover her mouth to stop from choking after taking a very long draught. "Water?"

"Well yeah what were you expecting." "Well wine." "Seriously. How would I carry that much wine on me?" Flynn laughed.

"I haven't had a drink outside an inn since we met." "But why did you let us think it was wine. We all thought you got drunk every night." "Because no one pays attention to what they say to or around drunks. Plus, it was funny" Flynn added as an afterthought.

Vashti just sat in silence going over every conversation they'd had around the completely sober Flynn. She realised just how smart he was, not just for a human and it was a little intimidating. "Just don't tell the others. I'd hate to ruin the illusion they have of me."

They sat in silence after that, passing the water back and forth staring out at the blackness together.

Vashti awoke when Ailish came to take over the watch. Flynn was right the water somehow worked and she slept. She slept right through her watch while Flynn sat and did both. He was already carrying the saddle over his shoulder slumping away to his bed roll as she realised her watch was done.

It was just as creepy amongst the trees as Baird expected. Everything was dead. Grey trees stood rooted in dry soil free from of mould. Dry leaves littered the ground crumbling underfoot. Brown vines and creepers wrapped around the long dead tree husks.

"Everything's dead" Ailish said, giving voice to the obvious. "Yes, we can see that" Vaike snapped angrily, obviously out of place amongst all the dead trees. 'No, I mean its dead but not rotting. Like it all died yesterday."

She was right. It was like everything was frozen in time at its moment of death, even the air while smelling stale didn't carry the stench of death with it.

"How is this possible" Garrett asked. "Magic obviously." Flynn snapped, his turn to be irate.

"We had best keep our guard up." Vaike said putting an end to the bickering.

They saw a deer, the first living thing they encountered amongst the skeletal trees. How it survived in this waste land was made apparent when a twig snapping underfoot startled the creature causing it to flee. Its left flank was mauled exposing bones and organs.

Baird threw up, and the sound of retching told him he wasn't the only one. "So, the rumours are true. The undead stalk these shadows." Vaike said face deathly pale.

"We had best be careful even if they are only animals I don't much like the idea of meeting an undead wolf or bear." "And if it's human" Baird found himself asking, feeling sick and even more pale then Vaike. "We had best hope we don't have to find that out."

With no discernible road the horses chose their own path, avoiding roots and uneven ground. They lost a full day doubling back trying to avoid a large bog that barred their way.

Even Flynn wasn't crazy enough to suggest trudging through that murky water when they saw the surface churn as something struggled beneath the thick darkness. Man, or beast no one seemed keen to find out but Baird could swear he saw a rotting hand break through the surface for only an instant.

With no leaves overhead they used the sun to guide their way north west. The third day ended with them bursting from the shadows of the dead trees as the sun dropped low in the horizon. To everyone's relief with no one sleeping much the last two nights.

"There it is" Vaike said pointing to the west. "Maroxis tower." Eyes clearing as the sun dropped behind the mountains Baird saw it. Nestled at the base of the tallest mountain with grey smoke curling at its peak, standing alone and proud was their destination.

Chapter 8

THE END, THE BEGINNING

Yawning, Baird stretched out his cramped muscles, enjoying a good night sleep considering what they stood between. His good mood disappearing with dawns first rays of light.

Last night Vaike spoke of the mountain that was actually a volcano filling the sky with grey smoke and ash. The plains they now stood on were called the Ash lands.

Dead forest and now Ash lands. Not creative names but accurate ones. The ground was hard with little vegetation. A thick layer of ash coated everything. A trail of hoof prints followed them, stretching back to the horizon. Disturbing its century long slumber, they rode with the sun at their backs.

"The woods must be full of bodies, how did we miss them?" 'An odd question to be asked out of the blue especially from Flynn' Baird thought.

"The bodies aren't from this battle. This was fought when it was discovered Maroxis was practicing black magic. Three other wizards watched over the four corners of Thaldesa. Fearing him they gathered an army and marched.

"I have never heard of this battle, or of the other wizards" said a puzzled Flynn. "No record of it exists outside of my mother's library. Maybe a copy exists somewhere in a dwarven library lost to time as well.

The four wizards, North, east, south and west were created during the Hallow wars to watch over, guide and protect. The order of four, more commonly called the guiding wind. It didn't even stand for two centuries before the betrayal.

The other three gathered allies when they discovered the goals of their lost brother. Leading an army, they marched through the Borah woods still very much alive and green then. Maroxis won overpowering his brethren.

United they were powerful, but they also believed in peace. Still discovering his new powers, Maroxis couldn't raise the dead at this stage but they were still sufficient to carry the day.

In the passing years, the Borah woods died, the volcano woke and the immortal elves hid in their woods while the long-lived dwarves retreated underground.

Now that he was looking for it, Baird saw the evidence of battle all over. Rusted armour and swords. Axe heads and spears, hafts long since rotten. The ash covering and protecting, stopping the forgotten from fully disappearing Baird thought picking up a skull bleached white by the sun.

"So did the elves fight with the wizards?" Baird asked Vaike as they sat around eating lunch. "No. The elves and dwarves were still recovering from the wounds they suffered during the hallow wars. It was only men, short lived and with even shorter memories who were ready to relive the horrors of war.

❧

Scouting out an entrance is dangerous during the daylight but once darkness falls it was deemed even riskier to stumble around blindly, so while the sun sank low and the shadows were long Vaike and Flynn crept closer.

The encircling stone wall lay a crumbling wreck. Boulders strewn around its base once much larger and flung at the great black stone wall creating the breach that Vaike and Flynn now crept through. Large ballistae sat atop the walls, each fitted with slots for twenty javelins to be fired at once.

A frightening siege weapon that looks like it required magic to fire. Matching the wall they rested on, they too were long neglected.

Defences no longer needed when you can level armies with just a wave of the hand.

Fifty yards across the open field the same black stone stretched to the sky. Not a wall but now a tower. The towers outer wall merged with the mountain, making any estimation of the interiors scale impossible.

Following the exterior wall as it circled to their right, they found the main door. The words, abandon all hope ye who enters, was carved in large letters above the opening. "So, he thinks this is hell" scoffed Flynn. "It comes of arrogant and cliched" Vaike agreed.

Grunting and cursing in foul accents echoed from the dark portal as they crept closer. A solitary goblin stalked into the waning light. No weapon or armour, just a simple loincloth.

With his back to them, he faced the wall as the sound of liquid splattering on stone was heard. A shake of the head from Vaike had Flynn sheathing his knife. They waited around the bend in the wall as the goblin finished its business and returned through the entrance.

They returned from scouting quicker than expected. Bringing good news with them. Getting into the tower was going to be simple, between the breach in the wall and a rusted portcullis that looks like it hasn't moved in centuries they couldn't keep a cow out.

The problems will be once they're inside. With no idea how many goblins are inside or how large the tower is. It could be larger than the dwarf mines or the size of the fort at red cliff. They needed to be prepared to spend a week searching inside the tower if necessary.

A cold breeze flitted down from the north as they rested waiting for the sun to set. The ocean scents missing from the breeze, as Maroxis magic took even that little shard of life as well.

Sneaking in was easy, even with Baird tripping over the loose rocks in the breach. Inside was colder than outside like an invisible barrier separated the two. The air felt heavier and the darkness thicker. Baird froze halfway through, paralyzed by fear he was unable to move.

The twins passed unperturbed by whatever spell affected the humans pinning them in place, except for Flynn. Flynn strode on with the twins without missing a step. The spell ended, either a deterrent to scare weak willed intruders or broken by those who walked through Baird could only guess.

It lasted a heartbeat but felt like hours. Even the vampires scream didn't produce that level of fear in him. Sharing a brief look with Ailish and Garrett they continued on after the others. All asking the same question, how did it not bother Flynn. Was he not afraid, or does he just not understand what it means to fear?

Weapons drawn Baird followed down the dark corridor after the others, stealing silently towards the only source of light. It was a guard room twenty strides from the entrance.

Ten goblins in various stages of inebriation occupied the small room. Some asleep at a table with finger bones and cards scattered about, while others dozed in a corner or nodded off struggling to finish the drink they nursed.

Sneaking past, not much stealth was necessary with all the snoring they crept deeper into the abyss.

Straight. Always heading straight. Vaike would occasionally look inside rooms as they passed by. Others would be ignored completely, "it felt off" is all he would say when this happened.

The stoned floor gradually climbed higher into the mountain, and unlike the perfectly straight tunnels of the dwarves these would twist and bend. Baird had no idea if they still even faced west.

Stairs led up and some passages went down. Vaike stayed straight, exploring with methodical precision.

They found a huge mess hall this way, 'unfortunately' Baird thought. Ten huge tables cut from stone each fifty yards long lined the floor. Light flickered from roaring fires scattered unevenly around the walls and between the tables. Huge oaken doors stood open at the opposite end inviting the inhabitants to dine and seated at the tables were the inhabitants. A horde of goblins. Unlike those in the guard room these goblins were very much awake and very well-armed.

To make matters worse, the passage they followed here stopped at a crumbling staircase that once provided servants access, now it was barley more than a single step at each end. Across the open space stood another door and another ruined staircase similar to the one before them.

Thick oaken supports stretched across the hall. Reaching wall to wall. Large chandeliers thick with cobwebs hung from the rafters, long since they were last lit. The rafters themselves looked in good condition and after hauling himself onto the nearest one Vaike deemed them sturdy.

The blood pounded in his ears as he crawled across the rafter. The coarse-grained fibre of the timber snagging his pants, Baird was glad he had gloves on. The sound the goblins made was deafening, but welcome as it helped mask the sounds made above them. It was relatively dark, but Baird prayed they didn't look up, not positive that he was hidden.

The others all walked, or ran in Flynn's case to minimise that risk but even crawling felt too fast for Baird across the beam no wider than his hand. Only Vashti remained, her and Vaike being the only ones tall enough to reach the beam unaided she stayed behind to boost him up.

After a few minutes but what felt like an eternity Baird dropped onto the opposite landing as Vashti pulled herself up with feline grace. With one fluid motion she swung her legs around hauling herself onto her feet. Smiling like it was the easiest thing in the world she walked across the open space.

Bow slung over her shoulder she followed the path of the other five. Halfway across was a rope passing through the rafter reaching towards the ceiling from the chandelier below. Baird hated that rope having to stand up just to get around. He now hated it even more.

As she stepped around, the bow strung across her back snagged something hidden in the shadows. Pulling her off balance Vashti fell, silent screams from the five companions as they watched on in horror.

It happened in slow motion, her hands grasping around the metal ring of the dusty chandelier below. The relief was temporary as the momentum of her fall continued to the chandelier, swinging it like a pendulum. Candles and centuries of dust rained down upon the goblins below.

Cries of rage, shock and fury rose up from the rabble below as Vashti's added weight caused the rope holding the chandelier to slip. First an inch, then a foot. "Guide him back home". Her last words before the rope gave and she plummeted.

"We have to get down there, we have to save her" Baird screamed. "No. We continue on" Vaike said fear and grief splashed across his face. "But she's not dead."

Jumping free just before crashing to the ground a goblin broke her fall with the heavy chandelier crushing a few more. She now fought sword in hand, against impossible odds.

"I know" Vaike said tears running down his face. "But we must go on, there is nothing we can do for her." Understanding Baird nodded, his voice failing him.

"This is it for me, it's up to you now runt." Baird looked at Flynn as he stood at the precipice looking down. "You will die. You know that" Vaike said, chocking over the lump in his throat. "Aye. But she won't die alone.

In yore deina heura wenn the damonen koomen." "Ruffe on oir bruder und we kombatter les gemesien" Vaike finished for Flynn.

Turning his head to face the others he smiled. Ear to ear, a more genuine smile then Baird thought possible on that scarred face. Then he jumped.

"He smiled" Garrett said astounded. "When death comes be happy because it's the last thing you can do." Vaike said turning his back on his sister and friend. No not friend, brother. He never expected Flynn to know that verse from an elven battle hymn. 'In your darkest hour when the demons come, call on me brother and we will fight them together.'

Baird ran on with gritted teeth. No sounds of pursuit followed them as Vaike led them on at a run, all thoughts of stealth now gone. The looks on his companions faces telling him their thoughts reflected his own. Each time they go after Maroxis they lose someone and this time it was two of their strongest already.

Garrett snatched his shirt collar, choking him as he tried to run past. Lost in thought, Baird didn't notice Vaike stop outside a tunnel listening. "Still no pursuit, I don't like this."

"Is it possible they didn't see us, and think it was only Vas.. Only two of us?" Garrett asked Vaike, unable to say their names. "I think it's more likely this tunnel doesn't connect to the main hall directly, if at all. We had best hope it's not the later" Vaike stated.

Passing rooms full of weapons on shelfs and old tattered blankets on the floor confirmed these tunnels were still used, supposedly as sleeping quarters they guessed. Vaike started taking any path that led up, putting as much distance between the mess hall and them as possible. Even Baird noted the flaw in this plan, unless they found a secret back door, they still needed to escape the way they came.

Up stairways, along passages, down stairs whenever they had no choice, they ran on through the tunnels. Tunnels that gradually became more illuminated. Tunnels that showed more evidence of habitation. Yet other than the occasional rat scurrying into holes upset at having its meal disturbed, they saw no living creatures.

They ran until a wooden door barred their advance. The door was clean and well maintained, the lock giving only when Garrett and Vaike threw their shoulders at it.

Behind the door stairs spiralled up. Stairs cut perfectly into square blocks of black stone. Candles recessed in the wall spaced every six steps. Fourteen steps making a complete revolution. The staircase like the outside looked dwarven. The interior up too now was a mixed assortment of hobbled together craftsmanship by comparison. "It has to be this way" Vaike said leading the charge up.

Was it five minutes or twenty. Two hundred or five hundred candles. A thousand steps? Baird had no idea. Sweat drenched their shirts, making it hard to clench weapons as they raced on. The steps were perfectly spaced apart. Creating the minimum number of steps without placing huge strain on your calves. So, while they burned from exertion, they didn't tremble with exhaustion only fear as they stood before black iron doors.

The doors were twenty feet high with rings of gold the size of cart wheels hanging at head height. More marvels of dwarven engineering for despite their size, the doors opened at a gentle touch. Breath leaving his body as Baird marvelled at the sight.

They stood outside a chamber that was a living representation of the heavens. Moving across the ceiling controlled through some magic. Looking past the stars, the whole chamber was domed with a flat floor. All made from the same perfectly cut black stone. The chamber however was empty save for a stone desk covered in books, parchment and laughter.

The room was filled with blinding light as the heavens changed from night to day. A grating sound echoed around the chamber, originating opposite where they stood. Blinking as their eyes adjusted to the light, Maroxis stood before them. Robed, staff in hand and smiling.

Taking a step forward, Baird was barged aside by Vaike, sword drawn and levelled. The second vampire, he had completely forgotten about it, yet once again Vaike's quick reactions had saved them.

Maroxis confidently retreated, cloak swirling around him as he turned and exited. No order given, yet his meaning was evident. Unlike last time, this vampire wasn't letting himself get stuck in an engagement with Vaike, no matter what he tried. Four on one and completely unfazed as he focused on preventing anyone from giving chase.

Circling back and forth, door always behind and distance never closing. If it wasn't so frustrating Baird would've laughed at the irony. Two vampires each with personalities reflecting their opponents. One brash and impulsive, the other calm and collected. Unfortunately, it's the later one they now faced.

Still the numbers advantage didn't help as everyone could only block with Vaike swooping in to save them every so often. Exhaustion was starting to show on Vaike's face but the vampire was also starting to slow slightly. While only one threat to himself existed, he still had to waste energy not letting them past.

The question was who would reach exhaustion first. The vampire would mean they could continue on or Vaike, in which case they die.

Baird had only blocked two or three blows yet his arms shook from the impact. Flynn or Vaike didn't swing that hard and he suspected it wasn't the vampire's full power. It truly was a foe beyond him.

Through the swapping of positions, Baird now stood between Ailish and Garrett with Vaike slightly in front. It happened so quick he missed it, but the Vampire slipped by Vaike's guard. Vaike fell to his knee as the vampire came straight for Baird.

A loud thunk reverberating in his ears, as Ailish caught the sword with her shield. The strength of the blow allowed the sword to penetrate the steel rim and embed itself between the wooden panels. She was folding under the pressure applied as the sword continued to be pushed down, red blood staining her furs as the sword cut across her left shoulder.

Baird ran. As hard as it was to flee, he knew he had to get to Maroxis. The vampire changed target immediately pulling his sword and shield from Ailish's grip sending her sliding across the floor. Garrett's spear whistled through the air, aimed straight for the back of that bat like face. A slight tilt of the head and the spear flew past clattering to the stone floor.

It bought time for Vaike to tackle the vampire to the floor. A tangle of flailing limbs as they fought for position. Baird was already in full stride, sprinting towards the open door. Garrett hesitating a second before following.

&

Baird raced onwards and up another spiral stair case identical to the previous one. He could hear footsteps following him Garrett or Ailish he supposed, or hoped more accurately. He couldn't see them for the turns and he wasn't slowing to check.

Light was shining around the curve ahead. This staircase significantly shorter than the last. Blinded by daylight, real daylight, Baird burst through an open door. Standing atop the tower, open to the elements and sky.

Parapets encircled the unobstructed view of the ash lands, smoke from the volcano drifting upwards from the mountain ranges to their left. The sun shone almost directly upon them as noon approached. Maroxis leaned against the parapets, arms crossed completely at ease.

Baird drew Harbinger and slowly stepped around to his right. Whatever little effect it might have, it was still better to put the sun in his opponents' eyes not his own, exactly as Vaike taught him.

He hadn't taken more than a few steps before his legs froze. Not just his legs he realised as he became unable to move his upper body and arms. Only his head remained unaffected.

Maroxis hadn't moved an inch, not even so much as a twitch of the finger and his magic had him trapped. Baird was concerned, what kind of magic would require effort.

Maroxis now slowly approached, carefree swagger in each step. Black energy forming at the tip of his staff, energy that felt like darkness. That black bolt of energy shot fourth, aimed straight for his heart as Garrett reached the top.

A wave of his right hand had Garrett thrown backwards, the same spell used on Baird in the cave. Maroxis then rounded on Garrett. Baird crumbled to his knees. Released from the spell that was holding him, Maroxis believing him dead.

By all accounts he should be, that bolt of energy dissipated when it hit Harbinger. If it wasn't for Garrett bursting in distracting him, Maroxis would've just launched another bolt.

Picking up Harbinger, Baird charged in, Maroxis completely oblivious as he continued to throw Garrett around, like a cat toying with a mouse.

Learning his lesson from their last encounter Baird was silent as a jumped, sword swinging in a downwards arc. Maroxis saw him but too late to cast a spell. Blocking with the only thing available his staff.

A black staff made from obsidian steel was no match for the Dwarven masterpiece that was Harbinger, the staff shattering as the swords arc carried the blade downward crashing against the stone.

Stepping back, discarding the useless shards of his staff, maniacal laughter reverberated around them. "It has been far too long since I had a challenge. Do me a favour and don't die too quickly" Maroxis said snapping his fingers.

Instantly his robe was gone, replaced with black armour and sword. Everything was made from the same obsidian steel and unlike the staff, actually made for combat.

❧

Garrett stood panting shoulder to shoulder with Baird who beamed with pride, feeling the confidence felt in him now. Spear laying forgotten on the cold stones of the heaven room, Garrett firmly gripped the sabre gifted to him by Flynn those many moons ago.

Maroxis was no gifted swordsman but with centuries of practice he was competent enough. Harbinger in the hands of Vaike or Flynn and it would be no contest but against him and Baird, exhausted as they were.

His sabre couldn't even mark that obsidian armour that encased Maroxis in a protective shell. The only opening the face, even the joints at the shoulder and elbow couldn't be pierced. Baird managed better with Harbinger leaving a few long thin scratches across the otherwise unblemished chest piece. However, slashes don't cut it, he needed a thrust to go unguarded.

Baird knew it too, so they checked, thrust, parried and stabbed. Most blows swatted away harmlessly with that armoured fist. Maroxis only using his sword anytime Baird attacked. He had a good read on Baird anticipating his feints and thrusts. The longer the fight lasts the worse it looked.

A feinted slash from Garrett drew blood from the necromancer's face. A thin slash across his right cheek, magic already mending the scratch. But a start.

Wiping a single drop of blood from his face. Scowling as he saw the crimson drop of life force on his thumb. A drop of red as vibrant as the sun upon that black background.

❦

Garrett was sprawled on the floor spitting out teeth and blood. Maroxis punching him in the jaw with a gauntleted fist. Struggling to regain his footing, concussion, possible broken jaw and sword nowhere in sight. Baird was now alone.

A steady calm began to set over him, the battle calm Flynn often spoke off. Baird could feel breeze as it wound its way around their feet, cooling him as it found the sweat drenching his exhausted body. Taste the coppery tang of blood in his mouth, see every twitch and muscle move as Maroxis surveyed him. He could feel the blood pulsing in his ears and hear footsteps echoing up the chamber below them.

Hands slick with sweat gripped Harbingers leather wound hilt, its familiar weight comforting, slowing his breathing. Friend or foe approaching, it makes no difference. It will soon be over.

Taking a deep steadying breath his heightened senses noticed one last thing. Snow berries. He could smell snow berries. Grinning he realised it was perfume, Ailish's perfume to be exact.

Putting an exclamation point on his deduction, an axe whistled through the air from somewhere to the left where he knew the door was. Like a lumberjack swinging at a trunk Maroxis batted the axe away, clattering against a parapet. Eyes glancing to the top of the stairs where Ailish knelt against the top step. Gripping her shoulder as fresh blood flowed through her fingers.

❦

Garrett saw his moment and seized it. Maroxis had completely ignored him and was now distracted by Ailish. His Ailish.

His sword hung loosely at his side after deflecting that axe while Baird's was still at the ready. Grinning he offered a silent prayer, thanking muscle memory before jumping and grabbing Maroxis in a bear hug.

Pinning both arms, sword trapped helplessly at his side. Garrett's hands only just clasping behind his back, slick with sweat and body raked with exhaustion he may only be able to hold on for a few seconds.

A few seconds was all Baird needed.

❦

Garrett was playing possum, taking Maroxis by surprise. Giving him one clear shot by sacrificing himself. Baird didn't hesitate. Harbinger plunging through them both. Pulling Harbinger free Garrett collapsed bleeding out as Maroxis fell dead, his heart pierced. No blast of power, no death wail not even a body that disappeared into ash. He just died. Like any mortal.

Chapter 9

THE FALL

'A sudden plunge into a sullen swell, ten thousand fathoms deep.' The wind tore at his clothes as the ground rushed up to meet him. Rolling to break his fall, Flynn stood swords drawn, limbs already flying.

He had no idea how many goblins surrounded them, or if they noticed the others. Eyes only for the woman trapped in the opposite corner.

Dead goblins littered the ground at her feet already but they kept coming, slowly pushing her back. Running through the horde, cutting down some and barging others aside.

"What are you doing? You're supposed to be helping him." Words shouted over the din of battle. "Vaike has him. I have you." "You fool" Vashti screamed at him as her eyes betrayed her, eyes full of hope and gratitude.

Fighting side by side they were a force to be feared. Yet through sheer numbers they were slowly shepherded around the hall. Slipping and stumbling with each step. Fallen weapons, corpses and blood making the floor treacherous. Their feet battling the ground while their arms fought the horde.

Alone neither would've survived. Together they worked as one, protecting each other if they fell. Teamwork, the concept foreign to goblins as they trampled the fallen. Eager to fell the intruders.

Flynn thanked the gods, all of them. Somehow, they stood before the large doors leading clear of the mess hall. At least a hundred goblins lay dead or dying. Panting, covered in sweat and blood the stood tired but otherwise unscathed.

Left, or right? The passage headed both directions both the same black stone illuminated with torches curled out of sight.

Pausing long enough to have a drink and wipe the blood from their hands and blades. Waiting in silence, nothing needing to be said.

Catching their breaths, they decided upon the left path. It being the same direction the others took. Cobweb infested rooms, full of dust and crates, while other rooms completely empty littered the corridor.

Only a few showed signs of recent occupation, but they continued to check each room they passed. No longer concerned about enemies, but not wanting to miss a stairwell. Assuming they aren't hidden.

Standing before the final wooden door, a fire crackling in a hearth could be heard on the other side. The passage ended here, with no other choice they entered. Vashti the first through fell to the floor as something heavy smashed into the wall.

Her elven hearing and reflexes saving her as it missed Flynn's head by inches. A wooden chair flung across the room by a beast of a man who stood opposite them.

"Careful. This is the one who killed Foden" cautioned Vashti. Flynn didn't notice the square tables spaced evenly around the room. Or the wine and ale bottles neatly stacked on shelves behind a bar. He even missed the dead goblins, crushed heads staining the floor with black blood. All he saw was the man who stood before them. "Edward" Flynn snarled. "Come now boy, is that any way to greet your father."

"I haven't seen you in six years." No outstretched arms offering an inviting embrace accompanied those words. Just cold indifference as facts were stated.

"Everyone thought you dead, and now. Now I find you working with that bastard. You've gone against everything you taught me."

"Look out for number one. Or did you forget that lesson. I'm guessing you have considering you're here too." "I signed up for gold. I stayed, for my family" Flynn screamed.

"Family hey. I guess that means you've turned your back on your old family." "You're one to talk" Flynn said removing the sash from his head letting the coins fall free. "You're no longer a pirate." "Would you look at that, you added to your collection since I saw you last. Still not as many as I had before I joined the big guy.”

“Something I’ll make you regret.” The time for words was over, Flynn drew his swords redcoat falling to the floor, as Vashti did the same.

“I’ll do you an honour. For old times’ sake.” Throwing back the black coat draped over his own shoulders, worn in the same fashion as Flynn, revealing the large, worn cudgel hanging from his waste. The same cudgel he never even used to kill Foden.

“Hull breaker. Never thought I’d see it in use again.” “Your life changed when you met me twelve years ago. Mine changed when I met him. Now let’s see who’s changed for the better.”

Flynn grinned. Excitement plainly written on his face for all to see. More excited than crossing blades with Vaike, or testing his mantle against monsters. This is the man who trained him. Who raised him. The person who made him who he was today. The titanic shadow that has loomed over him his entire life. Now was his chance to get out from under it.

Tables splintered under the weight of Edwards blows. The stone walls cracked and chipped whenever that cudgel crashed into it. Dodging was the best choice, even parrying sent shockwaves through your arms making it nearly impossible to grip his swords. Bloodfist it seems held back when training even at the end, just like he did with Baird. Flynn chuckled to himself, noticing the similarities.

He was still no match for their speed, a few deep cuts already marked his legs and left arm. However just like Vashti said months ago, he shows no recognition of the pain and he doesn’t bleed.

❧

This monster is incredible. Incredible strength, evident by his sheer size yet still light on his feet despite that. Someone else raised in combat, someone used to fighting for their survival. He only toyed with them last time and Foden still died. She fared little better.

Even with Flynn this time, they weren’t making much headway. Sweat dripped down her face, making it hard to see. Shoulders bruised from hitting the stone floor to avoid the crushing weight of his blows.

He was tiring. But his blows still carried that incredible strength. He only slowed. Just not enough as he grabbed Flynn by his shirt and tossed him away.

❧

Sliding into the wall, rolling to direct the impact towards his shoulders. Flynn stood groaning rolling his arms. Not broken, but he'll feel that later. This not feeling pain thing was becoming a nuisance. The only reason that he hasn't died yet is the months on the road sobered him up. Forcing him back into the best shape of his life.

Still it will take more. As Edward taught him when trapped. Kick your way out. And if your feet are taken from you, use your hands. When they take your hands, use your head. If your head is bound bite your way free. The message being to never give up.

The memory giving him new life as he tore free the scraps of cloth that used to be his shirt. Throwing it at Edwards face, his other sword lying forgotten under a table somewhere. It was enough for Vashti to attack, swinging for his head.

Whether on instinct or anticipation Edward stepped back out of range, stopping his head from being separated from his body. Left hand grabbing the back rest of a wooden chair as he did. Using the chair as a makeshift club, it swung around in a huge arc whistling through the air.

Jumping in, Flynn took the blow side on. Chair breaking on impact along with his right arm. Crashing into Vashti they both slid across the floor.

"I'm disappointed boy. You've gone soft. There was once a time you would have let her get hit so you could strike me down."

"Caring about others doesn't make you weak" Flynn said through clenched teeth. Pain wracking his body as they both forced themselves to stand. Right arm hanging useless. Broken in several places and a dislocated shoulder. Left arm bleeding heavily from where Vashti's sword cut him as they tumbled together. "Protecting those you care about helps you find hidden strength."

❧

This might be their last chance. It's amazing Flynn is still conscious, let alone standing. Judging by the look on his face and the shaking of his knees, he must be close to passing out from the pain.

But they have a chance. A slow trickle of blood seeping from the small gash she just put on Edwards face below his right eye. Flynn saw it too, steeling himself hunting knife gripped firmly in his left hand. Edward seemed to be the only one oblivious to it.

In perfect unspoken unison. Something she couldn't even perform with her brother without planning they attacked. A last-ditch effort.

Forcing stiff legs to obey her she ran, wrapping behind Flynn attacking from his left. Flynn sluggishly following her lead, as they ran head on. Edward let them come, entering his range. Swinging at Vashti's chest when she was in reach. No need to aim for her head the hit would suffice, crushing her arms and ribs while driving the air from her lungs. One hit and she'd still be as good as dead.

Dropping to her knees, the cudgel whistled over her head. Strands of her hair dragged along by the vortex of trailing air. Flynn used her as a stepping stone and jumped. Knees pinning Edwards arm as his knife plunged into his chest. With a roar he flung Flynn off and stepped forward. It was a few seconds before his cudgel fell to the floor hands going limp.

"I don't believe it. That bastard died."

❦

Edward slumped back in a chair. Knife still imbedded in his chest slowing the bleeding. He was dead it was only a matter of time. The only reason it wasn't now was the words he spoke as Flynn approached. "I was already dead." Vashti stood back giving them space, sensing questions that needed to be voiced.

Flynn just stood and listened as Edward told his story "I had an incurable disease that was destroying my body. The crew left me as I was no longer strong enough to lead. I spent everything, even the coins in my hair trying to escape deaths icy grip.

Nothing worked, eventually I was confined to a bed, trapped, wasting away, without the strength to even move when an old man in a black robe approached me. He promised to cure me. Give me back my old strength, my old body. The chance to sail again in return I had to serve him."

After a coughing fit Edward continued. "True to his word he cured me. Sort of. As you saw my body was suspended, not quite alive but unable to die. Not true immortality but close. When he achieved his goal and became a lich lord, he could grant me true immortality and I could leave his service. Not forced to stay close by so his power could keep me alive."

Flynn stood emotionless as the man who was like a father to him poured out his heart. Although that was probably due to the pain.

"Here" Edward said offering out his hand. A single gold coin, a pirate coin sat inside his pan sized palm. "No matter how desperate I got, I couldn't part with my coin. All I wanted was to sail again.

I've made a mess of my life and failed at a lot of things. I'm glad I did one thing mostly right despite being a horrible father."

"You weren't the best father yes. But you weren't the worst either." Flynn said reaching for the coin. "If you head down that way, you will find your way out." Indicating with his head to a small doorway beside the bar.

"Take care of her Flynn, she's better then you deserve" Edward said gripping the knife with both hands." "I know" Flynn said, barely more than a whisper.

"Goodbye... Father" Smiling, the first genuine smile in his life Edward ripped the knife free.

❧

Despite giving them space, her elven ears still heard most of what the two said. So, she wasn't surprised that Flynn sat in silence as she tended to his wounds as best she could. Processing everything he had just heard was sure to take time, she was here if he wanted to talk.

Still the distraction was good, taking his mind of his physical wounds. The cut caused by her sword was deep and caused some grief. His right shoulder needed to be popped into place and a sling made for his fractured humerus.

❧

Vaike dragged himself up the last few steps. The staircase wall stained with a trail of his blood as he leaned against it for support. Complementing the crimson droplets on the steps from Ailish's shoulder wound.

Injured knee causing him grief and a deep gash on his side that won't stop bleeding. With no idea what he will find at the end or what help he can offer now. But he will share in his companions' fate.

Pleading, grief-stricken crying reached his ears as light filtered from the end of the passage. Baird leaned dazed against the parapets, staring at his own bloody hands. Ailish knelt beside Garrett's prone body lying in a pool of blood, as her own blood flowed freely mixing with Garretts. Applying pressure to a wound on his chest blood leaked between her fingers as the pool of blood continued to grow. A through and through wound, Vaike grimaced.

Hand pressed against his own wound he stumbled over to Baird. Gripping his shoulders shaking vigorously, bringing him back to the moment.

After giving instructions and sending him away, Vaike knelt opposite Ailish. Ripping his own bloodied shirt off and pressing it against the wound.

In the brief glimpse he saw of it, the wound missed his heart and possibly his lung also. Passing cleanly through his shoulder, blood loss was the immediate issue. If his sister was here, or if they had proper supplies, he would've been fine. With what they have to work with he wasn't so sure.

Every second that passed felt like an eternity while they waited for Baird to return. Baird tripped on the top step as he came charging through the door. Barley staying upright and keeping the torches in his hands from falling. Vaike asked for one but Baird brought three. Hopefully he didn't waste too much time getting the extras.

Removing the knife from his belt used for skinning animals he took one torch from Baird. Placing the other torches on the ground, Baird took Vaike's spot next to Ailish, assisting her in applying pressure to the wound.

The torch didn't have much heat. Eventually he piled all three torches together and built a small fire.

The added flames helped heat the knife up, hopefully enough as they lifted up Garretts shirt. Hands now removed blood flowed freely. Ordering the others to pin him down Vaike pressed the heated metal against flesh. Blood sizzled and hissed. Not as much as he hoped but Garrett still kicked and thrashed trying to break contact. The first movement he'd made since Vaike arrived.

Two second bursts is what he was taught. Vaike gave it four, just to be safe. Removing the blade Garrett slumped back down again motionless. It worked. The bleeding stopped on the front. Rolling him onto his front they prepared to seal the remaining wound.

Garrett thrashed even harder this time but once completed he collapsed, passed out. Baird followed his instructions, tending to Ailish and his own wounds. Sacrificing his own shirt for the cause making bandages for them both.

Exhausted and out of danger as their wounds no longer bleed, they enjoyed a hard-earned break. Even though every fibre of his being screamed for him to run back to the mess hall. Praying his sister was fine, he knew he had to remain here. Not that he could do much while he struggles to even walk.

❧

He meant to stay awake and alert instead he fell into a deep sleep. After the strenuous events of the day, and wounds that needed healing exhaustion won out.

Eyes heavy with exhaustion, and stomach light with hunger Vaike awoke. Stars shone down on them as insects buzzed across the night sky.

Despite the hunger gnawing at him or his parched throat, Vaike laid there enjoying the serenity. Flesh burned on his side as he stretched, knee groaning in protest as pain rattled through his whole body.

Memories flooding his mind as his body remembered all their little and major injuries. "Vashti." Jumping to his feet to quickly he staggered light headed, almost collapsing to the ground again.

The others all began to stir from his outburst. As their bodies remembered their own pain, they too remembered their missing friends.

Garrett stirred, temporary relief washing over the others. Helping Garrett to his feet he stood, legs wobbling but supporting his weight.

With Baird supporting Garrett they began the long slow descent. If he wasn't grief stricken or in so much pain Vaike would've laughed at the rag tag group who stood upon deaths door.

They passed through the heavens chamber without lingering. Headless corpse littering the cold stone floor surrounded by a puddle of black blood. Deeper black then the stone of the tower. Head lying a few feet away, dagger buried to its hilt. 'No, not dagger, a broken sword.' Baird casually noticed as he and Garrett gave it and the corpse a wide berth.

Somehow, they found themselves looking down upon a bloodbath. Vaike managed to lead them back to the mess hall, following the same route they took. Food and drink littered the tables, all spilt during the chaos that was Flynn.

Goblins lay dead all over the hall. The floor stained black with blood, barely a stone left uncovered. Some piled high as they climbed over the fallen, others on the tables or trapped between the benches. A few even near the door or in the corners missing limbs.

Baird being the least injured climbed down first. Dragging, lifting and cursing he stacked up the corpses of goblins reducing the drop from the broken stairs. Then one by one, they climbed down into the bone yard.

Look as they might they found no sign of Vashti and Flynn.

⚬

Behind the door was a passageway cut from the earth. Tool marks evident and not neatly cut stones, an obvious addition made after the tower's construction. With weary minds and wounded bodies, they trudged along one uneven step at a time.

Vashti led flaming torch held high, despite Flynn's contesting. Water dripped down the walls, allowing them to refill their water skins and grant a reprieve for their raspy throats.

It was slow going with Flynn's injuries hindering them but eventually they stood in a large natural cavern. Even with the oil braziers lit they couldn't see the far side. Walls stretching into darkness, stalactite's steadily dripping water into the ice-cold lake. Ripples rolling across the flat surface.

Sitting in the lake, only just visible at the edge of the light was a moored ship. Even from this distance Vashti could tell it was huge. With multiple decks and four sails it was twice the size of the rose. "Executioner." Flynn whispered in awe.

Deciding this was the way out Bloodfist spoke off, they boarded the boat tied to the shore and Vashti rowed out into the darkness towards the galleon.

Chapter 10

THE HOMECOMING

Tossing another scrunched up message across the floor Olaf slumped in his heavy oaken chair. Another lord complaining about taxes. There was nothing more expensive than maintaining an army in peace time.

Opening another missive from a southern lord it promptly joins others scattered across the marble floor of his private study. More of the same, poor crop yields, people starving, taxes to high.

His father and grandfather, the cowards they were maintained only small armies. Keeping the lords happy by using the army to build roads during peace time.

Olaf himself used this method as a way of disciplining conquered soldiers in his captured territories. Roads now stretch across his empire, aqueducts stretched across farm lands. With his army preparing to invade the west, then other lands he would prefer they train.

Maybe it was time for a few of his nameless to pay these lords a visit. Worst case he can always replace them and their families.

After acknowledging a knock on his door, a scout stood before him. Dirty from a long ride, probably famished also, the scout brought his report to the king first before seeing to his own needs. Just what Olaf expected of his subordinates.

Turning to leave after delivering his news Olaf just grinned, a solution to his problem has just presented itself. Olaf headed to his war room, ordering Duke Ivan to join him.

The horses all grazed where they left them two days ago. Using Vashti's politicises and salves Ailish dressed everyone's wounds. Supplies were low and Vaike admitting he didn't know how to make more. Using it sparingly, Garrett was the only one to receive liberal amounts off it to prevent infection spreading from his burns.

It was slow going, with them managing a few hours a day in the saddle, and sleeping exuberant amounts at night. The horses remembered the best path through the dead trees. The air now thick with death, but also life. At the reduced pace it still took a nerve wrecking three days to break free.

The first morning after leaving the dead forest Kallen and Sterben were restless and kept gazing to the north, back the way they'd come. Eager to be off and unwilling to wait they headed south while the others buckled up their own saddles. 'A good sign. Only lost, not dead.' Vaike noted. Not wanting to get everyone's hopes up only to crush them he kept the thought to himself.

It was another week before Garrett could spend a full day in the saddle. They had journeyed less than half way, but only Vashti and Flynn's mounts seemed to be in a hurry.

Enjoying dinner around the fire after a full day of riding Baird asked Vaike about his sword. It now had a black hilt and a blood red ruby set in the base. The blade was something between Flynn's katanas and Vaike's Yanyue. Black steel gleamed down the blade with the wave pattern being more jagged. Not obsidian steel like Maroxis used but something unique, like Harbingers star metal.

Ancient and strong the sword was. Where the vampire got it and who made it Vaike had no clue. But the sword proved stronger than what the elven smiths could make, snapping his own in half during their battle. Leaving the broken remains in his foes head he claimed the spoils for himself.

❧

Flynn walked across the timber decks of the replica, of the fake executioner. It wasn't the ship of his childhood. His first real home.

It was a perfect copy complete with broken figurehead, only those who had bled on the original would know the difference. No two trees are exactly the same so no two ships can be identical. A knot in a board, bulge or imperfection in the mast, even joins in the timber. All slight differences.

Nostalgia still present despite it being a different ship. Vashti was awestruck by the sheer size of her. "She can hold near two hundred souls when not overburdened with cargo. An experienced skeleton crew of fifteen can sail her but thirty-five or so is more ideal."

"Well it begs the obvious question. How do we sail her then?" Vashti asked. "Well how did Edward sail her?" Flynn mused.

"You're not the captain" cried a voice from up the main mast. In response to the cry feet could be heard charging up the wooden steps below deck quickly followed by the hatch in the centre of the deck being flung open.

People stormed out one after another in varying stages of dress. Thirty or so sailors formed a ring around the wounded companions. "Where is Edward?" One asked, Flynn supposed was the leader.

"Dead by my hand." Flynn answered with as much resolve as he could muster. It was pathetic by his normal standards.

"I'm now the captain" Flynn said adjusting his sling to show his tattoo. "Whatever. So long as we get paid the lads and I don't care who's in charge."

'Mercenaries' Flynn thought. 'That makes this easier. "We'll talk payment later, for now get us underway."

"Fair enough. Your cabins that way" indicating to the room below the tiller. "I'm guessing you're after a rest, I'll come wake you when we reach open water."

Flynn managed a nod then silently trudged of to the cabin, Vashti trailing behind much to his surprise.

The attention to detail continued inside as well. The cabin as Flynn remembered it when Edward was Captain. A large mattress in the corner with a desk in the centre littered with charts and navigational gear. The right wall when you entered was covered in books on various topics including history, language, medicine, wildlife, military tactics and seamanship.

Sitting down on the bed he struggled trying to kick of his boots. "You can go watch you know. These guys are mercenaries not pirates."

"I know, but you're not the only one who needs to sleep." Vashti said helping Flynn with his boots.

"Thank you." "For what?" Vashti asked. "For everything" Flynn answered lying down under the sheets. "For never giving up on me."

"It hasn't been easy but you also haven't given up on us." Blushing Vashti climbed into bed beside the now snoring Flynn, unsure if he even heard her reply.

❧

Garrett developed a fever keeping him bed ridden. Vaike was unsure if it was a result of his wounds or burns. They had been healing fine and after inspecting the healing skin it didn't appear infected. Without his sister's expertise they made do as best they could. Ailish playing healer in Vashti's stead.

Through the exhaustion and stress of their journey, compounded with injuries and healing it seemed Garretts body had reached its limit. Vaike couldn't blame him, they were all on their last legs.

A day of rest worked its magic with Garrett's fever breaking and everyone feeling reenergized.

Three days later the wooden buildings of Dernst broke above the horizon. The same weather worn dirty buildings, housing the same misfits they did a month ago. But now that they are passing on their way home it felt less dejected.

It was late in the day with the sun close to setting, so Vaike led them on a bee line straight to the Foreshore inn.

The owner remembered them giving them the same attic room, with the same five beds and the window overlooking the ocean. The same young boy brought some food up to their room and promised to watch the horses after asking after Flynn.

Thinking on his feet Vaike explained he was exploring and will be by later but he appreciates the continued effort. Tossing a few coins to the boy he hurried away excited.

While the others enjoyed a few mugs of ale in the common room downstairs Vaike sat alone in silence. Planning their next step. 'Truth be told, he missed Flynn.

Despite their difference he was good to bounce ideas off. Garrett could only help so much. He had travelled a lot yes, but he lacked the leadership skills of Flynn.

Even Vashti usually followed his lead without too much question, it was nice to have someone to fight with and call him out on every decision. Well most of the time anyway' Vaike grinned standing up and heading down stairs. If he can't make a decision his way, he'll try Flynn's way and get drunk. What's the worst that could happen.

With the dawn came no new brainstorms other than do the trip to the blood cliffs in reverse. Well that and a ringing headache. With a dry mouth Vaike headed out taking only Baird with him since he knew the ports better than he did. Garrett and Ailish still slept deeply when they left. Both smelling strongly of alcohol.

A bearded man greeted them at the base of the stairs. He was seated at the table closest to them facing the stairs. Normally the worst seat in the place, unless you were waiting for someone. He was eating a plate of sausages and eggs, drinking what Vaike guessed was ale. Draped over the back of his chair was a brown leather jacket with large brass buttons and brass epaulette's.

He introduced himself as Benni, captain of the cargo ship, Gilded Gull and pointed at the empty seats opposite him. Benni got two more plates and mugs brought over. Baird feverously dug into his own plate, Vaike looking at his own with distaste.

Reaching for his mug instead and drinking deeply. Benni grinned before speaking. "The boy brought me a message last night that you had finally arrived. Klein was right that you would stay at the same inn. Only arriving later then he guessed."

"Klein isn't with us any longer" Baird spat out through a mouthful of egg. "He said that was a possibility. Well no matter, so does that mean there are five of you now?"

"You seem to know an awful lot about our group." "You must be Vaike then" Benni answered. "Klein said you were uptight, and that must be the boy. He didn't have anything flattering to say about him either.

Vaike's hand gripped the handle of his knife concealed under the table, wishing they hadn't left their swords upstairs. "Now there is no need for that" Benni said noticing Baird follow Vaike's lead with less subtlety.

"I'm a friend, I'm just guessing Klein didn't fill you in on his plan." "Klein's not his real name. If you didn't know that then I won't trust you" Vaike answered standing up from the table. They were halfway across the common room when Benni spoke. "I may not know his real name but I know he is the pirate captain, Twin blade." Vaike and Baird stopped in their tracks.

The three now sat in the captain's quarters aboard the Gilded Gull, a three masted Barque. Something that meant nothing to any of them now that Flynn was gone. Benni told them how he made a fortune a few weeks back betting on twin blade, enough so that he could retire. We had one last shipment to take to Cruzwigg, setting sail the same day they set off. As a favour to Klein, he agreed to take them all to Haven. The port town north of the Blood cliffs."

Ailish's face burned red when Vaike and Baird entered the room after making plans to depart. Both her and Garrett were awake but hadn't ventured downstairs yet. Sitting down in a corner of the common room Vaike filled them in while they ate lunch. Not having to ride all the way was great news that came as much needed relief. Especially since the arse was wearing thin on everyone's clothes. Spirits high they enjoyed an evening of drinking and merriment, Vaike even participating. The journeys end in sight.

The next day, four people and six horses boarded the Gull, setting sail for home.

❦

Waves crashed over the bow. Water spray glistened across the timber deck, it's salty tang mixing with the sweat rolling down his bare back. The ship might look like the Executioner but she handled nothing like the original.

Faster than the original yes, but Flynn likened steering her to leading a three-legged bull. Making her faster ruined the balance and made her harder to control. With the helmsman fighting the rudder in a never-ending struggle for dominance while at full mast.

Still the challenge was exhilarating and they made good time. Vashti proved a quick study, learning the ropes quicker than any of the others did on the rose, even having a go controlling the tiller arm at the wheel.

Vashti loved it, smiling ear to ear as she climbed the masts or shouted orders from the tiller flat. Even taking command at times, giving orders to Flynn. Something she found greatly satisfying.

At her request they sailed further north than they needed to. They sailed until the birds stopped keeping them company and giant sea creatures replaced them as companions.

A giant fish that blew water from a hole in its head greeted them one morning and followed them the entire day. A whale Flynn called it. A peaceful and harmless creature. Unless you hit it or it breaches on your ship.

After a month of enjoying the feeling of euphoria from complete freedom, Vashti felt it was time to head home. Flynn agreed plotting a course to the mainland.

❦

Haven was unlike any port they had visited yet. With soldiers patrolling the wharves and checking the cargo manifests of every merchant. Banners flapping in the morning breeze depicted a howling wolf on a field of black and red. Evidence of Olaf's control of the town.

With a bag of coins passing hands between Benni and a guard they disembarked unchallenged. Saddle bags full of fresh food and new clothes they rode out of Haven, heads high.

It was a week's journey north east to reach Vaike's home traveling on the highway as it circumvented the grass sea. After three days the road turned eastward travelling towards Gism and the cross roads.

Here Vaike led them north across open fields and plains, spotting the Sea wall to the east early the next morning. Giant cliffs that the waves crashed upon and the occasional unfortunate ship. The cliffs follow the coast right through to the northern border of the forest.

As the sun set on the fourth day, trees began replacing the small shrubs and bushes of the previous days.

Atop a hill eating lunch the next day Baird looked upon the southern end of the Nibban forest, Vaike's home. His elven eyes spotted hours ago but now the three humans eyed it.

Entering the forest mid-afternoon they followed Vaike down ancient, overgrown trails as the trees surrounded them on all sides. Vaike lit three fires that night, surrounding their camp in a ring of light and warmth.

Ghasps being the least of their concern in the southern portions of the forest. With his mother's city and influence in the northern section the shadows and darkness were strongest here.

When he asked why they don't hunt and kill the creatures, Vaike only laughed. Saying some of the nastier creatures can't die while others are too dangerous to hunt unless they leave their lairs. Besides they work wonders scaring away humans who venture in to deep trying to cut down the older trees.

Baird slept soundly, not even noticing the noises made in the darkness just outside the firelight. In the morning Vaike showed him the trails made by some creature. Footprints not of a human or any animal Baird new.

It was like a wolf's paw only two or three times larger but then stretched back to a heel, long like a human. A Lycanthrope, a humanoid wolf, the origin for the stories about werewolves.

The forest grew denser the further north they journeyed. With some areas they passed appearing to swallow what little light penetrated the leaf ceiling. Vaike stayed well clear of these areas, saying they are the lairs of dangerous shadows.

Three days they journeyed through the thick undergrowth of the ancient woods. The horses picking the best routes along long forgotten paths. Proceeding at a leisurely pace, potential dangers now existing behind them.

Stopping for lunch alongside a flowing river, Aniteena. The same river they reached months before when fleeing the vampires. At Vaike's suggestion they sampled the water. It was unlike anything Baird had ever tasted. Fresh and pure like the streams flowing from the Veluca mountains, but also sweet.

They all drank deeply as Vaike stood by and smiled. They camped beside the river that day soothing tired feet in its cool waters. No one even considered bathing in it, not wanting to destroy its purity.

❧

While they relaxed a doe approached the bank with her fowl in tow. Ailish mere feet away watched on as these creatures were completely unperturbed by their presence. Weather they knew no threat humans posed to their kind or Vaike's presence soothed them, she didn't know.

The doe seemed more curious of her than drinking its fill, choosing to sniff her side instead. Satisfied the fowl curled up on her lap, its mother walking away to graze completely at peace.

"They are comfortable around elves the same way sheep and cows are for you." Vaike said in response to her look. "They are raised with us as a constant presence the exception being, they're wild. They know few predators and will flee them. Humans are unknown to them, but obviously they don't think of you as a threat."

Smiling, happier than she'd been since the destruction of her home she stroked the head of the sleeping fowl.

❧

The doe slept snuggled tight with Ailish that night, its mother disappearing from the camp during the night before returning at dawn with several more deer including a large white buck with horns four feet long.

"A rare treat indeed." Vaike said before sweeping into an exaggerated bow, rising only when the buck stooped its head.

"I present to you, the King of the forest." Vaike said as Baird and the others bowed low also. While bowed the fowl hoped over bleating, joining its mother.

At a word from Vaike they stood, the deer's all having disappeared. "He rarely even shows himself to us elves outside of certain festivals."

He has given you permission to come and go throughout the woods as you please, a judgement even my mother recognizes." "How long till we reach your home?" Baird asked.

"This evening if we rush, but I'm planning late tomorrow morning. It's been a long hard journey so we might as well relax. While we can."

'While we can.' Baird didn't like how ominous that sounded. But he trusted Vaike enough not to ask.

❧

It took a week for Flynn to find somewhere without Olaf's ships skulking around where they could land. Halfway between Voldengird and her home, he found a secluded beach. Too shallow to approach with the executioner's draft so the two of them piled into a long boat with what supplies they could take.

The executioner given as payment to the mercenaries who could sell it or turn to piracy for all Flynn cared. Just glad to get off the ship. Despite his love of the water the ship was an insult to his memories, growing up on the original. His father, Edward had to have felt the same.

Flynn rowed the distance after her brief attempt resulted in them spinning in circles. She watched on in silence as his muscles strained with the exertion of each pull of the oars. Calloused hands gripping the handles polished smooth from countless strokes. Broken arm fully healed while they explored the seas.

With a light fog and a waning moon providing little light Flynn snuck the boat towards the shore.

Feet on solid ground for the first time in weeks, Flynn stood panting sweat dripping of his face. Vashti watched as the executioner disappeared over the horizon.

Without a word, Flynn slung his pack over his shoulder and walked away from the beach. With one last look towards the horizon, Vashti followed.

"How do you do it. How do you walk away from the sea?" she asked catching up to Flynn. "You don't.

Some say they outgrow it. But I think the sea beat them, or scared them. Others like your brother never see the beauty in it. But the true children of the sea are forever cursed. As land-based creatures we are lost on land and at home on the sea. It's why all sailors drink and party ashore. To try and fool ourselves."

"And the violence and depravity?" "That's just a pirate's idea of fun" shrugged Flynn.

❦

Baird stared on, awestruck. Words failing him as he took in Vaike's home. The city of the Elves "Zardelfan", an elven name with no translation into the common tongue.

The city was built as one, in harmony with the forest. Structures built around the bases of giant trees with giant roots forming archways. Some living up in the boughs with houses built high up in the branches. Walkways built connecting them to other trees.

"We shape the trees to suit us, and we shape our buildings to suit the trees." Vaike said smiling at the awestruck look on the humans faces. "We all live up in the trees with the ground structures providing the stairways up to the higher levels. The only dwellings on the ground are barracks for scouts and guards. No longer used in times of peace for us. Only a few elves who prefer their isolation stay in them.

Vaike dismounted before a giant archway with a vine of white roses wrapped around it. Letting go of the reins Kjorgen wandered off. "We have no need for a stable here" Vaike said before stepping under the arch.

Dismounting Baird and the others followed along as their horses followed Kjorgen. It was dark behind the archway, following the sound of Vaike's footsteps. After fifty steps or so Baird blinked as they stepped back into sunlight. Having walked through the centre of the tree, they now stood at the base of a staircase, winding around the outside of the ancient tree. Having travelled upwards, the bottom step stood fifteen metres of the ground.

The wooden stairs were attached in a method that was lost on Baird with a few branches shaped into the occasional step. Every step was carved depicting a different image. Some featured scenes of battle or hunting. Animals, dragons, rivers, sunrises each different and masterfully done. A hand rail wound itself around the outside of the steps. Grown Baird decided, gripping a long vine that was as hard as steel.

Sweat ran down Baird's face and his legs burned as he struggled, step after step. He could hear laboured breathing behind him as Ailish and Garrett struggled also. The gap between steps being higher and further apart then the humans were used too. With no kick boards tripping was common place with the guardrail saving them on more than one occasion as they climbed onwards.

Exhausted and out of breath Baird collapsed on the wooden floor. The spiral staircase behind them they now looked upon the elven city. No metal or stone in sight, everything was timber.

Some dwellings were built on higher or lower levels with stairways leading to them. Armed guards blocked their path, withdrawing after welcoming their prince home.

Standing on unsteady legs, Baird followed as Vaike led them deeper into his home city. Leading them to the palace Baird supposed. Elves went about their business all around them. A few offering greetings to Vaike who returned them with a warm smile. With no mention of the humans or Vashti absence.

The elves were all as different from one another as humans were. Longer noses, more pronounced chins. Short, tall, blonde, black, red hair that was straight and long, short and wavy. All of the men missing facial hair like Vaike. Despite the varied appearances Baird couldn't spot an elf that he wouldn't call beautiful.

"Almost there" Vaike said addressing his exhausted companions. Placing his foot on another flight of stairs. With no guard rails on these steps the four walked in the centre of the stairs that narrowed as they climbed. These steps being much shorter and less steep made them manageable and after a few minutes they stood under an open sky.

Surrounded an all sides by the crowns of trees as old as Thaldesa itself, they stood on a plain wooden floor roughly a hundred square feet. Thirteen identical seats placed in a half circle with thirteen elves seated upon them. Each of the thirteen gave off an aura of power and wisdom. None more so then the one seated in the middle who was the first to greet them.

"Welcome visitors, how did you find the ten thousand steps?" "They barely made it. Mother." The last word hanging in the air as Vaike dropped to one knee. Baird dropped to his knee's forehead pressed firmly against the rough timber floor. He could feel Ailish and Garrett kneel likewise.

Chapter 11

THE FIGHT NEVER ENDS

Olaf rode out to join the soldiers he dispatched weeks ago. Duke Ivan riding beside him, the order of one surrounding them both as they journeyed south with two thousand soldiers.

The order was his elite guard. Trained from the time they could walk completely loyal to him and devoid of emotion. The perfect soldiers. Thirty rode with them wearing full plate armour and visored helms. Helmet design and pauldrons identifying rank.

A month ago, he received word of a rebel host marshalling to the east of the Nibban forest. He dispatched three thousand soldiers a fortnight ago as a vanguard with the orders not to engage unless provoked.

⚔

Flynn only knew directions inland via highways, forcing them to take the scenic route. Following Vaike's directions on the rare occasions she actually left the forest made her even worse than Flynn.

The towns they passed through swarmed with soldiers passing through on Olaf's orders, all heading somewhere east. Not looking for recruits or supplies, just looking to blow of some steam before reaching their destination.

To avoid detection, they passed through town portraying a newly married couple travelling south to help an unwell uncle. A convenient story to pass through without question and one Vashti enjoyed.

Playing the doting lover, getting to hug Flynn and share a bed when they spent the night at the local inn. Flynn even avoided the inn's common rooms to prevent fighting with the soldiers.

Wearing hoods or scarves to hide their identities they journeyed through town after town on the main highway south.

❧

'Mother. Then this must be Queen Yisolde.' Her face, almost the mirror image of Vashti's while Vaike's yellow hair fell around her shoulders. Simple white robes that seemed to sparkle adorned her graceful figure.

While the twins looked to be in their young twenties the Queen looked no older than thirty. With no wrinkles or age spots tainting her skin. Only the depth of wisdom and pain in her eyes betrayed her youthful visage.

"We didn't expect you so soon. It's been barely a moon since we learnt of Maroxis demise." The queen said standing. "I have much to tell you mother." "You most certainly do. Like where your sister is?"

Vaike looked up at his mother who stood before him. With a gentle hand under his chin she guided him to his feet. Vaike stood looking down on the queen who came to his shoulder.

"I'm glad to see you again" she said sweeping Vaike into her arms, a mother's embrace.

Pulling apart holding him at arm's length she looked Vaike over. "You need to eat more" she tsked before striding back to her seat.

Seated she told the humans to rise. "Welcome to Zardelfan. Make yourself comfortable, I'll have a guide show you to a room or give you a tour of the city. While the prince debriefs the council and myself."

Baird looked at the other twelve elves for the first time. Eight men and four women all looking young but bearing eyes deep with age. All robed in similar attire as the Queen but in twelve different colours. Some bore scarred faces or wore weapons at their side. Others had perfectly manicured hands and un-calloused palms. A council of warriors and scholars.

Silently and without a discernible order an attendant stood behind them, leading the three humans away.

❧

Vaike stood before the council feeling self-conscious of their stares, of standing all alone. Regardless of how often he has stood in this very spot it still unnerved him.

He recounted the story of their adventure beginning at Voldengird and his meeting with King Olaf in his throne room.

Eyebrows were raised when he reached the Fiddlers green, the point that Flynn joined them. His elders however kept silent as he continued on.

His mother sent for refreshments around the time they reached Reyvadin. Vaike's stomach growled as he watched the council eat bowls of fresh fruit but he continued to recap the journey, unable to eat and talk.

He skipped the part on the sea voyage to the maw when he threw up several times. His sister was even unaware of this, something he wished to keep from Flynn.

When Vaike spoke of Maroxis fleeing in the Tower of heaven after Baird cut down his ally a few elders started. At a wave from the Queen they sank further into their seats, questions will come later.

The air cooled as he spoke of them reaching the dead forest. Like he did, his own home also rejected the name of that cursed place. Vaike swears he saw tears shine on his mother's eyes when he spoke of Vashti falling and Flynn following after.

By the time Vaike finished the story hurriedly brushing over the return journey the sky was ablaze with stars as evening had set in.

He found his way to where his companions were, his mother having dismissed him after a few questions so the council could discuss what they had heard. After his mother promised to see him tomorrow, no doubt to discuss Vashti.

❧

True to her word his mother stopped by the next morning while the four of them ate breakfast. Vaike preferring to stay with the humans rather than alone in his own room.

To his surprise his mother didn't ask about his sister. Rather informing them that Olaf's troops were on the move, preparing to engage the rebel force just to the east. "So, they came" Garrett said looking towards Ailish, only Baird was as shocked as he was.

"It was Flynn's idea after our little incident in Koyake. Guessing it was Olaf after Harbinger he suggested we contact some of our friends since Baird would likely need an army to deal with the king. We messaged mercenaries, former pirates, other tribes in the Veluca mountains and even the nomads from the Sulthard desert, Foden's people."

"Yes, we surmised as much" his mother answered. "They await their commanders and king" she continued gesturing to the humans. "Your next mission Vaike is to guide them there."

"What about Vashti?" "I wouldn't worry about your sister. Our sentries reported Kallen and a black horse leaving the forest heading north during the night. You'll likely see her soon."

Relief flooded through him as he looked to his friends. "Shall we?"

They lost three days heading in the wrong direction. With the soldiers clearing out of the area the local bandits became emboldened. Tampering with the signposts at a crossroads, leading travellers unbeknownst to an ambush.

Twelve bandits, little more than desperate farmers got more than they bargained on. Flynn cutting them all down while maintaining a bored expression.

This action was regretted when it became apparent that they were lost. A point that Vashti made quite clear. Still the best action was to be continue along the highway towards whatever town lay along it.

Reaching the next inn down the road, they were advised to take the long way rather than double back. They should count their blessings they avoided the bandits that have been praying on travellers.

Maintaining their cover meant they stayed silent about the bandit's current state. They did pay for their room and meals with what coins Flynn found on their corpses.

Feet sore and swollen from weeks of walking they debated staying longer at the inn. Deciding against it, with Vashti wanting to get home they set out after breakfast. Packs once again full of supplies they trudged along on tired feet.

They camped that night under the stars, keeping watch more from habit then necessity. The fire was a pile of glowing embers, having burnt itself out long ago when Flynn stirred.

Vashti scanned the darkness around them, searching for the source of the noise that caused her to grip her sword. The night sky was clear but no moon shone lighting up the night.

Flynn threw some sticks on the fire, kicking it into life. A snorted breath through large flared nostrils answered the roaring flame. The expanding circle of light grew to encompass the silhouette of two horses.

Standing up swords drawn Flynn and Vashti watched for the riders. The closest horse took a whinnying step forward, face encircled in an orange glow from the flames.

"Kallen" Vashti cried dropping her sword and running to embrace her horse. Sheathing his swords Flynn stepped towards Sterben as he too entered the light.

⤌

It was a shamble in complete disarray. A scrounged together, rag tag army with no discernible leadership. Most factions having a leader but no one was in direct command. The camp was set up on a rise with a ring of sharpened stakes encircling half the camp. The wrong half Vaike sighed as the open side faced the tree line a hundred yards away.

To make matters worse they rode right into the camp unchallenged. Entering the largest tent in the centre they found a group of men arguing like children. After gaining some semblance of order Vaike declared who they were and called for all the leaders to be summoned.

The four now stood in the tent with seventeen others. It took two hours for all the leaders to be summoned. Various leaders of different groups ranging from twenty to a hundred plus people.

Nobody wished to forfeit what power they had so Vaike listened as each leader introduced themselves and informed on the numbers they brought.

Just over two thousand men rallied to Baird, most little more than armed peasants but an untrained spear in formation can still be deadly.

After discussions Vaike broke the army off into four battalions. Four different mercenary groups made up over half their number. Rork and Blaine commanded the largest two groups so Vaike left them each in command of their group and one of the smaller groups.

The last group of mercenaries joined up with the mountain folk. Garrett was to lead this group with Ailish and Milne the mercenary leader as his seconds.

Vaike was to command the smallest battalion comprising of nomads, farmers a few hired guards and former pirates. He intended this battalion to be Baird's shield.

Order now restored, Vaike started directing commanders to build better defences, dispatch scouts and post sentries.

☙

With the return of their horses the last leg of their journey home breezed bye. They would ride miles in silence just to speak non-stop of an evening like long lost friends.

It was one of these evenings when Vashti breached the topic of Edward. Something inside her sensing it was the right time, like Flynn was ready.

Keeping it simple at first just testing the waters, she asked what was one memory he liked of him.

Flynn's face lit up as he enjoyed retelling a fond memory. A memory completely true of the two scoundrels.

"There was this one time after I had left his crew where by chance we berthed in the same port at the same time. I arrived a few days later and saw the executioner in port and naturally set out in search of the dirtiest dive in the place.

The revelries were in full swing by the time we arrived. It had been a while since seeing each other so naturally we celebrated like pirates. We got black out drunk, or at least I did.

Despite having already been at it a few days, Edward drank me under the table. He's one of the few people to ever manage this by the way. Anyway, the real fun began later when a squadron of soldiers entered the town.

I'm not sure why they came into town or who they were looking for but they started to swing their dicks around.

I was so drunk I couldn't get my sword out and ended up loosening my belt and wearing my trousers around my ankles.

Edwards problem was similar. He couldn't find hull breaker. I mean it was right beside him but rather then search he just grabbed the nearest chair and ran outside. I chased after him holding my pants up trying to not fall over or crash into anything.

Bursting outside I saw Edward sprawled on the ground. Chair a splintered wreck underneath his vast torso.

He stood up laughing, patting the dirt of his stained clothes holding onto a single chair leg. It looked like a twig in his hand.

He used this twig to beat up seven soldiers. Seven armoured soldiers before they all fled. It wasn't pretty, it wasn't spectacular it was hilarious.

The most feared man on the sea flailing around like a drunk bear, using a stick to obliterate everything in its path."

Smiling ear to ear, feeling joy after reminiscing Vashti handed Flynn a gift. Flynn stared at it speechless. Vashti unsure if he forgot about it or hated it.

Quick as a viper Flynn closed the distance between them. Arms pinned to her side as he embraced her. He obviously liked it.

"I wasn't sure I dreamt it" Flynn said placing the leather strap around his neck, Edwards gold coin resting against his bare chest.

"I'm sorry for taking it and for holding onto it for this long. I was just." "Its alright" Flynn said cutting her off. "In the state I was in I probably would've lost it. And besides I wouldn't have known what to do with it.

Edward was no longer a pirate so it couldn't go in my hair, even if it didn't feel wrong. But this, this is perfect. Thankyou."

Vashti smiled, eyes welling up with tears as Flynn sat staring at the coin.

❧

A few days later the Nibban forest came into view. The horses finding their own way across the plains, travelling at a steady trot.

An hour into the forest the trees began to engulf them. Closing in on all sides reminding Flynn of being underground.

Flynn asked questions as the trees grew denser and the light dimmed, curious about the number of elves and cities within the trees.

Vashti explained that all elves live in Zardelfan, the only elven city in the forest. The Dusk watch being the only exception to this as they patrolled the boarders of their land, protecting it from all threats.

"In fact, they are probably following us now. Their motto. Never seen, ever watchful. Any threat is littered with arrows without any warning."

"I think they need a new motto" Flynn said reigning in Sterben.

An elf garbed in leather armour and wearing the green cloak emblazoned with the seven-point southern star of the Dusk watch stood before them. Hood pulled back revealing a male of average appearance and a long scar running from his left ear too his chin. The tip of his ear cut off, making it more human than elven.

"Greeting princess, it is good to see that you're well." "Thank you, Captain." Vashti answered seeing the red horse hair tied to his spear head, signifying his rank. "I am very much looking forward to seeing mother and sleeping in a bed."

"Well I'm afraid that will have to wait. By order of the Queen you are refused entry beyond this point.

"What" roared Flynn, swords already in hand. Vashti quickly moving beside him, placing a calming hand on his knee. "You'll be dead before you can move an inch" she whispered towards the short-tempered warrior.

"So why am I refused entry. Is it the company I bring? I've never known mother to turn away guests."

"No princess, the pirate is welcome when you are. By order of the Queen you will be granted entry when you return with your brother."

"That's a fool's errand. I have no idea where Vaike is. We parted ways over a month ago." "Yes, we know. The prince left here with some humans a little over a week ago." "So, he is alive." Vashti was glad she was sitting otherwise she might have fallen over out of relief.

"Yes. They travelled east to where the human King Olaf has gathered an army and is preparing to crush the rebel force." "Very well Captain, we will travel there now."

In nine short days the camp began to resemble something of a structured military unit. Hopefully it is enough with enemy troops setting up their own camp and trenches across the open field.

The wooden stakes and trenches began being built three days ago, when a thousand soldiers arrived. Since then their numbers had tripled with the fortifications only growing. No other sign of movement had come from the enemy camp.

Baird navigated his way through the camp bustling with activity. Completely anonymous, no more than another young boy risking it all for an unknown leader. He's no king yet they intend to crown him because of his long dead ancestors. It's crazy.

The camps paths, already turned to mud from the thousands of feet trekking through the same pass, Baird made a bee line for the command tent. He ran into Garrett and Ailish who were always together these days. They too were summoned by Vaike. With the probability of bad news awaiting them they hurried along the last few steps.

The look of despair plastered on the faces of everyone in the tent confirmed their suspicions. "The scouts have just sent word. Olaf has arrived." Vaike said. His expression telling them there was more news to come.

"He's not alone, bringing a further two thousand soldiers with him. We are outnumbered more than two to one with a large percentage of our number being made up of militia who will likely flee when the fighting starts."

"Put em' on the front lines then" growled Blaine. The hardened mercenary leader was not well liked by his men. Everyone else seemed to think him extreme and Baird could see why.

"No, they'll be crushed instantly. Better to keep them in reserve portraying greater strength" Garrett responded, the voice of reason.

"War is mostly deception." Vaike interjected taking control of the conversation before senseless bickering broke out.

They debated for hours. Discussing every viable option from withdrawing to a fortified position and an ensuing siege. Flee with troops circling back around to try and attack from two fronts. Dig in and wait for them to charge. Covering every option, regardless how impossible they might've been.

It all came back to three things. Numbers, equipment and skill. Sadly, they were worse off on all accounts. Meaning no great solution existed. Best choice was to stand and fight. Better to die now then too starve in a siege or picked off one by one in a mad retreat.

Olaf's army was still marching into their camp the next day. Two thousand people moving at once don't go very fast or cover much ground. Especially travelling with the supply train. Still they rode out, Baird and his companions with three mercenary leaders.

`Olaf was seated in a wooden chair in the middle of no man's land between the two armies. Another man stood idly beside him. The white banner of truce blowing in the breeze behind them with a dozen heavily armoured knights flanking them.

Dismounting they walked the last thirty yards, their own banner left with the horses. Olaf didn't even deign to rise from his chair. The man beside him just stepped forward and addressed the seven leaders.

"Well you saved the cliffs, killed the Necromancer and found Harbinger. To acknowledge your achievement's his majesty has decided spare you and your men. All you have to do is surrender to him."

"What no pleasantries. Just straight to business then." Vaike directed to the King. Olaf smirked as the Duke continued to speak for him.

"The terms of your surrender are simple. Lord Vaike you will return to your forest and remain there. You and your people will not meddle in the affairs of mortals.

Your soldiers will all enter into the royal army, even the mercenaries. Thirdly the boy will surrender Harbinger to the one and only king and disappear from Thaldesa never to return. Lastly his majesty wants the woman."

"Like hell he will" challenged Garrett as he Indicated to Ailish. Vaike held out his arm In-front of Garrett as the Duke continued despite the interruption. "His majesty will wed her and unite with the tribesmen of the mountain bringing them all into his vast kingdom."

"And if we refuse?" Vaike asked already knowing the answer. "Then we will crush you all on the field of battle. The survivors will be enlisted. Commanders executed. Women raped and your forest burnt down. Your corpses will become dog food and your skulls will become part of the king's new throne in the south."

"Well we shall meet on the field of battle than, pray you don't cross swords with me." Vaike said turning on his heels.

"Disappointing, but not surprising. Very well we shall cross blades." "Wait you value military strength right" interrupted Baird. "What are you doing?" Vaike whispered.

Ignoring him Baird continued on looking Olaf in the eyes finding some hidden courage. "Why risk the lives of thousands, weakening your own strength when a single death could resolve this." Baird had no idea what gave him this idea or where it came from. His mouth was moving but the words didn't feel like his own.

"You dare speak to his Majesty like that. You insolent." "Ivan." Olaf said in a booming voice. A voice that demanded obedience. "What is it you propose?"

"A dual. Single combat, a fight to the death between champions of our choice. If you win, we'll accept your terms." At those words Vaike once again needed to stop a friend with his arm, this time Garrett. "And if we win, you leave Thaldesa, for good."

Olaf was silent for what felt an eternity before he answered. "I agree. Tomorrow at noon our champions will fight on this spot."

❧

The troop movements made sense if Olaf was gathering an army. Vashti voiced her confusion as to why he was, resulting in Flynn bringing her up to speed on his and Garretts plan. Even showing his own amazement that it bore fruit.

The horses chose the path they took journeying across fields, avoiding the forest completely. Knowing they weren't welcome.

Passing similar hills to the ones they saw months ago after their first encounter with the vampires. Heading further east they knew they would soon reach the highway.

Cresting a hill, the highway came into view. No travellers or soldiers for as far as Vashti's elven eyes could see. Travelling along the highway would allow them greater speed but could present dangers of encountering soldiers in large numbers.

Agreeing to take the risk, trusting in Vashti's heightened senses and the speed of their horses they trotted along the cobbled stones making up the main road throughout Olaf's lands.

The third day after leaving the forest they were riding before dawn. Well rested, having set up camp behind a rise in the ground. Shielding them and their fire from the highway but close enough that they could still hear steps echoing off the cut stones.

The sun was barely over the horizon when they stopped to inspect an abandoned camp that encompassed both sides of the road, spilling out onto the hard stones.

It was impossible to tell the number of soldiers but it was in excess of a thousand and soldiers they were. Broken packs and gear discarded on the ground. Footprints left in the dirt from armoured feet and a flag bearing Olaf's wolf sigil trapped in the branches of a nearby tree. Flapping in the breeze like it was atop a conquered battlement.

They searched for an hour before setting off at a mad gallop. Guessing the camp was two weeks old judging by the grass starting to grow over the fires. With the straight level ground, they maintained a frantic pace, some unknown sense of urgency hurrying them.

Pushing the horses for three days straight had their nostrils flaring in exhausted huffs as they stopped to dismount. The horses taking a chance to graze and recover strength while Flynn and Vashti proceeded on foot. They passed ten more camps on the way here that they saw. Not stopping to check if any were fresh.

Which they know they weren't with it evident they had left the highway. Long lines of steel boots trudging through the grass turning it to mud. Cart tracks trailing behind presumably making up the supply line.

The mud was still wet in places so they were getting close. They spared the horses, proceeding with caution on foot. Spotting sentries they doubled back heading further north until they stood on a rise a mile back from no man's land.

Flynn could make out two encampments on either end. One entrenched with a ring of defences and the other too his left vastly larger. Knowing Olaf's troop lay to the east they continued onwards to the smaller camp and Vaike.

The sentries posted on the western entrance refused entry even when they said they wanted to fight. Fearing Olaf was sending spies in to sow discord and confusion. Flynn scoffed at the idea with his superior force it was unnecessary.

Refusing them entry still Flynn knocked out both sentries without the alarm being raised and they rode into camp.

❧

The ride back from the parley was long and awkward. Made awkward with Garrett staring daggers at him and Vaike sitting in silence.

It wasn't until the flap fell shut behind them and they were alone with the other commanders being dismissed did Vaike deign to speak.

"I'm not sure that was the smartest decision." Holding up a hand to silence Baird's protests he continued on. "I understand why you did it. You are trying to save countless lives on both sides. I applaud you for that but I fear its futile. Olaf will fight himself and we have no one here to face him." "But. I thought you?" Baird stammered. "I know what you thought but I won't fight as your champion. This is a human matter, to be resolved by humans." Dismay, hopelessness, fear, panic. Baird didn't know what to think or say before their attention was captured by a disturbance outside the tent.

A guard tumbled through the tent flap, prone body lying helpless in the middle of the floor. Weapons were out, guards were up before the cloth flapped shut.

Vaike stepping to the fore, waiting for Olaf's men to come. 'He wouldn't even honour the bargain or was this put in place before the parley?' Thoughts spiralled through Vaike's mind while he stood before his friends. He will be the first to fall. "When you get a chance to escape take it."

No response forthcoming as a second guard tumbled into the tent face first and in strolled the last person he expected to see.

Flynn and Vashti stood in the entrance, tent flap blowing in the breeze. Light shining behind, encircling them with a heroic glow.

Weapons clattered to the floor as Ailish rushed forward embracing his sister. The two females crying out of joy learning everyone was alive. They broke apart, Ailish admiring Vashti's skin and how good she looked tanned, as the tent again opened. Armed soldiers ran in swords drawn and pointing at Flynn.

Rushing footsteps and the clanking of weapons sounded just outside revealing the presence of even more soldiers. Ready to protect the commanders and avenge their fallen comrades. Expecting a large powerful force since the eight guards posted outside fell so quickly.

Completely unperturbed by the threat Flynn strode toward the table occupying the centre of the tent and stood with hands splayed on the roughly hewn timber. Not in a sign of submission, but in thought studying the map spread across it.

Vaike ordered the soldiers to withdraw and to post more guards after taking the wounded to the healer's tent.

"The outlook is bleak. I can't see how we can win this fight. Olaf brought more strength then we anticipated he would."

"I completely agree with you" Vaike answered Flynn walking to stand opposite him as the other four took up positions around the table.

"We may have a way." Baird said, so quietly it almost went unheard. Vaike went over their encounter earlier today with Olaf and Baird's bargain. The whole time he spoke Baird just stared at the table unable to meet Flynn's eyes. Unable to ask him the one question that could save them all.

"I guess you refused to fight then?" Flynn asked as Vaike finished his recollection. "No. He said it needed to be a human." "What. Speak up boy" Flynn ordered of Baird. "He said it needs to be a human" Baird shouted, finally meeting Flynn's eyes. Eyes that are still the same pale grey they were when they met but no longer so lifeless. Something filled them, like a spark of joy or hope.

"Good. It means I don't have to argue with him about fighting. Delight, joy, relief, hope, Baird was overwhelmed.

"Don't look so surprised, I'm happy to help my friends. Well that and Olaf is a strong opponent. It should be fun" Flynn grinned. Tears wetted a few cheeks in the tent not only Baird's. Even Flynn couldn't ruin the moment with his attempts to play down the significance of his actions.

❦

Wigni Kai. A tradition of the royal family for generations. A trial all children have to first pass in order to be recognised as royal heirs.

The same trial that he and his elder brother Vorid survived. Their other siblings weren't so fortunate. He had just learnt that his most recent offspring to attempt the trial failed. That made five.

Olaf new of four other siblings who attempted the trial before he himself did, however despite his constant questioning his father never told him how many of his siblings actually died before him. He was the third youngest that he knew off. His father siring no more offspring after his sister Diann died.

He always regretted that she died. Diann was the gentlest person he'd ever met. The room immediately felt brighter whenever she entered. The only person in his family he loved. He remembered the beating he was given after he attacked his father with a knife. Trying to convince him not to send her.

The trial consists of sending the child out into the wilderness on the winter of their tenth year. Taking no supplies with them other than the clothes on their back, which are more suited to warm summer weather. A knife and six feet of rope.

The goal, to survive using your own wits and strength until they come and get you. Fighting off hunger, cold and wolves. A month for boys to endure and survive, half that for girls.

Vorid who was set to be king instead of himself never truly recovered from the trial. Constantly getting sick each winter eventually dying his seventeenth year when Olaf was fifteen. Olaf often found himself wondering how things would've turned out if he survived.

He was always the weaker swordsmen and despite being two years older was smaller. He was still the first born however, so he received most of the education and grooming. Olaf focused on martial matters assuming himself to be the commander to his brother's army.

Primogeniture. A tradition of his family that he did away with. A tradition that could've ruined them at worst. At best their kingdom would still be a small piece off the north not encompassing the entire east with plans for more growth.

Preferring instead to name his successor as his most capable child. Educating and training them all equally. Hell, it could even be a daughter of his, as unlikely as that would be.

With the remaining children married off for alliances or made commanders, supporting the heir.

First however he needs to find a woman to give him children strong enough to make it through the Wigni Kai. Concubines don't seem to cut it.

Hopefully this mountain girl can.

❧

A hand gripped the open edge of the canvas tent that Flynn was given. A tent on the far side of the camp away from the others and all to himself. Giving him space to prepare for his dual tomorrow.

"I told you not to return or the consequences will be dire" warned Flynn. "Is that anyway to great a friend" Vashti answered pulling the flap open and stepping inside the small tent.

Flynn was sitting crossed leg on a bedroll, swords on the floor before him being methodically sharpened and polished.

"Sorry I thought you were one of the camp followers." "I doubt they'll return. They looked quite troubled when they ran from the tent before joining a group of mercenaries. They'll make plenty of money tonight. Although I must say I thought you'd entertain the pair all night."

Flynn moved the weapons spread around him making room for Vashti to sit opposite before answering.

"I surprised myself also. As a pirate drinking and whoring were the pleasures we chased. So, we would drink and fuck before facing death. I'm not sure if it was to not think about it or to blow off steam but it is an ingrained part of pirate life."

"So, what's different now?" Vashti asked picking up one of Flynn's knives and running it against a whetstone.

"I think its fear. Not a fear of dying" Flynn hastily added in response to the look of shock sprawled across Vashti's face. "I'm mortal so I could die in my sleep tonight, I'm still at peace with that. No, I fear failing tomorrow. Of what will happen to Ailish and Garrett. What will happen to Vaike and the boy. And what will happen to you should I lose?"

Flynn just sat in silence, staring at the sword in his hands unsure what to say or do next. Vashti took his face in her hands with more gentleness then Flynn had ever known, forcing their eyes to meet. "You have things you care about. People you fear to lose. It may be a new concept for you but it is not a weakness, it's a source of great strength. Remember that tomorrow."

The pair talked late into the night before falling asleep side by side.

They sat in the saddles waiting to ride out into no man's land. The six companions, commanders followed by two hundred soldiers on foot.

Eventually the order to move out passed down the line. Cracking the reigns and they moved out in formation. The seven from yesterday out front with Flynn and Vashti blending in with the other soldiers.

Olaf stood waiting for them with two hundred of his own soldiers forming a half ring a dozen deep around them. Two young squires stood a few feet behind him. One holding Grimsever arms shaking from the weight of the massive sword. The other held Olaf's shield bearing the wolf upon the black and red field. They assumed correctly. Olaf will fight himself.

"So, who is your champion. The elf? It might actually make things interesting" taunted the king. "No this is a human matter I'm here to observe." "Hmm that's too bad then. I guess this will be boring after all."

"Perhaps I can help with that." Flynn said riding to the front joining the others, Vashti riding on his left. Red coat draped over his shoulder's, hanging flat in the breezeless air, as if it too felt the weight Flynn bore on his shoulders. Hair uncovered, displaying the coin braids, his legacy to the world.

"Ahh twin blade. Its good seeing you here this might not be a total bore now." "I couldn't agree more" Flynn answered flashing a wicked grin, channelling the inner madness he will soon need.

"My lord, I'm not sure this is a good idea. Twin blade has killed every bounty hunter and assassin that has gone after the price on his head. I mean just look at him, he wears the proof of his victories for the world to see." "Shut up Ivan. If I wanted to hear the bleating of lesser creatures, I would visit a farm. Besides" Olaf continued, this time to Flynn. "I still owe you for the Koyake princess."

Squaring off across the cleared area, encircled by soldiers and friends. The two as different from each other as night and day.

Olaf completely armoured in steel plates from head to toe, polished to a lustre sparkling in the sun. A shield hung limply from his left arm with Grimsever gripped firmly in his right. The blade that the squire could barely lift he swung with ease, proving with a few test swings after being handed it.

Across from him was Flynn. Half the size even before the armour which Flynn chose to forgo. Vashti held his red coat, removed before entering the ring he now stood wearing a light leathered tunic and pants. Supposedly strong enough to protect against sword slashes but with the weight and size of Grimsever Baird doubted it would do anything. Flynn thought the same deciding agility and speed was more important to win against the king.

❧

Flynn breathed deeply as the controlled calm overcame him. Completely sober and focused he slipped into a calm frenzy. Not noticing the clear cloudless sky or the sun that shone directly down on them.

No thought of Vashti or his friends. No thought of the stakes, as he directed his complete attention to the giant before him.

"Now tell me pirate. Why you are willing to die for this? Surely you'd rather be back in your tavern drinking and whoring." "Why that's simple. So that the world may know peace."

Olaf was almost as big and strong as Edward but his father was a brute. Fighting more like a berserk. Nothing like the skilled swordsman Olaf was known to be.

He needed to overwhelm him with his speed advantage and wait for that armour to tire him out. Wait for his opportunity, wait for an opening.

With that in mind Flynn rushed in first. Ducking under Olaf's first slash dancing away. Feint, duck, pivot, roll, repeat. The dance went on, repeating in the same sequence until Olaf stepped back an inch too far. With his balance and centre of gravity off, quick as a viper Flynn lashed out with a kick.

It was like kicking a fucking mountain. Jumping with momentum and throwing his whole-body weight into the kick. Raising his shield Flynn struck dead centre of the dented steel. Olaf didn't even budge. Flynn's right leg went numb as he stumbled away from the king's counter attack.

Luckily his leg wasn't broken but he was caught on the back foot as Olaf now pressed his advantage blows coming from both sword and shield.

Feeling quickly returned to his leg and with it so too did his speed advantage. Unfortunately, one of his swords now lay in the mud behind Olaf on the far side of the clearing. Having to check a blow from Olaf sent it spinning from his grip. He was having better luck with a two-handed grip but every collision of steel left his hands and arms shaking from the force.

The king was no pushover. Sweat ran freely down Flynn's face and back now, yet Olaf didn't slow. His attacks didn't weaken.

Avoiding an overzealous shield bash allowed Flynn to draw first blood. His sword tip piercing the join in his shoulder. Olaf's shield dropped to the ground, spinning to a stop as blood dripped from his gauntleted fist.

They circled each other like vultures, waiting for an opening. With no shield and two hands behind it Grimsever whistled through the air at even faster speeds. Almost as fast as Vaike swung his own sword but with double the force if not more.

❧

Vaike stood transfixed, watching the two human swordsmen fighting at a level that rivals his own. Knowing Flynn's abilities first hand he expected this to be a quick fight. It seems Olaf more than lived up to his reputation.

Dirt rained down covering the onlookers every time Flynn dodged Olaf's sword. Flynn's sword whistled through the air, blade a blur trying to find its mark only to explode in a shower of sparks when steel met steel. Olaf's sword countered with a howling rage, more likely to crush then cut. Folding opponents and armour under the sheer force of the blow.

If asked Vaike would say Flynn was losing. Olaf's shield lay forgotten, the wound under his shoulder already clotting, stemming the flow of blood.

Flynn's injuries were more subtle, something only a master would notice. Like the shifted centre of gravity favouring his left leg ever since kicking the shield. Or how his arms shake after blocking Olaf's strikes. They were incredible powerful with only one arm bearing down, with two hands he could probably crush a mountain goat's skull, horns and all with a single blow let alone a human.

Turning his head to look away from the fight, Vaike focused on his sister's presence beside him. She was pale as death, eyes wide in horror.

Clasping hands, his fingers interlocked hers, offering his strength trying to reassure her it will be fine. Even if he didn't believe it himself as the fighting continued.

⚬

Panting, finally Olaf seemed to be tiring but he'd already spent most of his own energy also. Having to dig deep into his reserves just to block those strikes.

Still the moment he'd been waiting for had arrived. The question is does he have enough energy left. 'Only one way to find out.'

After a few more exchanges Olaf retreated to create distance, Flynn stepped forward to close the distance and stumbled.

Grinning ear to ear knowing the fight was over Olaf halted and swung downwards, aiming for Flynn's exposed back. Swinging down with enough force to break bones and pin his broken form against the ground.

Olaf took the bait hook, line and sinker. Like Flynn knew he would, the king was greedy and bloodthirsty after all. At the last second Flynn spun up and outwards balance never lost. Sword slipping between Olaf's hands and twisting breaking his grip on his sword.

The normal follow through from this position was a hip throw, planting the opponent on their back. Olaf's size and weight of all his armour made that impossible, so Flynn settled on disarming him removing Olaf's reach advantage. A flick of the wrist had Olaf's sword falling to the ground, Flynn between it and the king.

To his credit Olaf didn't even baulk headbutting the crown of Flynn's head with his armoured skull. Used to the beatings he received from Edward allowed Flynn to remain conscious. It still hurt like a bitch, dazing him long enough for Olaf to drive a gauntleted fist into his stomach. Driving the air from his lungs, the blow lifted his feet from the ground.

Winded and sword forgotten Flynn struggled to find his feet. Olaf grabbed his tunic tossing him across the clearing. Rocks cutting up his face and hands. Olaf strolled across the clearing with a predator's gait, not bothering to reclaim his weapons. A hunter stalking his prey.

Hand closing around the knife in his boot Flynn slashed at the hand that Olaf stretched towards him. Iron met bone as Olaf smashed Flynn's hand, knife dropping free. Right arm going numb, the impact breaking bones as his left gripped the dagger sheathed on his waist. Stabbing at the Kings face, sharpened tip aiming for the exposed eye.

Caught off guard Olaf instinctively protected his face with his own left hand. Blade piercing the unprotected palm and penetrating through the gauntlet, momentum carrying the tip forward. Stopping a hairsbreadth from its intended target. The king's eyelashes gently caressing the daggers tip.

Pulling the blade free was impossible as Olaf clamped down. His hand completely engulfed in the king's meaty fist. Olaf's blood ran down Flynn's arm staining his shirt as his grip tightened, slowly crushing his hand.

❧

Vashti hugged him tightly now. Head buried in his shoulder averting her eyes from the scene unfurling before them. Burying her head to drown out the sound of Flynn's Scream. Crying out as Olaf broke his hand and wrist. The distraught cries that rang through their ears didn't come from Flynn's lips however. It was his sister who cried out.

The sound silenced, turning to deep sobs as Olaf kneed Flynn in the face. Sweat spraying as his head whipped back. Nose crunching as it broke beneath the knee, blood already flowed from its shattered remains.

Releasing his right arm Flynn completely slumped on the ground, gurgling on his own blood. Olaf kicked Flynn's exposed ribs as Vashti sobbed into his shoulder. Not daring to look, not wanting to watch as Flynn was gruesomely beaten to death

Rolling into the foetal position, coughing up his own blood. The king stood either side of him, feet apart, right hand wrapped around the dagger still implanted in his hand. With a wrathful cry he ripped it free, blood dripping down its blade as he decided how best to finish his prey.

Vaike spared a brief glance in Baird's direction and despite the paleness of his face the boy stood strong. Wide eyes transfixed on the scene before them. Taking Vaike's words to heart, spoken as Flynn entered the ring. "Whatever happens, don't you dare look away and dishonour him. He is doing this for you."

❦

Wheezing unable to breathe through his own blood and broken ribs. Completely helpless. He felt Olaf's bloody left-hand reach down and fingers thick as sausages wrap around his throat, fingers meeting at the back.

He began kicking and punching, right arm flailing uselessly. Olaf brought the dagger still coated into his own blood downwards, stabbing his exposed thigh. The tip punctured bone as the grip on his throat tightened. Left hand searching for something, anything, a way to fight. Grimacing in pain as Olaf twisted the knife in his leg.

Vision fading, he locked eyes with Vaike. Vashti's head buried in his shoulder. 'Well at least she will be spared from seeing this' he thought blacking out as his fingers tightened around a worn old hilt.

Chapter 12

THE FORGOTTEN HOPE

Thoughts were confusing and strange as his mind was shrouded in fog. Stuck in some kind of hell, unable to move, unable to remember why. Unable to even remember who he was, what he was.

Drifting in and out of short moments of lucidness, offering brief respites from the darkness. The confusion.

Eventually the fog lifted allowing clarity to slowly return. With the clarity came pain. Incredible pain, everything hurt, no particular injury claiming dominance.

Sounds began to filter in through the pain. More accurately voices. Muffled voices speaking rapidly making it difficult to comprehend what was being said, but he knew those voices.

The voices stopped, replaced with the sound of dry gravel crunching underfoot. Hearing cloth ripple he forced one heavy eye open. "I really must be in hell if you're the first person I see."

Vaike stood in the tent's threshold smiling. "I can assure you, you're very much alive. Despite, your best efforts." Vaike stuck his head outside the tent and spoke some inaudible words before approaching the wooden table in the opposite corner. Filling an earthenware cup from the pitcher beside it.

The sound of water filling the cup made Flynn realise just how thirsty he was. He struggled to sit, body complaining in protest with each movement. For every twist and turn, he received a fresh jolt of pain in return.

Vaike stood and watched, water cup held extended just beyond reach. Knowing full well Flynn would never accept the help.

Half way up three more pairs of boots shuffled into the carpeted interior of the tent. "Great, more idiots to watch me struggle" Flynn rasped. Each syllable causing pain and discomfort as Garrett, Ailish and Baird skulked to the corner.

Crashing down onto the pillows now situated underneath his shoulder blades. Exhaustion and discomfort too great to try and crawl any further. Left arm reaching out to take the cup from Vaike's hand. The deep throbbing in his right arm provided enough indication to not use that arm. Rolling onto his side enough to reach the cup caused a groan of pain to squeeze past his cracked lips.

Stiff fingers wrapped around the rough clay of the mug. The weight was greater than his tired body anticipated. With Vaike releasing his grip only to see the cup slip from Flynn's outstretched hand.

Water soaked into the thick carpet as Vaike tried to disentangle the jagged shards of clay. Plucking the last piece from the carpet's woollen fibres as the tent flap was thrown violently aside by the figure swooping in.

Flynn braced and struggled to move as they charged straight for him. Brain still trying to place the intruder, the other four complacently standing by.

Silver hair pooled across his torso as he was caught in a rough embrace. Vashti squeezing him tightly as she buried her face into his chest crying.

Flynn settled down deeper into the straw mattress beneath him, reassuringly placing his left hand on the back of Vashti's head.

Lifting her head to look him in the eye. Black rings formed underneath each eye. Eyes red from crying. "You reckless idiot, I thought you'd died."

"Don't weep for the stupid, you'll be crying all day." His snide remark earning him a play full punch on the arm. Play full it may have been but with his body in its currently battered state it still hurt.

"She has barely left your side in the last five days" Vaike said as Vashti once again buried her head in his chest. I finally convinced her this morning to get a proper meal and rest, if only for a few minutes.

Unable to find the words to express what he was feeling, Flynn just stared at the immortal princess who embraced him more tightly then any lover. Choked up on a lump in his throat he managed to utter a single word, "Vashti."

Lifting her head at the sound of her name they locked eyes. No words spoken but her eyes told him she understood what he meant. The emotion in his voice telling her everything he wished he could say.

When they finally broke of their gaze Vashti helped Flynn into a sitting position. Not taking no for an answer and Flynn, still wounded and tired couldn't resist her. While she forced Flynn to drink from a new cup, she now held against his lips Vaike asked what was the last thing he remembered.

"Let's see" he started. Speaking easier now that he'd drunk something. "I remember duelling Olaf. It went downhill and he was strangling me and, and.. And how am I alive now? I lost." Confusion plastered across his bruised face.

"You didn't lose that's how" Baird cut in unable to contain his excitement as it pooled out of him like a physical presence, filling the tent.

"What. How?" Flynn asked confusion turning into complete bewilderment. Vaike answered, placing a hand on Baird's shoulder calming him before he pissed himself like an over excited puppy. "Well as you so accurately remember, the fight was going poorly."

"That's putting it mildly" Garrett muttered loud enough for all of the tents occupants to hear. "He performed far better than you would've" scolded Vaike.

"Yes, but unlike him I don't chase strong opponents. I don't base my self-worth on my arrogance of being undefeated."

"Apparently I still am" smirked Flynn. Vashti pinching his side at the quip. "There it is" grinned Garrett. "Lying in a hospice, on the verge of death and you still act like your better than us. I can't believe I missed you." "Well only idiots enjoy war" Ailish added in support of Garrett.

"Well not that this isn't heart-warming but can we continue on." Flynn said changing the subject, already overwhelmed with enough emotions for one day. "Well as I was saying you were backed into a corner.

I thought you were lost when I saw the light leaving your eyes. But whether on instinct or muscle memory I'm not sure, but either way you stabbed Olaf with that rusty blade you carried everywhere. You stabbed him underneath the jaw where no armour was protecting and the blade penetrated his brain. Olaf died instantly, but your injuries were, severe. We didn't know if you'd, recover."

"The blade?" Flynn asked concern in his voice. "Your swords are fine. They were collected after the fight." Vaike answered. "I'm not sure what that dagger meant to you but it is gone. The blade snapped off inside of Olaf's skull and in the confusion of the retreat the hilt was lost."

"That's unfortunate" Flynn said settling down further into the mattress. "Get some rest. We'll fill you in on everything later" Vaike said leaving the tent with everyone else following.

Vashti last to move. Standing to leave after speaking softly enough so the others couldn't hear. "Maybe now the knife's gone you can finally let go of Jenna and your past. Remembering what you have, not what was."

Fingers lightly brushed against her own as she stood to leave. Pausing she looked back and saw Flynn. Left arm outstretched, eyes closed and a face at peace. Smiling to herself, she adjusted Flynn's pillows then curled up beside him.

Vaike found them later that evening. Sleeping peacefully side by side, Flynn snoring loudly due to his broken nose and Vashti looking happier than he could ever recall seeing his sister as she held the scoundrel. His friend and brother.

Leaving a tray of fruit behind, he left them alone. Vaike returned over the next three days with more food and water. His sister was usually present but she left more regularly to see to her own needs then she did the first five days. Nine days after his fight with Olaf, Flynn finally left the tent.

It was good to see him moving around but being out of bed made him appear even more lame. Right arm in a sling and left arm wielding a crutch as his left leg shook under what little weight it took.

Vashti walked beside him, offering a hand should he need it as they walked. Needing to stretch his legs and get out of bed they walked nowhere in particular, eventually arriving at the clearing where they duelled.

Blood still stained the ground in two puddles. One significantly larger than the other, blood belonging to Olaf. All that remained of the strongest opponent Flynn had ever fought. His own puddle was still shocking large. Having lost more than enough blood himself to have died. Probably the cause of Vashti's concern.

Vaike found them as they stalked amongst the tents. Now significantly fewer than when they arrived. Sitting on a tree stump around a fire in the centre of the camp. A stew of rabbit bubbled over as flames licked the iron pot above it. Vaike briefed Flynn on the happenings of the last few days.

Duke Ivan fled with a few loyalists to Voldengird after Olaf fell. Most of the soldiers surrendered joining their own numbers. Forced into Olaf's service, they held no loyalty to the king. The Kings elite guard were all executed, receiving orders not to interfere in the dual they just stood still refusing to move or speak after he died.

They sent a thousand mercenaries with two thousand of the deserters to give chase and begin the siege of the city a day later.

Three days ago, Baird, Garrett and Ailish followed with the remaining two thousand. It was time for Baird to claim his birthright. His throne. Garrett and Ailish followed as his advisor's. The only people remaining are those who were wounded in the retreat their healers and a few guards. Their numbers were decreasing daily.

"What now then?" Vashti asked. Only knowing the basics told to her in the short moments when she wasn't tending to the wounded idiot that was Flynn.

"Well we are to return home. Our task is complete." "And me?" Flynn asked as fear entered Vashti's eyes. "You are free to do as you wish. You can return to your tavern and whoring. Head to Voldengird and fight for Baird. Or" Vaike continued after a pause. "You can continue to travel with us."

"I'd like that a lot." Flynn said as Vashti squeezed his hand. Her fingers grasping his own while Vaike spoke.

Chapter 13

THE TASK

Two days later they stood silent as the remains of the camp were disassembled around them. Canvas rippled in the breeze as tents were pulled down. Horses whinnied impatiently while the carts they pulled were loaded with any remaining supplies. Guards unceremoniously scoffed down a breakfast of clumpy porridge preparing to protect the convoy as they followed north.

A few of the medics and camp followers will drop off at villages and towns they pass, most will continue on towards the capitol. If they pushed themselves and the horses the loyalists should have reached the capitol by now. An army can't travel that quick especially with most on foot so it'll take Baird another fortnight or so.

Sterben proved difficult to mount with his left leg still unable to bear his weight and right arm in a sling. Having to grab the saddle horn and place his right foot in the stirrup, then haul himself up and over. Easy enough with a cooperative horse, Sterben was anything but. Enjoying himself as he turned and pulled away causing Flynn to fall on his arse yet again.

Sterben eventually let him mount on his third attempt as the twins approached from overseeing the last of the evacuations. If they saw or heard his struggle they didn't let on. Vaike however made a remark about how horses personalities reflect that of their owners. Scratching Sterben behind the ear Flynn couldn't agree more.

The ground was still soft mud, slowing the horses down much to everyone's chagrin. Especially Vashti, who was eager to get home. When the horse's hooves stomped on the hard cobblestone of the highway Flynn decided he missed the mud despite the delays. The mud cushioned the impact that now reverberated throughout his many injuries, causing him to grit his teeth several times throughout the day.

Rest stops for meals and personal needs granted respite but presented a new set of challenges. Namely remounting Sterben who could be helpful or difficult. He gave up caring if the twins saw, despite already suspecting that they had.

Regardless of Vashti's desire to get home, they travelled at a slow pace. Flynn suspected for his own benefit. With each day his strength improved with Vashti continuing to change dressings and apply fresh tinctures each evening.

The destruction left behind from the army they trailed behind was less than when Olaf commanded. Like his soldiers had no respect for their own countryside, or none for their king. Now the tell-tale signs were harder to spot. They were still there. Three thousand people can't travel without draining wells and trampling the ground but none of it was senseless.

At the steady pace they travelled it took seven days just to reach the point where they needed to leave the highway and head west. Turning left with the sun following them across the sky they started the final leg. Each step bringing them closer to the forest. Closer to the twin's home.

Twice before Flynn had journeyed this leg. Travelling in the opposite direction he felt excitement at the journey that was yet to come. Now. Now he felt sore and tired. So very tired, ready to rest.

Flynn noticed gradual changes over the following days. The grass slowly looked darker and thicker. More and more birds and small game crossed their paths keeping them well fed each night.

Four days travel from the highway and they camped overlooking the forest. The smile that graced Vashti's face spoke volumes about how excited she was to see her home.

❧

"Welcome to Zardelfan" Vashti said to Flynn her face lighting up like the sun. They were met at the tree line by several members of the Dusk guard who escorted them to the city. Unusual for her mother to order them out of her borders, and any escort was normally comprised of her own guards since they have no army. Most elves will fight in a war but very few actually soldier professionally.

Flynn limped beside her awestruck. Trying to take in everything but not knowing where to look or focus. Eyes roaming over everything like the world was a blank slate and he was trying to find something to focus on.

He had given up the crutch before entering the trees. Wanting to enter under his own strength, his own volition. The wounds suffered had all finally closed up over the last few days and no longer bled. Only his broken arm and leg were left to fully heal, the knife's tip piercing the bone.

A splint was still strapped to his right arm with the sling deep in her own pack. He didn't want to look weak in front of her people or her mother. Flynn wouldn't say but she guessed so.

"Shit" Vashti swore stopping at the base of the ten thousand steps. Red roses wrapped around an arch caused by an ancient root pushed up out of the ground. The Northern staircase up to the city spiralled around the monolithic tree. With the first dozen steps carved out of stone before transitioning over to timber.

"How's Flynn meant to climb this?" He isn't. He can wait here with the dusk guard and we'll have them lower the travel lift when we get there." 'Like hell I will" Flynn growled. "I refuse to be treated like an invalid. Like luggage."

"It's ten thousand steps. Steep steps." Vaike answered. "It takes one step at a time to reach the top" Flynn responded, taking a limping step towards the spiralling staircase. "Very well we'll see you at the top. Vashti mother is waiting." With that her brother stepped past Flynn striding up the ten thousand steps. With an encouraging smile to Flynn, Vashti followed.

They quickly passed beyond the point of hearing Flynn struggle up the steps behind them. Vashti kept pace with her brother as they climbed. She supposed her brother picked the northern entrance on purpose just to mess with Flynn. The western entrance was roughly the same distance to reach as the north from where they entered but with three hundred steps less.

The northern staircase they climbed was the oldest and longest with the western being the most recently one built. They were all referred to as the ten thousand steps but with the archaic trees having variations in trunk circumference the total steps all numbered differently.

As they climbed the last few steps sweat beaded on her forehead. Vashti wasn't sure how Flynn was fairing but a glance from Vaike confirmed her suspicions about his choice in entrances.

Guards welcomed them home as they passed through the northern entrance. Several guards even falling into step beside them as an honour guard they marched towards her mother's throne. The elven seat of power.

The guards didn't falter as they climbed the steps towards the council. Even as they marched inches from the narrowing edge overlooking a drop straight to the forest floor and an untimely death.

The captain marched out front, kneeling as he took the last step. Announcing that the Prince and Princess had returned. One look at her mother and Vashti lost control. Squealing with joy she rushed the council embracing the Queen tightly who stood to meet her daughter. The announcement dying on the captain's lips who was dismissed with a wave.

Whatever the council was discussing, whatever report they expected would wait. As mother and daughter strolled away arm in arm. Heads buried together like a pair of ladies in waiting catching up on castle gossip.

Vaike was left dumbstruck still on the top step staring at the twelve council members, all just as shocked as he was by the Queens display.

Pausing on the bottom step the Queen turned to her brother ordering him to give the council his report. She'll seek him out with any questions later.

❧

Stars shone through the gaps in the canopy above his head. The cool evening breeze causing him to shiver as it mixed with his sweat soaked shirt. His leg was swollen and couldn't support his weight as he dragged his exhausted body up the last few steps.

Legs shaking from exhaustion he found himself reaching for the cane he had become accustomed to. Four elves stood guard ten metres away and out of pure willpower he took a step towards them.

Head held high, he took a second, a third. Refusing to fall or accept help. They merely watched him, amusement on their faces as he limped between the gap they opened up. Flynn swore he saw coins change hands as he passed, like they took bets against him making the climb.

"If you'd follow me please sir, i'll show you to your quarters." Standing just to the right of the entrance a well-dressed elf greeted him. Light brown hair and a green tunic, slippers resembling the style worn in Olaf's court covered his feet.

Unable to find enough spare energy to speak, to challenge the sir slight, Flynn only nodded. With a smile that seemed almost to perfect, like he'd practiced for centuries to master he turned on his heels and strode away.

Not slowing for Flynn rather he dictated the pace they would walk at. Jaw clenched and knuckles white Flynn followed. It took five minutes to reach their destination. Flynn new they passed some remarkable sights that existed nowhere else in the world but he noticed none of them.

He didn't take in the three-story house they stopped outside. With the ground floor where they stood being the middle of the three floors. Or the door that was carved with scenes depicting the sea and the creatures within it, decorated with a silver border.

No as soon as the door opened Flynn staggered through, nodding his head in thanks to his guide who shut the door behind him. With the echoing boom of wood on wood Flynn collapsed from exhaustion. The wooden floor of the threshold as welcoming as any bed at the moment. His snores echoed around the foyer before Vashti could come down and greet him.

The sun shone onto his face causing him to stir. Confused as Flynn tried to figure out where he was for, he found himself in a strange bed in his undergarments. Not for the first time either. Sliding his tongue around checking for cottonmouth expecting a bender the previous night to explain his current situation.

A creaking floorboard had him sitting upright looking for a weapon as the door opened. Vashti entered wearing a stained apron over her tunic carrying a platter of food. "Good your awake" she said placing the tray on the bed beside him.

Flynn's stomach growled with hunger as he looked at the plate piled high with toast, eggs, bacon and tomato. "You collapsed from exhaustion so you missed dinner last night, Vaike has already left to answer some questions for mother so I thought to let you sleep in." "Much appreciated" Flynn said taking a bite of toast.

As he ate Vashti pulled back the quilt to inspect his leg, complaining the whole time about how it had gotten worse again and insisting that he needed to use the cane for the next few days. After much quarrelling Vashti won out fetching the cane from the corner while Flynn struggled into some pants. Plate now empty of food.

"You know It's not like my brother to bother with shenanigan's. He really likes you." "He did pick those stairs on purpose. I thought so." "Yeah. There are three entrances and that one is the longest and hardest." "Still it has its advantages." "How so?" "Well I would say its responsible for how you got those legs and arse" Flynn said winking.

Blushing Vashti grabbed the empty tray and wordlessly left the room, Flynn following behind.

Flynn's face hurt from smiling so much. He spent a week exploring Zardelfan. Vashti showing him all over the city. It was indescribable, reminding Flynn of the first time he sat in a crow's nest, gazing out over the horizon seeing only blue in every direction. Wonder, beauty, majestic. Centuries spent building, perfecting the city and they were never satisfied.

They ate lunch at different spots throughout the city. Small shops able to seat twelve customers. Tables outside under the open sky, birds perched on backrests as couples ate. Only to have the next tree housing an indoor eatery that could feed fifty plus.

In the city the possibilities were endless. Every elf works, but over centuries of existence many grew bored. Trying new things and exploring other cultures. Some elves are master craftsmen in several trades. Allowing them to create imposing works that are completely their own or work in whatever trade took their fancy that decade.

Even the army was basically a militia. All elves can fight but other than those few that desire to serve most are content not taking up arms. Even those in the guard can leave whenever they wish, only needing to serve fifty years minimum. Barely a drop in the ocean for immortals.

Vashti continued to impress Flynn with her cooking ability each night. Each meal better than the last. Even simple dishes tasted amazing with everything fresher, healthier.

❧

The last week with Flynn was incredible. She saw the amazement in his eyes that she shared on the Executioner. She showed him her favourite place in the city today, feeling confident he was healed enough to handle the climb. For climb it was.

On a small landing built high up in one of the tallest trees in the forest they sat on a plain wooden bench. In this city of art, the bench was basically a stump. Building the entire landing, bench and walkway herself.

Taking her nearly thirty years to complete it was solid but unimpressive looking like something a child would build. Well she was a child when she started it, she supposed. At least by their standards.

Crossing along a rope bridge, one of many in the city they then climbed upwards. It takes five ladders to reach the lookout forty metres above the nearest building but the climb was worth it. Vashti discovered it when she turned fifty. It was the best place in the forest to look out over the ocean.

She used to spend all her free time here, gazing longingly towards the sea. Even from this distance you can see the vastness of it. Breathing deeply Vashti imagined she could smell the faintest traces of salt in the air.

They sat together for hours, silently starring off into the distance. Hands so close the tips of their fingers touched. Peaceful bliss. So naturally, the moment her mother decided to visit. Vashti silently groaned hearing her mother climb onto the landing.

❧

"That's no dignified way for a Princess to move about, never mind a Queen." Flynn jumped to his feet with the haste off man who was just caught laying with another man's wife. Which was weird because that has happened to him more than once with no response other than to continue.

"If it bothered me mother, I would've ordered its construction and not built it myself. But then it wouldn't be a secret spot would it." "It's not as secret as you think" laughed the queen. "Now I'm here to steal your friend away. Don't worry he'll be fine. Probably. In the meantime, the council has a few questions for you."

"Very well. I'll see you back at the house later." Dismissing herself Vashti grabbed the ladder and with all the grace of a dancer climbed off the landing.

Flynn was frozen in place. Watching on as the queen strolled towards him, hands clasped behind her back. The landing was lucky to be ten square paces. The queen made it feel like fifty with her gait and poise. "So tell me. What are your intentions with my daughter?"

Flynn couldn't speak over the lump in his throat. All of his encounters with death and this felt closer. Like death was here waiting to collect what was long overdue.

"Come now, don't be shy." The queen said, commandingly patting the bench beside her. "Sit." Slowly Flynn lowered himself back down like he was a weathered old man. "So. Do you love her?"

Flynn guessed she already knew the answer but he still gave it. "Yes." The crushing weight on his chest lifting with the honesty. The first time he had ever said it allowed or even admitted it to himself. "She loves you also" the Queen stated.

"Yeah I know." The words flowed freely, the lock on his heart freshly opened. "But she is immortal so I can't give her what she wants. At best I'll live another thirty years but most likely twenty." "Is that why you did nothing. She wanted you to kiss her while you were at sea."

"I've ruined the lives of countless women that I've laid with. All done without a second thought. But in twenty years they'll be dead so what does it matter. Regardless of how I feel about your daughter. One night of passion will beget centuries of pain for her."

"That's what I was hoping to hear. So how do you like my city?" "I don't have the words to describe it." "How would you like to find those words?" "How?"

"I am giving you two choices. Firstly, you can leave the forest with more gold then you could spend in a lifetime and believe you me Vaike has told me how you spend it." Colour filled Flynn's cheeks at that. "Or, you can earn your place amongst us and live out your days in the city."

Staying true to his character Flynn chose to be selfish.

⚔

Vaike rode deeper into the forest. Needing to clear his head after mother gave him some big news. She has finally decided it was time for him to take the throne. His father dying before he ever met him, mother was the only ruler he's ever known. For five centuries she has guided their people, including the years she watched over during the war.

Herself close to half a millennium old when she took over for his father. The king ruling for barely a century before war erupted. His grandfather stepping down on his sons eight hundredth birthday. He himself was barely two hundred and fifty. A young adult by his people's standards. An unheard-of age for ruling.

To show he is ready mother has tasked him with finding his father's crown. Buried with him in a tomb that has never been entered. A task that Flynn is accompanying him on.

An impossible task for two different souls. Two different purposes. One to be crowned a king and the other seeking acceptance.

Still if mother feels I'm ready to lead I must be. She's never been wrong.

Chapter 14

THE TIES OF FAMILY

Garrett sat in the saddle, watching the sun rise behind Voldengird. Their camp encircled the walls of the city, besieging the loyalists. The command tent situated atop a rise on the western edge offering the best vantage point.

Garretts mount shifted with impatience, his left-hand twitching as he tightened his grip. He could feel the tendons in his hands stretch as the fingers tightened around the old leather.

A strange sensation that Garrett still found bizarre he thought glancing down at his bandaged stump. Left hand missing halfway to his elbow.

Two weeks since he lost it and it was now relatively pain free, just the phantom sensation remained. A sensation that could last the rest of his life according to the stories he'd heard from seasoned veterans missing limbs of their own.

"Are you feeling your hand again?" Ailish asked. She had barely left his side since the incident. Blaming herself for the loss of his hand despite whatever he had to say. Afterall it was the loyalists who ambushed them. Sneaking into their army, disguised as those that defected when Olaf died.

Then striking at the head, sacrificing themselves to kill the leaders and allow Duke Ivan to claim the throne. He shoved Ailish aside, the sword designed to split the back of her head open missing her just to take his hand. A trade he would gladly give again.

Since the attack security has been increased with lists kept of everyone who leaves the camp. Anyone who tries entering camp and is not on the list is hanged. They unfortunately executed over fifty soldiers the first few days while everyone adjusted to the change.

Only three since then that Garrett guessed were loyalists. A hefty price to pay but one that most understood as necessary. Even amongst the footmen, especially since four officers joined them on the noose. No favouritism, Baird's main focus. He'll make a good ruler for that alone. But first they need to take the city.

"Well, are you?" "What? Oh right." Garrett started remembering the question. "Yeah just a little. Looking at it helps remind myself that it's not there.

❧

A month after talking with the Queen, Flynn was completely healed and eager to be off. He had barely spent a minute alone with Vashti since his talk with the queen. Not that he wanted to. Every time he looked at her now his chest ached in ways foreign to him.

They stood at the landing of the southern stair case. Queen and Princess coming to see them off. Both wearing finery worthy of their station. Vashti looking more like a princess and less like the warrior then Flynn had ever seen.

The Queen saw them off with a wave and words of encouragement while Vashti squeezed both men in a strong embrace. Offering Flynn a quick peck on the cheek as he pulled away. Unable to even look back, he took the first step down.

The trek down the ten thousand steps was taken in silence. Both men trudging along with sealed lips, lost with their own thoughts. Sterben and Kjorgen were saddled and waiting at the base. No stable boys holding them, they grazed around waiting completely untethered.

The wordless procession continued all day as Vaike rode ahead on Kjorgen, Sterben following along. The silence was finally broken after dinner when Flynn declared he'd take first watch. Despite the fact they didn't need to keep watch till they left the forest Vaike remained silent. Figuring Flynn still wanted to be alone with his thoughts.

Not that Vaike could blame him, he too was still was working through the gravity of what success meant. Give him villains and worlds to save any day, the responsibility of ruling still scared him.

For three days they rode south through the forest with barely a dozen words spoken between them. Not that this was strange since they were both two of the quitter ones.

No what bothered Vaike was Flynn's sobriety. Since leaving he was yet to drink from his ever-present wineskin.

Breaking through the trees they camped under an open tree that night. The third evening together when Vaike finally broke the silence.

Staring down at his bowl of half-eaten stew he spoke five words. Five words that changed everything.

⌁

Flynn was lost deep in thought. He didn't taste the potato or rabbit in the stew he merely ate for the sustenance. He sought silence and solitude the last month in the forest, preferring to be alone with his thoughts. Now the silence was crushing, getting worse with each mile travelled. But the silence was also safe. Breaking it meant opening the door to unknown places.

"You love her, don't you?" "What?" "Vashti. You love her, don't you?" "It's alright" Vaike continued while Flynn just blankly stared at him. "I watched how close you too grew all those months we journeyed together. And I saw firsthand how it hurt her when you almost died fighting Olaf."

"Yes" Flynn spoke so softly the slight breeze swallowed it up. "What was that?" "Yes. I love her" Flynn shouted. "But it can never be." "Why? She feels the same it should be simple."

"Because you said so yourself" continued Flynn, eyes sparkling with tears. "It almost destroyed her to see me near death. I'm human, so even if blade or sickness doesn't claim me the years will. What could we have together twenty, thirty years? Even forty it makes no difference I'll die and it'll be like a blink of the eye to her."

"Why do this then. Why risk death to stay? You could be back in your tavern drinking and whoring away a kingdoms wealth." "I'm tired" Flynn said in a weary voice. "Tired of the chaos and waste. There is no one left to fight. I have no ship and crew and I'm weak. Yes, I am too weak to leave your sister" Flynn continued over Vaike's protestations.

"So, I have decided to be selfish, even though it will be painful for Vashti with me staying." "If anyone has earnt the right it is you my friend. But don't give up hope yet, you never know what tomorrow may bring" Vaike said standing beside the sitting Flynn. "And regardless what happens I am honoured to call you my brother" Vaike finished before strolling off to take first watch.

By some unspoken agreement neither man spoke off the previous night's discussion. No longer riding in silence however they discussed the journey ahead. Eventually Flynn asked what was so important about this crown and why his mother couldn't just commission another one or if it was all about the journey. Was it designed to teach him a lesson? Vaike told the tale of the crown and its significance.

"Long ago, before the darkness that was the hallow wars the dwarves delved. Deep into the roots of mountains they tunnelled. Building and expanding. In their expanse they stumbled across an empty cavern in the heart of Cullnurna. Empty, save for a boulder. A boulder that had no business being there.

Dwarves are the foremost experts on stones and ore but even they couldn't place it. Eventually deciding the rock came from the heaven's millennia ago. Lying here forgotten while the mountains swallowed it up.

Believing it a sign the dwarves chose that cavern to be the seat of their power. Replacing the star with a throne. Filling the cavern with statues and the skull of the star's guardian.

With the completion of Reyvadin the star was melted down creating a new metal. Stronger and lighter than anything the dwarves had ever worked with it shone with the unmatched lustre of a star itself.

Two crowns were made, simple and without jewels. Crafted to adorn the heads of those in the two greatest seats of power. The dwarves and elves. Both crowns resting with their last owners, heroes lost in the dying days of the hallow wars.

The star no longer remains. The dwarves used the remaining ore to forge Harbinger. Choosing to entrusting their legacy with men.

As for the journey and any lessons that I am meant to gain I have no idea."

The bandits that roamed in the north spread fear. Filling the void left from the soldier's absence they continued their reign of terror down south. Farms were abandoned and left as smoking cinders. Fields torched and livestock chased off or slaughtered. The actions of men blinded by rage, by loss they lashed out at the world with no thought to their own future.

Sticking to the main road out of convenience made them the target of frequent attacks and ambushes. Proving to be a nuisance on par with the fly that circles your face, neither bothered to even give chase to any survivors that fled. Few that they were.

It was after one such attack with two survivors throwing down pitchforks and fleeing after their six companions were cut down in the blink of an eye. Vaike, casually leant from his saddle catching his last victim by the scruff of his coat while pulling his sword free. Staining the shirts shoulder red with the blood from his sword before letting the corpse collapse on the ground. Blood quickly pooling together with five other corpses.

"I've been meaning to ask, what happened to your Yanyue blade?" "I know we haven't spoken much about what happened in the tower but didn't mother or Vashti mention it to you?" Vaike asked with a bewildered look on his face.

"They both did. But other than Maroxis and the vampire being defeated and everyone else surviving I didn't really care so I just zoned out and stopped listening."

"You sat in discussion with the oldest and wisest ruler in Thaldesa if not the world and you zoned out. You truly are one of a kind" Vaike laughed like it was the funniest joke in the world. He laughed until his sides hurt and a gasped for air.

❧

A week after her brother left with Flynn and Vashti found herself once again enduring another council meeting. She hated sitting in on these monotonous meetings. Well standing since she wasn't on the council so, she stood of to the side. Listening, watching, learning.

At least that's how her mother put it, declaring she needed to learn how the kingdom was governed. Her brother dutifully stood for hours on end silently learning, he was after all being groomed to take over.

Vashti had never seen the need to or cared enough to bother. Suspecting the Queen's sudden interest in teaching her has more to do with keeping her occupied so as to not dwell on the ruffian Flynn.

The next report grabbed her attention, despite her best efforts to ignore the councils talks and sulk in the corner. Shifting her weight on tired feet, Vashti straightened her back and listened as the discussions turned to the necromancer.

"Our spellweaver's have little comprehension of dark magic and the spells construction is beyond them. Based on the prince's report however and with what little they could interpret they have made an educated guess.

To become a lich lord, he had to give up his physical shell allowing his soul to enter the void. No longer just being able to control the dead but becoming one of them, becoming their lord.

To achieve this, he couldn't be killed by just anyone. It must also be during the ritual and as far as we can tell, by someone he's resurrected. His death required an aspect of betrayal even if staged, to enter the right level of the void.

He then needed a willing vessel for his soul to escape the void. We have been unable to discern if his previous body was an option or if he required a living body. Nor could we glean if he did require a living body what happened to the host.

Based on the reports we assume that the human was to be the vessel and killed. Probably promised to be revived in a new vessel, gaining immortality in a sense as a reward.

We guess the human titan was not a viable option for some reason. Perhaps he was already dead or perhaps the victim had to have died recently or been a descendant from someone of note.

This is mere conjecture however. It could simply be Maroxis needed a human sacrifice or a new body and the human was brainwashed or that he missed a narrow timeframe with your intrusion."

'So, a whole lot of nothing' sighed Vashti to herself. A lot of theorizing and guess work. Her mother usually prefers hard facts to conjecture but it matters little, Maroxis is dead and with the current level of ability amongst gifted there is no one capable of reproducing the spell.

Haven was a completely different town with Olaf's influence gone. Far removed from the chaos of a pirate port but no longer run with the efficiency of a military camp. Somewhere in the median.

Merchants still traded, but now free of scrutiny and taxes they openly traded in contraband and extortion. Whores more openly plied their trade instead of behind doors and Vaike and Flynn walked openly through the streets.

The tavern seemed the worst off, with the soldiers leaving most of the regular clientele disappeared also. The loud and jubilant common room replaced with a few sailors drinking their earnings. Quiet and dull, the inn waited on the soldiers to return or more ships to enter the currently free port.

The pair quickly offering a particular inn compensation when Flynn decided to rest his saddle stiff arse spending three days binging on grog.

The inn keeper was grateful for the business offering them both separate rooms for the price of one.

Vaike joined Flynn for the first two days, enjoying the casual pace they were able to travel at. Leaving the inn early morning on the third day to buy enough victuals to last them the next leg of their journey. Flynn already starting on his second jug of ale refused to accompany him.

Vaike dragged Flynn from the inn before dawn. Not wanting to let him start drinking, preventing their departure for another day. Not that Vaike wanted to leave today either. He too felt miserable joining Flynn for some drinking games after returning from shopping. The games and merriments lasting long into the night.

Other than the black rings under his eyes, Flynn however seemed fine. Ripping into a loaf of bread he mounted Sterben and led the way out of town. If he was indeed fine, he respected Vaike's pounding head riding in silence. Perhaps not choosing the best path as Vaike was jolted around in the saddle making his stomach roil in protest.

By midday Vaike had recovered. His elven vitality having sufficiently passed the alcohol through his system.

"Feeling better?" Flynn asked when he started eating some strips of salted meat. "Yes. But how were you okay. We went drink for drink?" Vaike asked in between bites.

"Because my ale was watered down. That was a game we would play on new pirates the day before sailing. It was a tradition, and until they figured out to water down their own, they would be forced to suffer the consequences."

Vaike didn't know why but he laughed. In centuries it was the best practical joke that had ever been played on him. A joke he couldn't wait to take home.

⚓

It had been a difficult two days. Two days full of confusion, chaos and death. All thanks to the new weapon the defenders brought to bear.

Deafening booms reverberated around the city walls, echoing through the valley as three iron balls barrelled towards the attackers. Propelled by some unknown method the balls carried momentum equal to a ballistae bolt with significantly increased destructive capabilities.

The soldiers had taken to calling them Dragon shots. An apt name Garrett mused as he watched three more iron balls roll through tents, timber barricades and men. Blood, splinters and timber rained down on the lucky bystanders.

Metal balls embedded in the earth showed the inexperience off the crews who only have one in three shots fall on target. Still each Dragon shot fired five times an hour resulting in five or six balls ripping through their men in the same time frame.

Unlike boulders from catapults that crush whatever is unlucky enough to be standing in the wrong spot. These balls bounce across the ground like children skipping smooth stones across a pond.

Resulting in swathes of destruction up to fifty feet behind the initial point of impact. Then the fallout from timber structures shattering, throwing debris outwards like the ripples formed once the stone sinks.

⚓

The two men travelled at a slow pace, heading towards the Blood cliffs. They were attacked by bandits once again two days out of Haven with Flynn prying a pair of spears from their lifeless grips.

The reason becoming apparent later that evening when Flynn tossed a spear across the camp, landing at Vaike's feet. Flynn already standing with the second gripped firmly in his hand.

For whatever reason Flynn wanted to learn to fight with another weapon and he guessed Vaike was at least competent with the spear.

Competent was an understatement with Vaike being almost as good with the spear as he was with a sword. Now Flynn was the one repeatedly picking himself up from the ground each night.

Two weeks of riding at a relaxed pace set by their mounts and they looked down on the walls guarding the eastern end of the blood cliffs. Walls aflame with an orange glow as the sun sank below the towering keep.

Chapter 15

THE LEAP

The moon shone down upon the men as they camped in the valley. Still a few hours ride from the keep and what they expect will be an awkward encounter with Commander Black.

"How do you think the Siege is going?" Vaike asked Flynn, returning with a bundle of wood cradled in his arms. "Poorly if they're listening to the kid." "True, but there are competent people with him" chuckled Vaike.

"But seriously, how do you think it is going?" "Hopefully better than the time King Ogstrim lay siege to his rival, King Adair's castle" Flynn responded. "I am versed in battles all across Thaldesa but I'm not familiar with that siege."

"It's a battle from a land across the northern sea. The land is divided into three nations but this battle took place a few generations ago when smaller nations were scrambling for power. In the east two main kings rose up subjugating the nations around them.

Both aiming to become high king, they waged many battles. Eventually culminating in the siege. Ogstrim had a significant troop advantage and pushed Adair all the way back to his castle.

The siege followed the typical pattern. Dig in and fortify your position, build scaling ladders, towers and siege weapons.

After three weeks or so the first boulders started hurling for the walls and the citizens revolted. Throwing open the gates allowing Ogstrim and his troops to flow through. Fuelled by greed and ambition they barrelled straight for the keep, leaving only their wounded and a few commanders in the camp."

"So far that sounds like a rather successful siege?" "That's exactly what Ogstrim thought. But while he bullied and threatened the other kings into following him, Adair convinced and inspired the ones who joined him. A brilliant tactician, every movement and battle over the year was all a calculated plan.

So, while Ogstrim's troops poured in, the citizens evacuated. Nothing strange about that when your city fell, except when Ogstrim entered the keep he discovered it to be completely empty.

His army chased one company of troops into the city. Meanwhile Adair's main army was encamped two days away, waiting.

When Ogstrim entered the walls, blinded by his ambition thinking he was now high king, Adair was killing those left behind in his camp. Chasing the last few towards his own castle, scaring them into closing the gates on his men. Exactly what they wanted.

Attackers now defenders. Besieged troops now laying siege. Ogstrim lost. His number advantage meant nothing without his cavalry and now having to charge into the defences built by his own men. No food stores were left in the keep and everything built and ready for Adair's men to scale the walls the moment his soldiers grew weak from hunger.

After five days king Ogstrim was driven through the gates at spear point by his own allies. The other kings turning on him the moment he was too weak to threaten them anymore. His own body guards lay dead in the keep.

Adair executed Ogstrim, dividing his lands amongst some of his most loyal commanders and became high king after the others all swore fealty to him before being sent off to see to their own lands."

"Well Ivan doesn't strike me as someone able to pull off a deception like that." 'Agreed. And either way they have enough mercenaries so it'll be fine. No self-respecting mercenary would abandon a siege with that much money available."

☙

Four hundred men dead with as many wounded after six days staring down those Dragon shots. That ends tonight Garrett thought, kneeling behind an overturned wagon.

They deduced fire was used to burn something dangerous causing the Dragon shots to expel their deadly load. With the regularity of the shots it must also be stored near the walls so a small team of volunteers is set to scale the wall. To find and destroy those caches.

The team stood holding a ladder between them, waiting on his signal. Five of the bravest, or dumbest soldiers volunteered, Garrett wasn't sure which as only the results truly tell.

Garrett waited patiently, learning the guard's pattern before signalling to his men. Silently cursing that he can't join them. His injury preventing him from scaling the ladder with them. A ball tore through Ailish's tent yesterday. Thankfully she was out and is completely unharmed but the near miss drove him to new levels of determination to end it tonight.

The five men scaled the wall with ease then quickly dispatched the Guards patrolling the wall up top. One donned the armour of a fallen guard taking up his patrol while the others split up into pairs.

Quickly enveloped by the blackness Garrett sat in silence waiting, taking shelter behind the wagon. Growing restless unable to do anything more than to count the minutes.

A shockwave rent the air wide open, hurling Garrett back. Unable to hear. Ears ringing, blood running from his left one pointed to a ruptured ear drum.

The ground was spinning, unsteady legs wobbled beneath him as Garrett tried to stand. The movement only caused him to double over retching instead.

Too sick to do anything else he collapsed on his side, sick splattering his cheek as he fell in the puddle.

Thick black smoke billowed upwards from the now gaping hole in the external wall. Stone chunks fell littering no man's land, the smallest even landing amongst the camp. Dust fell thick in the air making it difficult to see and even harder to breathe. Corpses lay around the base of the wall, bodies thrown clear.

The wagon lay in pieces around him, absorbing some of the shock probably saving his life.

⤙

"This doesn't bode well" Vaike said riding past the remains of pyres, reflecting his own thoughts. Charred bones and soot black mud, stained the land in several spots. Wagons parked nearby, littered with rotting corpses picked clean by scavengers.

The Fortress itself was exactly the same as they left it months ago. Wooden stakes protecting the rear entrance and stables. Timber doors thrown open to any visitors.

But no soldiers stood guarding the entrance. The stable was empty of mounts and an unnerving silence surrounded the keep. Reminding Flynn of Maroxis tower.

Looking at each other and shrugging, the pair dismounted and strode inside the walls. Hands resting on hilts, swords at the ready.

Upon entering the commander's office, they found it empty. No surprise given the mess hall and kitchen were both clear of soldiers also.

"Maybe they all fled when they learnt of Olaf's defeat." "That is possible but I don't think so" Vaike answered. "The dust is too thick in places and Black strikes me as someone more honourable then that. Either way we'll have to send word to Baird to reinforce the keep with more soldiers when he gets a chance."

"With the larder empty the rodents having picked it clean they decided to continue west. The stoned courtyard that flowed with blood months earlier was scrubbed clean. Evenly cut grey stone stretched wall to wall. Cliff to cliff. Wall stretching from north to south, stones haphazardly placed filling in the breached gate.

The whole place was silent and empty save for the spears mounted throughout the courtyard. Some toppled on their sides having fallen but all with a rotting head impaled on the tip. Some still wore helmets or fraying bandages. Most with their eyes pecked out by the birds.

"I bet if we count there would be sixty-four" Vaike said. "Sixty-three, for the survivors" Flynn countered. "I assume that's Black there he said pointing to a dismembered corpse hanging from the keeps upper windows.

Both men spent the remaining daylight burying the heads of the soldiers in the fort's graveyard. Short as it may have been, they were brothers in arms, deserving a warrior's burial. Surrounded by their comrades who have fallen defending the wall.

Blacks corpse proved problematic. Both men struggled to drag the heavy chains that it hung from up through the window. From here it got worse. Tortured and mutilated, the body was then displayed as a warning. A barbaric warning that was new to Vaike and Thaldesa. Something Flynn had only seen amongst the most bloodthirsty and hateful places he'd visited.

Dismembered, eyes gouged out. Tongue and teeth missing. One ear cut off, scalped and torso a complete mess. Burns from irons, marks from lashes and cuts from various weapons.

Large steel hooks were then driven through the shoulder blades and attached to the chains. From here a clear substance was poured over encasing and preserving the corpse. Clear like glass but solid like steel they couldn't break it open.

They buried black with his men, chains and all unable to do anything more. Knowing in a century the chains will rust but the disfigured corpse will still remain.

❦

It was pandemonium. Even worse than when the first Dragon shots landed amongst them. Troops ran everywhere gathering up weapons and armour thinking they missed some order to attack. The wall now open, mercenaries shoved others aside in an attempt to be the first through the breach. The first to riches.

Officers shrieking cries for order fell on deaf ears in an attempt to gain any semblance of control. Those closest to the wall staggered around confused, hands pressed against their ears.

Baird grabbed Ailish and his commanders. Giving chase to the crazed mob that his army had become. Ailish was concerned for Garrett. A fact she continually repeated. It's not that Baird didn't fear for his friend's safety, far from it.

He just feared what would happen to the innocent citizens if the soldiers were left unchecked. His citizens he thought glumly.

Mercenaries were already pulling people from their houses when they caught up to those first through the breach. One overly eager mercenary had dragged a woman onto her porch and was holding her down. Dress torn, exposing her naked breasts to the cool night air.

She scratched at his face while he tried to pull his own pants down earning her a back hand across the face.

Slumping back dazed, he continued on as everyone around him went about their own looting. Officers shouted orders were swallowed up by screams of fear and panic.

Ailish stopped behind the mercenary as he finished pulling down the woman's under garments. Plunging her own axe into his skull as he planned to plunge into the helpless woman.

The cold-blooded murder brought order to the mob faster than words could. Immediately taking control Ailish began ordering the soldiers around them to aid the citizens in dousing the fires that spread outwards from the breach. Several homes nearby were already fully engulfed in flames, thick smoke wafting into their faces.

The soldiers begrudgingly abandoned their looting to follow orders. The fresh blood dripping from Ailish's axe silencing any objections.

As more soldiers poured through the breach, the commanders began to take charge. Sending the most trusted to sweep homes for enemy soldiers and not to loot. Others left to search for survivors and wounded near the breach while the rest marched on the inner wall. Hoping it too wasn't protected with more Dragon shots.

◆

The two companions walked in silence. Tired, neither finding sleep the previous night in the fortress. Plagued by thoughts of the horrors that happened inside those walls. Horrors that even bothered Flynn who thought he had seen the worst of humanity.

They set off while the sun still sat below the horizon. Dim light from a waning moon guiding them along. Their horses left grazing outside the fortress. Wanting to put some distance between them and the graves they'd dug.

With the arrival of winters cold embrace, the land bridge appeared even more dead then the last time.

Pools of water now icy cold, piercing them through to the bones whenever a foot broke the glass like surface. Animals slumbered in their dens, while the flora looked withered and dead.

With the cold came shorter days and longer nights. Survival instincts told Vaike and Flynn to huddle together for warmth of an evening. An option both men were too proud to even consider, death was preferable.

The disappearing light from the setting sun had them both pulling coats tighter and wrapping woollen blankets around themselves. No wood to burn and too dark to continue walking. Each night was a struggle to find sleep. Each morning offering up silent prayers of thanks when they awoke.

Dawn's first light each morning greeted them. Still cold they shrugged of blankets and walked. Cold muscles protesting while blood was slowly warmed and pumped around their tired bodies.

Four nights of deathly cold. Four days of pushing unresponsive bodies onwards. Four days to find what they sought.

❧

The sun was well past its zenith, yet it was barely past midday. Vaike knelt consulting a map mere paces from a hole in the rocks. Actually, a crater Flynn thought standing near it. Twenty feet across narrowing as it burrowed into the stones. Disappearing into darkness.

Water laped against the shore below them. Wearing the rocks down over time eventually splitting the land bridge in two.

"This is it" declared Vaike. "The entrance to the tomb." "So, what are we meant to climb down there? My hands are so numb I doubt even I could manage that."

"Not exactly" answered Vaike as a tower of water burst forth from the crater before them. Showering them with cold water instantly freezing them to their core's.

"Oh great, a fucking blowhole" Flynn swore, teeth already chattering as he stood shivering from the drenched clothes. "Who's the moron who thought we should do this now, if the rocks don't kill us the cold will."

"It apparently is the only window. The water normally shoots out every few minutes making it impossible to swim through in time. During the winter it only shoots up roughly every ten or so and if we waited any longer the cold would definitely kill us.

"Here you'll need this" Vaike said handing over a leather pouch. The leather was abnormally thick, yet somehow stretched. An oily sheen glistened across the dark leather yet it was dry to the touch.

"One is for supplies the other is for your weapons" Vaike said pulling out a second pouch from his own pack. "Three days' worth should be plenty."

Muttering under his breath, Flynn opened the pouch pulling a second one from inside. Long and thin designed to carry a single sword. With a continuous stream of curses growing in volume, Flynn managed to force both of his swords inside and seal the bag shut.

Stuffing his dry clothes and some food into the other bag he stood beside Vaike. Mere feet from the edge of the crater. Water cascading back into the depths made the edge slippery and treacherous. Counting down the seconds the stood silent, rubbing themselves trying to bring warmth back into cold limbs.

Never before was Flynn happier to see a spout of water. As a sailor they would belong to giant fish and sea creatures capable of crushing ships. Something to be avoided. Now it meant no more waiting.

With the force of the initial upwards burst dissipating Vaike stepped to the lip and jumped head first. Flynn following a step behind. Water could be seen at the bottom. Yet even as they fell it was already starting to recede.

Despite being wet already, the shock from the freezing water almost drove the air from Flynn's lung as he broke the surface. Keeping his mouth closed on instinct the current tugged, dragged and pulled him along helplessly. Buffeted from all sides as the rocks tore at his clothes and cut up his arms shielding his head.

Too dark to see anything, regardless of the churning water and flailing limbs. Vaike's foot kicked his head, the only indication that he wasn't alone.

Eventually the crazy ride ended. Opening his eye's, a pale glow filtered around the underwater cave. Some sort of lichen provided the dim light that allowed them to see a few feet in every direction.

Vaike was turning around rapidly looking for something, trying to get his bearings while floating upside down. A fact Flynn had already noted, based on the directions the bubbles he blew out went.

A trick every sailor new in case you were ever stuck in a sinking ship. It is very easy to become disorientated underwater but bubbles always rise to the surface.

Worry and concern was plastered on Vaike's face when he locked eyes with Flynn. The pirate more comfortable underwater then the elven prince. Pointing up and down, left and right Flynn got the message. Emptying his lungs of more air then was probably wise, Flynn unleashed an eruption of large bubbles.

Eyes widening in understanding, Vaike flipped over and set of swimming after the bubbles. The light grew brighter the further they swam. Each stroke upwards harder than the previous as Flynn's lung began screaming for air. Eyes scrunched tight and head down forcing his mouth to stay closed he kicked frantically. Unsure if they were even close to the surface or if they will find a rock ceiling and be trapped.

Lightheaded and consciousness fading Flynn didn't feel it as his hand broke free through the surface. Finally breaking, his lungs opened trying to gulp down the much-needed air as his head broke free.

Never before had a breath of air felt so refreshing as it did then. Treading water Flynn continued to gulp down lungful after lungful, breathing deeply. Catching his breath, he looked around for the prince.

Lying on his back on the rocky shore still half in the water Vaike lay, chest rising and falling as he too filled his lungs.

Dragging himself up onto the rocky shelf beside Vaike Flynn forced himself into a sitting position. No longer panting but body wrecked with exhaustion.

Eyes snapping open Flynn sat up, cramped back groaning in protest. Startling Vaike awake who slept beside Flynn almost touching shoulders. Damp clothes clung to their bodies, encasing them while they slept. Unsure how long for or even what time of day it was.

Pulling open the bag containing his supplies, Flynn was amazed at how well they worked. Sailors use similar pouches when transporting delicate goods but sometimes water seeps through. Yet these bags made by elves were completely submerged and yet, everything inside was completely dry.

Something he was grateful for as he stripped off his wet clothes. The old tunic ripping in half as it stuck to his wet back. Discarding the rags Flynn changed into dry clothes then laid out his wet clothes on the rocks to dry. Vaike having the same idea they sat down for a meal.

Mindlessly chewing paying no attention to what he ate Flynn focused on the cave they sat in. The water glowed with a greenish hue from the lichen that didn't appear to live above the water line. The cave walls barren and surprisingly warm to the touch drying their clothes quicker than either of them expected.

The shelf they sat on was eight feet wide or so and five or six deep. The rocks themselves were dry with no signs of moss so the tide mustn't rise above them.

In the back right corner beside were Flynn sat was a hole. Large enough for a dwarf to stoop through but the two of them would have to crawl.

The floor was cut smooth, making it gentle on their knees. The same couldn't be said for the top and side with rocks snagging and cutting them every few feet. To narrow to allow them the light of a torch they relied on the glow moss. That light quickly faded away behind them, leaving the men in utter darkness.

Still they encountered no alternate routes, so they followed the path as it curved slightly to the left. Always to the left. After a few hours of darkness so thick Flynn thought he could feel the weight of it a small pinprick appeared ahead.

The tunnel slowly began to widen and straighten as they crawled closer to the light. Ten minutes after the light was seen they were able to walk along while stooping. The light seemed to grow disproportionately slow as they continued forward. Either the darkness or the tunnel straightening out made the distance deceiving.

Despite how cold it was outside, the cave it was too hot for the heavy fur coats they now carried in their bags. Now able to walk comfortably upright the ceiling half an arm's length above their heads.

It grew hotter as they followed the tunnel deeper in. Eventually Flynn discarded his new shirt also. Drenched in sweat so heavy it could almost be rung out.

The walls began to grow hot to the touch making it impossible to lean against them for more than a few seconds with them becoming unbearable as they stepped through into the light.

Chapter 16

THE SLEEPING HEROES

Blinking back tears, the source of the heat and light became apparent. Lava flowed down the opposite wall like a waterfall, a slow-moving waterfall. Hues of red and orange specked with black rolled down the wall dividing off into two paths.

Bellow the divide was another opening. Atop of which carved in stone was a triangle depicting three birds. A hawk, falcon and eagle each in a different corner but all faced inwards looking at each other.

Troughs either natural or manmade, Flynn couldn't tell directed the lava. Flowing around both sides of the chamber it continued around towards the tunnel exit behind them before disappearing below the rock. Thirty feet of molten rock radiating its heat down the tunnel and into the earth.

The light was generated from a giant diamond hanging from the ceiling. Ensconced in a steel bracket hanging from the ceiling, made it look like a giant mace. The light from the lava reflected through the clear surfaces of the gem, causing it to glisten with an almost blinding brilliance.

The pirate in him tried calculating a hundred different ways to steal and transport the stone. An impossible task he sighed, and even if he did manage to steal it, he would never find someone who could actually afford to buy it.

"The tomb of three kings lies ahead" Vaike said stepping through the next opening. Through the opening was another tunnel. This one was definitely made by dwarves. Fifty feet wide and as many high it stretched on as far as the eye could see. Lava flowed down the walls in small evenly spaced troughs, the regular intervals lighting up the path to the fallen kings.

Statues of the kings depicting different victories and battles lined the path. All spread out and jumbled together, no one king claiming supremacy over the others. All equals.

Each statue shone with the brilliance of the perfect golden ore used to create it. Perfectly cut rubies, sapphire's and other precious stones sparkled around them like a rainbow.

It was not Flynn's first time seeing the grandeur of the dwarves. Yet this tomb truly left him lost for words. Comparing this to Voldengird was how he felt comparing that city to human ones. Even accounting for the destruction caused by the goblins. The dwarves outdid themselves here honouring the fallen heroes.

The tomb was disappointing compared to the foyer. Grandeur replaced with simplicity. A round cavern untouched by dwarven hands. Stalactites hung from the ceiling, the occasional water droplet falling from their tips. Four identical stone caskets sat two by two inwards from the wall. Completely unadorned and unnamed.

Three statues of birds stood guard over the kings. Hawk and falcon either side with the eagle siting at the king's heads. The eagles and hawk's taloned foot curled over, clutching the crown of their king. The falcon's own talon stood raised, ready to guard their own crown if needed. Each with an inscription carved at the base of each statue.

Vaike walked over to the hawk statue on his left and knelt before it as if it was the king itself. "There is not one of us that is greater than all of us." "What?" "It's what the inscription reads" Vaike answered standing.

"This one is different" Flynn said squatting down before the Falcon reading it aloud. "The bonds of family transcend the boundaries of race."

"What are these?" Flynn asked aloud. "The king's feelings, their thought's, I think. An unnamed tomb, with no way to discern who's who from the parting words."

"So, who does the fourth casket belong too?" "Prince Vlathe I'd guess." "Ithiel's son." "The same. He fell beside his father but we had no record of what happened to his body. I would assume that he was awarded the same honour as his father but that is a complete guess."

"Maybe the Eagle can clear it up then" Flynn said following Vaike between the giant slabs of stone. Halting, Flynn stopped. Death before defeat. A fourth inscription carved on the floor, centralized with the four heroes.

"This one belongs to a human." "Huh" Vaike responded confused by Flynn's words. "The words, death before defeat. A rallying cry of the desperate, and usually young. I guess it's the prince's then." "All humans are young to me but I guess so."

"So, what does the last king say?" Flynn asked as Vaike knelt before the eagle. Turning around eyes glistening with tears the prince spoke. "It is my father's."

Sitting down beside his friend Flynn gazed upon the words.

> Here we lay, the honoured few
> Who led the many that risked everything
> To save everything we gladly paid the price
> Thereby ensuring that others wouldn't have to
>
> Here we rest for eternity
> Brothers in arms
> Brothers forged in blood
> From now to the end of time.

As he read Flynn felt the words speak to him. Placing a hand on the prince's shoulder gripping it firmly in comfort. Neither man speaking. Neither man moving. They stayed until they both understood it was time.

Vaike stood reaching up towards the crown. As if recognizing the prince and his authority the talon uncurled allowing him to claim it.

❧

The faint hint of smoke could still be smelt on the morning breeze as it kissed their skin. Half a dozen house burnt down before the fires were quenched. The remains still smouldered as the occupants knelt outside weeping.

One more thing he will have to deal with Baird thought as the sun rose high enough to illuminate the inner wall.

It seemed fortune favoured them with no Dragon shots coming to bear. Granting them enough time to route the remaining soldiers and regroup.

It was on the advice of Ailish and his other commanders when they arrived at the inner wall and saw it was only guarded by soldiers hastening to their posts. With no siege engines they could afford to take a breath, slow down and regain their composer.

They still didn't want to wait too long giving them ample time to regroup and compose themselves. Now they waited. Formed up in ranks behind the large wooden barriers wheeled in to protect against arrows. Already built but unused, useless against the heavy iron balls that tore through them.

The commanders all looked to him for orders. Baird was unsure what to do without his friends beside him. His friends who always took charge, making up for his inexperience.

But Garrett now lay gravely injured in a healer's tent with Ailish leaving to check on him not long after they began to secure the inner gate.

Looking around Baird tried to make a decision but he was terrified. What if they waited too long and the defenders had an ambush prepared? What if the strategy was wrong or the ladders were deployed in the wrong place's? The wrong decision could kill hundreds even thousands. The burden of command was indeed a heavy one.

Flynn's words from a lesson long forgotten filled his head like an echo. Cutting through the uncertainty.

Flynn was berating him for hesitating in attack. Unsure if it was a feint or not had him lying on the ground clutching his ribs trying to catch his breath, the air driven from his lungs with a punch. "The only thing worse than making the wrong decision is making none. Indecision will kill you just as easily and you have no chance of being right."

He was right of course. As usual Baird begrudgingly thought taking a deep breath then giving the order to attack.

❧

The cavern echoed with a grating sound. Deep and rumbling that could be felt as well as heard. Looking around confused searching for the sounds source Flynn taking a step back into open space. Vaike reaching out with his empty hand catching Flynn has he fell backwards. Left foot placed on solid stone right hanging over nothing.

The grating stopped and light filled the darkness below. The tile containing the prince's inscription had slid back revealing a narrow staircase illuminated by more lava flowing along the walls.

"Down we go I guess" Flynn said taking the first step. Fifty steps down and they levelled out into a narrow corridor. High enough so they could walk upright, the hall of statues somewhere above their heads.

Once again, the temperature grew to uncomfortable levels as they walked forward, pausing at the empty chamber near the end. They were directly below the diamond Flynn guessed wiping the sweat from his forehead yet again.

The chambers roof rose ten feet higher than in the tunnel. All shaped and polished stone completely bare save for the two holes at the far ends from which the lava flowed through from the chamber above.

There was no floor as the tunnel opened into darkness. A bridge wide enough for one person spanned the gap. The hollow beneath their feet so deep even the lava flowing downwards couldn't illuminate the bottom.

The bridge arched slightly reaching its peak halfway across the gap. Narrowing slightly also with it wide enough for only one foot at the top. A very slow and precarious walk across made all the more difficult by the heat radiating upwards from the hole.

'What was the point of that?" Vaike panted out of breath. The heat and concentration taking more of a toll than expected. "Security" Flynn answered between large gulps of water. "It's too narrow to carry anything large or heavy across preventing anyone from stealing anything if they ever broke in."

Hair slick with sweat, shirts drenched and sticking to their backs and waterskins drained they took the path onwards. Taking a sharp turn to the right the tunnel sloped downwards.

Lanterns hung from a hook in the wall, red light shining through metal slits. Similar to those found in Voldengird only portable. Each man claiming one from a hook, the metal handle cold against their wet palms. Despite their size they weighed less than Flynn expected.

The tunnel cooled rapidly the further down they journeyed. Soon the walls were slick with moisture and they began to shiver in their wet clothes. As the tunnel levelled out it opened into an empty cavern.

The lantern light couldn't reach to the far corners of the cavern. The trickle of water could be heard, punctuated by steady drips. Cracked lips and parched throats sent them searching for the source.

Water trailed down the wall nearby in a few places. Tasting revealed it to be fresh and while the flow wasn't strong it was adequate to fill cupped hands. The slight tang of salt and other minerals tainted the water, yet beside the taste it was safe to drink.

Thirst quenched they lay down to sleep, unsure what time of day or how long they would still be down here but too tired to care.

Vaike was the first to rise in the utter blackness, the nearby lanterns still covered shielding the darkness from their red light. Flynn snored loudly nearby. His human vitality having a harder time dealing with the heat then he did Vaike guessed.

Uncovering his lantern red light flooded the darkness around him. Red light not harsh on his vision causing momentary blindness like a normal torch would.

While Flynn slept, Vaike took to exploring and figuring out their next move.

Stretching, the hard stones wreaking havoc on his muscles Flynn woke up. Despite the tight muscles and growling stomach, he felt refreshed. A red light moved around in the distance. Too far away to make out anything more than a faint glow.

The light moved closer as Flynn dug through his pouch looking for food. Vaike joining him for breakfast Flynn supposed, they ate in silence. Stale travel biscuits and dried meat washed down with water.

After eating Vaike led Flynn over to show him his discovery. The cavern was huge with Vaike walking around following the wall, no other reference point existing in the black void.

Either by touch or sight Vaike noticed something on the wall Flynn didn't. Stepping left away from the wall they walked, light shining on more nothing.

Skeletons littered the ground just beyond. Red light giving an evil appearance to the lifeless bones.

Being careful where he placed his feet Flynn walked around. Judging by the size they were all dwarves. Some still seating or slouched against the wall. Others lay down on stone slabs, Flynn presumed to be beds. "There must be dozens" Flynn said.

"Sixty-seven" Vaike answered. 'It's all in here." Leading him through the tomb the lantern glow revealing a stone lectern. Atop sat a book. Flynn couldn't even guess at the age or materials used to make it as the pages crinkled, threatening to tear with each turn.

"The workers built the tomb for the kings. Spending years locked in here completing everything. Once they finished, they decided to stay beside their king forever, all having fought beside him during the war.

Some were even the remnants of his personal guard. They poisoned themselves here in their living quarters. The book lists the names of all the workers as well as position and ranks. Some even left messages for their wives and children."

"I'm sure the dwarves would love to have that back, wherever they're hiding." "Agreed but it has proved too fragile to move. I've made a list of the names, that will have to suffice."

Chapter 17

THE NEW KING FALLS

Baird's heart pounded in his chest in time with the battering ram. Bang, bang, bang, the hardened tip of the ram crashed against the reinforced door of the keep.

They took the inner wall with almost no resistance. Swept away in the tide of battle Baird raced ahead with the vanguard forgoing his position at the rear. He could hear the blood pounding in his ear and feel his heart beating so strongly it felt like it would burst from his chest.

Stalling at the door did nothing to kill their enthusiasm, as more and more mercenaries joined those on the ram. Adding their strength to each blow or raising shields over head to protect against any potential projectiles.

The doors started to crack and splinter under the sheer weight of repeated blows. The door split showing a sliver of the foyer behind the doors. The next blow opened the gap enough for arrows and spears to burst forth. A last desperate defence from the defenders. Defenders who know they've already lost and will soon be killed.

Part of Baird admired their grit and determination. But with one last swing the doors burst inwards. Baird charged straight in with those who held shields, the ground beneath his feet shaking with the impact of the battering ram falling. No longer needed hands now gripping cold steel.

Not even a dozen defenders greeted them. Three in front with shields held high while four spears poked and prodded over their shoulders. Four bowmen stood behind them, arrows knocked and drawn. Two halfway up the stairs firing from the high ground, while the others tried to protect the flanks.

A very effective strategy, if they had more numbers. The tide would be braking against cliffs, solid and immovable. It was more akin to the tide smashing people against the cliffs instead.

A few soldiers fell clutching at shafts protruding from their necks while others lay on the floor, red blood pooling underneath hands clutching at their sides. Spear thrusts penetrating armour.

The defenders could only bring down one or two attackers, most not even mortally wounded, before they were jumped on. Baird even claiming the left bowman for himself.

Soldiers and mercenaries scattered down corridors and upstairs. Wails and pleads of dying men, both friend and foe forgotten. Baird took off after them only to have a firm hand grab his shoulder. Ailish and the other commanders had caught up.

❧

They stood blinking back tears as the glare hurt their eyes. The tunnel exit swinging open, the sun greeting them shining directly upon them. The red lanterns of the dwarves maintaining their night vision but doing nothing to protect them against the winter sun.

A breeze stirred around their legs causing them to shiver in unison. Digging out coats and furs not needed underground but heavily desired in the morning chill.

The sky was relatively clear for this time of year and with any luck it won't rain for a few days. The snow was still a week or so away giving them time to leave the pass. Being stuck here when the snow falls would be deadly.

The cliffs stretched behind them in both directions. No identifiable land marks could be seen against the hard-stone walls. Their sense of direction lost underwater before they even entered the tunnels, they had no idea what direction the blow hole was.

East could be easily identified with the sun visible. But did their packs and supplies lie to the east. They had plenty of water but only enough food to last them today. With no better alternative they trudged off on tired feet towards the fort. Guessing worst case was three days with empty stomachs and any valuables left in their packs were not worth dying for.

The mercenary commanders took charge putting a stop to the looting and vandalism. Part of their agreement made with the Baird and the other leaders. No looting and they will be given commissions in the new royal army with their soldiers remaining under their command.

Steady pay without needing to find contracts which will be hard with no potential enemies for a while. As an added bonus during peace their job will be mostly ceremonial. An offer the mercenaries agreed to but old habits die hard Baird guessed.

With order restored they began a systematic search of the castle. Searching every nook and cranny for any loyalists and Ivan.

Room after room proved void of life. Soldiers and servants alike all vanished. No cooks in the kitchen or servants cowering in the larder. Just empty rooms and barren halls.

They found Ivan barricaded in what appeared to be Olaf's former bed chamber. No soldiers stood guard outside the doors. No servants shielded him. Just a chest of drawers pushed behind the door keeping it shut. A few mercenaries made short work of the shelf with axes. Finally carved and decorated it was probably worth more than they made in a year.

Ivan pressed a knife to his own throat as soldiers poured in. Eyes wide with fear and skin deathly pale he stood rooted to the spot. Unable to find the strength and courage to take his own life, remaining motionless while two soldiers pulled the knife free and dragged him to the dungeons. His judgement was to come later.

Completing a sweep of the remaining rooms revealed nothing. Servants all having fled or sent away, it made no difference now.

Instead soldiers were sent to guard the inner wall while others set up an infirmary in the castle keep. Ailish lead two hundred men back to the camp outside the wall. Wanting to get Garrett and the others inside the keep. They had won, but that didn't mean they were safe.

The next two weeks went by in a blur for Baird. At times feeling like he was watching events unfold through someone else's eyes.

Three days after taking the castle citizens approached the sealed gates. Nobody having ventured beyond the walls after the camp was cleared of supplies and the wounded made them curious.

Electing leaders to speak for them a dozen civilians entered the throne room to meet with Baird and the leaders. Garrett stood amongst them leaning heavily on a crutch, surviving the blast without sustaining any internal injuries thankfully. The external injuries were still severe he now resembled Flynn after tangling with Olaf even spending most of the time in bed.

The throne itself sat empty. Deciding it was too soon to have an arse polish the metal skulls. Baird was relieved by this after he first glimpsed it days prior. It was a monstrosity and in bad taste. Something few men would desire let alone sit on. Doubting even the Flynn they now knew would want to.

Much of the talk revolved around the question of what was to happen now that the city was under their control. Topics they themselves had spoken about in much detail already. Baird stood silent letting others address the citizens' concerns as much as possible. Still feeling uncomfortable with the whole notion.

After convincing them that they came as liberators not conquerors the group noticeably relaxed. Giving them a brief detail of their plan, including re-establishing the labour camps outside the walls, abandoned when their army approached.

However, agreeing on making it normal farms run by them with soldiers posted for protection not as task masters. Furthermore, the empty barracks will become emergency housing for any in need of it.

Any soldiers hiding among them had two choices. Lay down their sword and take up a plough or swear fealty to Baird. Giving up any rank or commission in the process, they would have to earn them in the new army.

They talked all day, stopping only to eat lunch. The dozen guests staring in disbelief at the spread before them, amazed they were being fed by the high and mighty. It was nothing special Baird remembered thinking merely a spread of fruits, bread and cheese. Even saying so, since no servants remained so the camp cooks were still performing this duty.

Over the next days the castle servants and workers began returning to work. Word getting around about the honourable and generous new ruler.

Everyone was still hesitant and sceptical but not wanting to miss out if their words proved true, they flocked. More and more each day.

Once the former major-domo stepped forward the process of managing the castles staff flowed smoothly. Fresh sheets were placed in the rooms each morning and three hot meals filled the mess hall every day.

Baird began emptying the coffers to hire labourers and builders to clear the rubble near the outer wall. Merchant convoys left to gather grain so the food would last until the farms were functioning again. Most of the castle's stockpiles were sabotaged. A final act of defiance from Ivan.

The most interesting discovery came when a fleet of ten ships pulled up to the docks. Olaf's personal flag ship with its escort sat of the coast, unseen during the siege.

Roughly half of the crew were former pirates, who swore fealty to Olaf rather than getting executed. When word of his death reached their ear's, they mutinied.

Wisely Olaf never offered officers to join so no commanders existed amongst the pirates who tried to escape on ships without supplies. Without captains and without navigators.

They sat of the coast gambling, watching and sleeping. They saw the dragon shots explode the outer wall and finally decided it was something worth investigating.

The new imperial army boarded the ships as soon as the mooring ropes were tied off. Taking everyone into custody. Since they were still garbed as mercenaries the pirates expected a warm welcome. Completely unprepared to clash steel.

Baird had already seen the good that a reformed swashbuckler could do. Pardoning the men of all past crimes he welcoming them to join his forces.

A few chose to remain but over a hundred sailors walked out of the city. Warned that the crime for any further piracy is death. Ailish muttered into his ear that they will definitely be returning to piracy. Baird didn't doubt it.

Baird looked over his new fleet. All ships looked impressive and imposing. Some narrow with two masts similar to the rose. Dwarfed by massive three masted floating fortress that looked impossibly heavy to even float.

Olaf's flag ship was the smallest amongst them all. No seaman himself, Baird couldn't identify what was so special about this ship. But it gave of an aura if that was even possible. An aura of power similar to what he felt when he met Olaf the first time.

With the black metal tubes of Dragon shots gracing the upper decks. Four in total, she bobbed alongside the wharf.

⚓

The snow arrived earlier than anticipated, nipping at their heels. The first snowflakes waking them from a sleep filled with dreams of meat roasting over an open fire.

With reality greeting them with empty stomachs and white flakes clumping in their eye lashes. Fearing the snow, they continued their trek eastwards towards the fort. Double timing it as feet groaned in exhaustion and stomachs gnawed with hunger.

The snow cleared with the dawn. No sun broke through the thick grey clouds overhead. Clouds that brought thick heavy raindrops, drenching the pair within minutes.

A sparkly sheen of water coated the rocky ground, making certain places treacherous to step. The cliffs rose in the haze as landmarks became visible. In clear conditions the wall should be visible from their current position. Cold, wet and miserable spirits lifted slightly with the prospect of shelter and a warm hearth to greet them. Still several hours, maybe more with the rain slowing them down.

Running through the open doors, Flynn collapsed onto the hard stone floor. Panting and exhausted having ran the last few miles as fast as their tired legs could managed. Just as the snow gave way to rain, it too was replaced by hale.

The frozen water droplets driving them onwards at a frantic pace. Vaike knelt beside him, as physically and mentally exhausted as Flynn was himself. Wanting nothing more to do then rest. Even thoughts of food driven from his mind. But sleep would spell death.

Forcing their bodies onwards, using the remaining dregs of strength. Each staggered step a battle. A battle for life. On instinct they found the kitchen. The closest sealable room to the doors with a fireplace.

The gods continued to favour them, or reward their desire to survive. Wood was stacked underneath the stone oven with the flint located nearby. The tinder catching with the sparks from the first strike of the flint. Thankfully, because Flynn didn't think he had the strength for a second.

❧

Ivan was escorted from his cell, flanked by two fully armoured guards just in case he tried to escape. Not that he could the chains binding his wrists and ankles were so tight the skin had been rubbed raw.

It had been seventeen days since he was incarcerated. Since then nothing. No interrogation, no torture. He was grateful for that last one.

He was completely ignored other than when they brought him food and water twice a day. He knows it ends now though. Dread building with each step, becoming a physical weight. The guards seemed intent to take their time. Walking up the cold stone steps from the dungeon. The sharp clanking of their mail echoing through the dimly lit corridor. No talking just an endless drone of clunking, creaking and screeching.

Blinking from the glare, the first time he has seen the sun in a fortnight. Eyes adjusting to the glare he saw his fate. In the castles courtyard a crowd of citizens had formed. At the sight of him they began screaming and hurling rocks, pushing against the barrier of soldiers separating him from the angry mob.

Without missing a beat and completely unperturbed by the stones bouncing off their armour his escorts continued on. In front of the mob stood a newly constructed platform raised ten feet off the ground. Steps from the back leading up to where a man stood rope in hand.

He made his bed and it was time to accept his fate. Ivan approached the steps head held high. Halfway up the stairs his body had second thoughts. Freezing unable to move his feet. A rough shove in his back had him sprawled on all fours, hands touching the roughly hewn timbers.

Jagged edges and splinters stuck out from the timber and the slight scent of sap still lingered in the wood. Freshly cut, the timber hadn't been dried or treated yet. It was amazing how you didn't notice the small things when you were climbing to the top Ivan mused.

Two strong hands grabbed him lifting him to his feet, guiding him the rest of the way. He didn't notice the executioner or the crowd. He didn't pay attention as the cross beam was lifted in place or the rope wrapped around it.

He now lived for the little things. Like the clear day that greeted them. The shapes that clouds made. The scent of fresh bread baking in the air.

A lever was pulled and the floor underneath him dropped away, then nothing.

Chapter 18

THE EYE FREELY GIVEN

Two days spent huddling in the empty fort. Drying clothes and staying warm while the storm raged outside. Hoping the horses were okay, unable to face the elements and search for them.

When the storm broke their fears were for naught. Two horses stood in the fresh snow outside of the fortress stables. Tracks through the snow leading away to wherever they took shelter. The sun shone bright behind a layer of cloud cover. Every now and then gracing the companions with its presence before being shut away.

The green tinged clouds of the previous few days were gone. The cloud canopy overhead looked like a patchwork blanket. White sheet intermittently broken up with grey and blue.

The ground was covered in lightly packed snow up to their waist in places. The horses finding their own path through the snow. Little faster than a trot but faster than either of them could manage on foot.

The snow cleared as they journeyed inland. Winter not having wrapped its icy tendrils around the land yet. It still rained most days and when the sun did come out it was usually joined by a cool westerly breeze.

They saw no merchants on the road to Haven as they made rapid time there. Arriving in five days despite the weather and the slow start the pair chose to stay at the same inn as before.

Remembering them from their previous visit, the inn keeper offered them the same rooms and full stomachs. He was disappointed to learn they would be only staying a single night and would be keeping the drinking to a minimum.

With dry clothes and saddle bags full they rode out of Haven, a cold icy wind speeding them along. The roads remained empty with minimal traffic. Only essential personal travel in winter and the bandits still present in the area forced many to travel in larger parties or take a longer route.

The second night Flynn drew the short straw. Vaike curled up in his bedroll, sleeping soundly next to the fire. Flynn sat on watch just outside the fires range. Coat wrapped tightly around himself hiding from the cold, his breath visible Infront of his face.

The fire had burnt down, now just embers glowing orange. Reluctant to add more wood trying to pass unnoticed. A full moon and unusually clear sky for this time of year granted surprisingly good visibility.

Flynn watched for five minutes as three man approached their camp. No strafing or scouting. Not even an attempt to flank. Like moths they were drawn straight to the flame. Stopping ten yards out observing the camp, completely oblivious to the pair of grey eyes following their every movement.

Cold and tired Flynn couldn't be bothered moving unless necessary so he watched. Two of them dropped weapons and began digging through their saddlebags draped over nearby rocks. Pulling out hunks of cheese and dried meat stuffing handfuls into their mouths.

They bought more food than was necessary to reach the Nibban forest. So even with what three people could carry away they were in no danger of starving themselves. Besides Flynn knows what it is like to truly be hungry. Having had food stores get contaminated once at sea and going nineteen days without eating.

Something he wouldn't wish on his worst enemies. Even the meagre scraps they picked up in the Sulthard desert made that trip as difficult as running by comparison. It was common knowledge that if you were doing it hard you could always get a meal at the Fiddlers Green. Something Franz was always given credit for. Flynn had his reputation to consider after all.

The third man was the problem. While his friends ate their fill, he began digging through the other bags. Tossing clothes, cooking gear and supplies on the ground.

Vaike opened his eyes at the sound of a frypan hitting a rock. Sleeping on his side facing Flynn he looked at his friend on watch.

With the slightest movement Flynn shook his head signalling Vaike not to make a move.

With mouths still full the two shushed the third telling him to be careful. Completely unperturbed he dropped the remaining items on the ground and strode towards the horses.

Picking up Sterben's bridle he approached the black horse. "Fuck" Flynn muttered to himself. Sterben allowed the bridle to be placed over his head. Obviously feeling as lazy as Flynn was. Only starting to show resistance as he was led away. Pulling against the worn leather.

The two eating now fought over a wineskin while the third pulled on the reins with both hands. Heels dug in trying to move Sterben.

A dozen steps from Flynn and a flash of steel saw him sprawled on the cold ground. Blinking in shock as his hands still gripped the reins hanging against Sterben's flank.

A fear driven scream escaped his lips as the pain shot up from his bloody stumps. The other two turned dropping the wineskin, its clear contents spilling out.

He was too tired to deal with this much noise. Stifling a yawn Flynn planted his boot. Pinning the foot of the wounded bandit as he tried to crawl to his friends. The screaming and crying increased in volume as the other two began backing away, pleading for their lives.

After kicking the blubbering fool in the head, silencing the annoying noise Flynn stared down the others. Putting an end to the pleading with a single gesture. Silence returned to the night with only the soft crackle of the waning fire heard.

Flynn let them go after making them repack their bags. Taking their wounded friend with them they disappeared into the night.

The next day Vaike gave him shit about it, talking about how he has come such a long way. Killing for the sake of it no longer carrying the same joy as it used to for him. Flynn protested that he just couldn't be bothered with the effort. Vaike didn't believe him for one second, neither did Flynn believe it himself if he was being honest.

Five more uneventful days had them standing inside the tree line of Vaike's home. The weather had grown colder the last few days with snow clinging to their coats as the entered the forest. Inside the forest was somehow warm. Difference between inside and outside as clear as night and day.

Clothes drying and layers quickly being removed. Vaike explained it was the magic of his people. While winter does reach the forest even snowing. It is less severe allowing the trees and flowers to grow year-round.

❧

Vaike was at unease. Six dusk guard greeted them a few hours after entering the forest. The Captain not asking him about his mission, even if he knew about it, it wasn't his place to ask.

They formed up escorting the pair for the three days ride to the city. Whilst not unheard off, Vaike normally comes and goes without one. He let it slide grateful for the reprieve resting in the saddle beside Flynn and sleeping deeply at night.

His unrest grew towards the end of the second day when he heard movement around the camp. With their escort not bothered by it Vaike wrote it off as a hunting party, probably after game for a feast when they return tomorrow.

The next morning the sound of feet scraping against bark in the trees, feet shuffling through the underbrush and breathing behind trees was still present. As they approached the city more and more appeared. What was going on?

❧

Vaike had been silent all morning. Deep in thought as they rode along. Flynn didn't care he had his own thoughts to wrestle with as the southern stairs came into view.

A wooden platform attached to ropes that stretched up into the trees was slowly being lowered. The travel lift that Vaike spoke of Flynn assumed, never having actually seen it before. Dismounting, he followed the Dusk guards lead.

Thankfully they walked towards the thousand steps. As difficult as that trek is, especially after weeks in the saddle he would prefer to walk into the city.

A hand gripped his shoulder as he took his first step. Vaike was looking at him with a look that Flynn had never seen on his friends face before. Not fear, no, more a cross between concern and intentness.

Something worried the prince but he wasn't sure if he was being paranoid. If he was reading into nothing. Nodding that he understood Flynn followed after their escort. The leaders who stood waiting a few steps onward.

❧

The pace was hard even for Vaike. Despite how many times he has made the climb himself, the weeks in the saddle had taken their toll. The dusk guard all in peak condition drove them along like cattle, sweat forming on their own brows, breathing becoming ragged.

No stops or breaks they marched up the stairs. Another six guards falling into step around them as they stepped into the city. His unease grew with eyes scanning as he saw the empty city. No residents walked around or waited to greet them.

Just them and their twelve escorts taking them straight to the council. A further four guards stood at the base of the council stairs. Stairs that have never been guarded in Vaike's entire life. Flynn's shoulders were tensed up but he didn't understand just how bad this was. What was happening. Unable to do or say anything he climbed the stairs, like lambs being led to the slaughter.

Head poking over the top step and Vaike relaxed. Maybe he was reading into nothing. The council were seated around his mother and his sister stood behind her. Six of the guards dismissed themselves while the others took up positions. Maybe this was some coronation tradition.

❧

Stopping beside Flynn, Vaike kneeled, bowing his head to the Queen. Flynn stood unmoving. No recognition towards rank and authority he looked ahead, not even deigning to tilt his head. "Who is this filth that comes before us showing such disrespect?" shouted an outraged council member standing.

Flynn lazily turned his head, fixing his gaze on the elf. "Who is this coward that questions his betters?" He almost frothed with rage, hand gripping the hilt of his sword. Goaded as all cowards are.

Seated with a sword at his hip, but no warrior. The others with swords all had scars and calloused hands. He was a politician wearing a sword for show, manicured nails wrapped around the decorative hilt.

"Kneel or I'll make you kneel!" "Try it. You'll never stand again" threatened Flynn as he made to move towards him.

"Andreas enough." "But my Queen, he disrespects you." "Does he. Do you think to know my mind?" "No, your majesty." "Yet you speak for me. I think that shows more disrespect. Don't you?" "Yes, my Queen. Sorry my Queen." The corners of Vaike's mouth curled upwards. Smiling as Andreas grovelled.

"Perhaps we should just ask him why he does not bow?" Turning her head from Andreas to Flynn as she spoke.

"Only men who fear for their lives bow. I do not cower nor do I quit." "With a snap of my fingers you would fall were you stand" the Queen responded.

Locking eyes with Vashti, Flynn answered. "I bow to no one."

❧

Vaike never liked Andreas much. It seems one look was all it took for Flynn to figure him out. He was one of five council members who carried swords with them. A sword he has never drawn with intent, unlike the other four. Three were veterans who fought with his father, all with physical and emotional wounds that haunted them from that war. The fourth now fought left handed. His right arm lost in a goblin raid while visiting the dwarves as an emissary before the hallowed wars.

Andreas was a politician through and through. The human equivalent to a high born who has never worked a day in his life. Not that he was incompetent. One of the finest swordsmen in the city but it is all for show, a visage.

Flynn however locked horns with his mother. A battle of wills that couldn't possible end well. It was getting out of hand. Vaike prayed Flynn would just let go of his pride.

Then the idiot enunciated those words. Clearly and confidently with no chance for a misunderstanding he uttered the words that would be his death.

"How did you fair on your task?" "What" Vaike blinked confused. His mother seeming amused by Flynn's defiance, she now turned her attention to him. Wordlessly Vaike fished the crown from inside his cloak.

"Congratulations. I was a little concerned when the snow arrived early but you have done well. I am very proud of you."

Holding out her hand Vaike approached his mother handing her the crown. "I can't even recall when I last saw your father wearing this Yisolde said examining the polished metal circlet.

"Now Flynn" the Queen said after Vaike took up the place on his mother's right side. "You have also proved yourself. So, I will keep my word you will be permitted to live out your days in my city. You will however, be living out your time confined in my dungeon."

Vaike was so surprised he couldn't react. The guards that took up position behind Flynn jumped him. Two guards pinned his arms to his side, while a third wrapped a gloved fist around his neck. The other three faced Vaike weapons drawn.

It was so fluid and efficient his mother didn't miss a beat. "You won't be harmed and you will be granted almost every luxury you could desire. You will however never see my daughter again." "No" Vashti cried in little more than a whimper.

Instinctively Vaike reached out with his left hand, finding his twins own behind their mothers back. Unable to do anything more for her then offer a reassuring squeeze.

It was a flash of movement so fast Vaike almost missed it. If not for the hours spent training with Flynn he probably would have. Everyone else just stared on in disbelief at the human who now stood cackling like a mad man.

One guard was down on the ground holding his nose as blood flowed freely from it. The other two still held his arms but staring on in disgust at the blood dripping from Flynn's right hand. Or more accurately from what he held.

If you could kill with a look his mother would have perished there as Flynn lifted his head. No longer laughing but grinning ear to ear, head tilted to the side staring down the Queen. Left eye socket empty and bloody. His sister gasped in shock along with several council members.

"I can't see her if I'm blind." "Mother stop this" Vashti pleaded as Flynn struggled to get his arms free, dropping the eye held in his hand. Optic nerve trailing behind like a comet tail as it fell.

Not caught unaware this time the guards struggled to restrain him. The four at the base of the stairs arriving in time to subdue the human. Bashing him across the head before he could remove his other eye.

He was dragged away dazed with two more guards taking up position with weapons drawn. Vashti knelt down tears falling freely as her emotions spilled over. No one else moved or spoke for ten long minutes, enough time for Flynn to be taken beyond their reach. Since Vaike has no idea where his mother has taken him.

At a wave of her hand the guards sheathed their weapons. "I will talk to you both later" the Queen said before dismissing the twins.

They weren't truly dismissed as they were escorted to their house. Locked in with guards posted at every exit, they were on house arrest. What has gotten into mother?

Chapter 19

THE GODS GIFT

"He saved my life." "I know." "He saved yours too." "I know." "Without him Maroxis would've succeeded." "I know" Vaike sighed for what felt like the fiftieth time. The same conversation they had been having on and off for the last three days.

Mother hasn't stopped by or sent word. The guards only leave when their relief arrives. Unable to do more than try and figure mother out. A seemingly impossible task.

❧

"He was fighting against the chains trying to get his other eye out" the guards told her when she arrived at the prison. "Once he was secured, the fighting stopped" "Very good captain, now leave us." With a wave of her hand the two guards saluted and left.

The heavy iron door swung open without a sound, feet barely making a sound on the hard, wooden stairs that flowed down. The prison built inside an ancient tree, designed to harbor the most dangerous or those guilty of the worst offences. Only one entrance high up in its boughs before spiralling down.

No elegant carvings or graceful designs, just practicality. Despite having held no prisoners for over a century the cells were all clean with well-greased hinges. Candles burned in scones along the walls casting shadows that would dance across the faces of the condemned.

She walked past dozens of empty cells. Cells that gradually got smaller. Less humane. Keeping the worst, the most deranged, the furthest away from the stairs. Slowing as her ears picked up slow ragged breathing. Stopping completely outside the last cell on the left.

For months her daughter regaled her with stories and praise for the human, the warrior that was before her. The stories seem little more than embellished tales, simple boasting, compared to this sad defeated wretch kneeling before her.

Unable to stand with shackles around his neck and wrists preventing even the tiniest movement. Shirt caked with dried blood and the ground between his legs stained black with it.

"I'm not hungry go away." Not shouted or spoken with confidence, more like a plea. "Good I didn't bring any" Lifting his head at the sound of her voice the Queen was taken aback.

Dried blood smeared across his face like war paint. Hair matted with his own gore, and a lifeless stare. One socket an empty void. The other looking at her with defeat. No fire, no anger or wrath. Just the look of a man who has lost the will to live.

❧

The footsteps of yet another person walking at a steady pace echoes down the chamber. Probably another guard coming to feed him. Until they force the food down his throat, he won't be eating a thing. There was no longer any point.

The footsteps stopped outside his cell. He tells them to go away without even raising his head. Once again why bother. It was the Queen that answered.

Looking into the Queens eyes he felt neither rage nor hate. Just a longing for her to finish it. She has ripped out his heart all she needs to do is crush it. End his suffering and let him be.

"Do you know how the elves became immortal?" A simple question. A difficult answer. A discussion for another time, another life. A time when he cared about knowledge, now it was more time. More torture.

Without a thought to his suffering the Queen answered her own question. "Long ago there existed three brothers, Ebsallom, Ascalon and Mordaqi. The brothers encompassed everything and nothing in their existence. Growing bored, they breathed life into the world.

Creating the heavens and earth. Once happy with their landscape they then filled it with creatures. Ebsallom created the elves, the first sentient race gifting us with the fruits of their labour.

The two younger brothers took offence to this and began creating their own races. Using less love and care then their brother. Mordaqi favouring life sculpted dwarves and various races of humans. Ascalon desiring chaos birthed darkness. Vampires, dragons the things that haunt your dreams.

With their creations came war and death. Ascalon's creations proving more destructive, more powerful they began to drive humans to the brink of extinction. Mordaqi fearing for his own creations began interfering in the mortal's war, thus starting the war between the brothers. The war of the gods.

The two brothers began creating lesser gods to fight for them. Only Ebsallom refrained himself content on ensuring his elves survived.

The fighting escalated as more and more gods were formed. Lesser gods began breeding with mortals to create demi gods. Foot soldiers in heavens war.

The destruction of elven cities saw Ebsallom intervene. Not choosing a side, instead focusing on ending the conflict by brokering peace between the two brothers.

Ebsallom who only knew trust and love, believed his brothers only had good intentions in stopping the war. Following their instructions for peace talks, only to be tricked.

His brothers made plans to betray him, trapping him away in his own paradise. Locked away from the outside world unable to escape, unable to interfere in worldly affairs.

The fighting escalated, culminating in his brother's mutual destruction. Neither winning out. The resulting fallout was worse. Lesser gods fought amongst themselves for position and command. Ebsallom watched on helpless as more and more elves died alongside his brother's creations. Finally caving, he broke the vow he made to never create another being.

Splitting himself in twain he created Mithras. His son and fourth high god. Not bound by the trap Mithras could come and go as he pleased however only Ascalon and Mordaqi could unlock his father's cage.

Mithras put an end to the fighting. Tasking each god with a role based on their strength before dispersing them.

This gave birth to the gods as we know them today, Grimmlocke, Aurith, Camilla and so forth.

Before joining him in paradise Mithras granted the elves with his father's final gift. Immortality, to all but blade and disease the elves have lived on and prospered since then."

Flynn grew tired of the Queens yammering. Head dropping to look at the floor not long into her story. Listening out of habit not desire.

"Do you know why I told you this story?" Raising his head not having realised she finished speaking Flynn answered. "To articulate the difference between our species. I get it. Now please kill me or leave me be."

"This has all been a test to see if you're worthy." 'Worthy of what?" Flynn asked. Despite his best intentions a little flame of hope flickered inside. A flame that if quenched would destroy him completely.

"Do you know why you're such a proficient warrior. Why you're superior in strength and speed to most human's? Yes, training is part of it but the natural talent and skill. That part is from the elven blood in your veins."

His face was frozen in shock. "It's impossible" he protested. "My mother would've known if my father was an elf. Beside elves can't breed with humans."

"That's not entirely true. It has about a one in a thousand chance of taking but it does happen. Besides, your fifth or sixth generation so it was probably unknown. Your father probably got an extra twenty years at most if he even died from old age."

"Once again, worthy of what?" Flynn asked. The tendrils of hope flaring up, giving him strength. "Why worthy of Mithra's, of Ebsallom's gift!"

With no further explanation the Queen placed a hand over his face covering his gouged-out eye with a perfectly manicured, blemish free hand. He had no idea when she opened the door or crossed the distance between them. The bare skin began to itch something terrible. He strained at the shackles trying to scratch at it, it was driving him mad.

The itching was then replaced by a strange burning sensation. It was weird, like when you hit your head and say ouch before realising it didn't hurt.

As quickly as it began it was over. Blinking he saw the Queen turn and leave without another word. The throbbing in his empty socket gone.

Flynn wasn't sure what happened but that night when they brought him food he surrendered. Loosening the shackle's, he ate his fill. Asking for seconds and thirds his guards obliging him, he was that famished.

⚘

They finally left the house. A week since returning. A week without a word from mother. Vashti losing the plot having trashed then cleaned every room of the house only to trash it again. They will need new furniture after this. If there is an after Vaike thought grimly. Not that mother would kill them but would they want to stay and where would they even go. They could advise Baird for a while, or find their cousins across the sea.

Escorted they were led to the travelators and out of the city. Without horses they walked down paths Vaike had never seen or ventured down before.

It was early in the morning when they left home yet the sun sank low in the sky as they entered a clearing.

Completely empty save for a white stone protruding from the ground facing the northern star. The clearing itself was such a perfect circle that even the elves couldn't shape it with their magic.

As the sun set footsteps scrapped along the path down the way they had come. From the trees walked the twelve council members followed by their mother.

Vaike placed a firm hand on his sister's shoulder fearing how she might react. He needn't have worried for she had eyes only for who now entered the clearing. Dragging chains, naked above the waist and missing an eye, Flynn walked in head held high.

⚘

Yesterday she came again. Not even entering the cell this time speaking through the bars. Telling him it will kill him if unsuccessful. It will also be excruciating either way so the choice was entirely his own. He could attempt the trial or leave the city a free man.

There was only one choice, the answer to which Vashti wouldn't be told. Flynn wanting to spare her if it failed.

❧

What kind of hell was this? Her own mother was going to force her watch the man she loves be executed. When his only crime was being human, it was absolutely absurd. Every fibre of her being was screaming to interfere, to free Flynn and escape.

But how, they were unarmed and outnumbered. Every elf here was completely loyal to their Queen. Why shouldn't they be, many having followed her lead for centuries and they owed this human nothing.

She could sense her brother's presence beside her. Feel the weight of his own grief and regret through their unspoken bond. The only thing keeping her grounded was the firm grip Vaike kept on her shoulder.

The procession for the condemned was dragged out. A pause between each step. The sky black above their heads. Stars lighting the clearing by the time Flynn paused at the white stone and his shackles were removed.

Rubbing the red marks on his wrists Flynn then grabbed hold of the white boulder and dragged himself up. It was a smooth surface with limited hand holds three metres high. Reaching the summit, he looked down at her and smiled.

Her heart broke as tears flowed. She knew for whatever the reason he chose this for her. The same as that broken face, that missing eye. He did that for her.

She knows what she must do. The only thing she could do. No matter how much it hurt she must witness his bravery once more. Witness his end.

❧

Vaike was at a loss as to what was happening. Having only witnessed human executions. Little more than fanfare for the masses, something to distract them. This was different. Like some sort of ritual, some sort of honour thing. His mother had never educated him on this side of ruling. The last elf sentenced was when he was in his twenties and he wasn't even aware of it at the time.

Flynn looked down upon them smiling and he felt Vashti stiffen. He could see the tears flowing freely as his own heart strained. Hurting for her, hurting for his brother.

Vashti interlocked their fingers together so tightly he was unable to pry his hand free if he wanted to. Vashti needed his strength to get through this. Like he too needed hers.

Flynn turned facing the northern star now shinning directly down upon them and knelt. No instruction from his mother, no prodding from the guards. Again, completely voluntarily, not out of fear for his life.

This triggered the next step in whatever this was. The twelve members of the council and his mother formed a ring around the stone. The Queen directly south, also facing the northern star.

With the council in position all the guards other than the four with Vaike dismissed themselves dissolving into the trees.

His mother began chanting slowly joined by the other council members. Vaike had no idea what they were saying. It was elven definitely, as he caught the odd word but some ancient dialect. Vaike was growing more and more frustrated with the number of secrets his mother had kept from them.

❧

The back of her sleeve was wet with tears having wiped her eyes. She needed to clear them as they were playing tricks on her. But still the stone seemed to be glowing, with the star seeming to focus on it. Like a light shining from heaven.

"Do you see that too or am I crazy?" The question coming from beside her. "I was about to ask you the same thing" she answered through sniffles.

"I don't want to get your hopes up, but I don't think this is an execution." "But what else could it be" desperation lacing her words. "I wish I knew."

The light grew in brilliance. Reaching the point that the twins had to shield their eyes with their spare hands. Vashti beginning to pray, to hope that her mother hadn't betrayed her.

Her hope built only to crush her as a scream ripped the air open. Cut, wounded and dying Flynn had barely uttered a whimper. Even the battle mad scream's she had heard him bellow against opponents was like stubbing your toe next to this.

Here he was screaming, crying, nearly begging. What horrors was her mother inflicting upon him. No blood flowed. No limbs twisted. Was this some kind of mental thing?

The next scream had the hairs on her arms standing up. She didn't care, she had to help, crashing through the guards who were too distracted by the light to stop her in time. Vaike relaxing his grip as she moved, knowing this was something she had to do.

The light was blinding, eyes squeezed shut she raced blindly towards the screams. Shouts ordering her to stop faded into nothing behind her. She crashed shoulder first into something soft.

One of the council members lay sprawled at her feet. Not knowing or caring which one it was she ran on. Stopping only when her hand felt a smooth stone surface. The screaming was near deafening this close. Flynn must be tearing his throat apart screaming like this.

She could see the light through her eye lids. Her ear drums felt like they were about to burst but she needed her hands to climb. It seems Cisty, the mother of good fortune smiled upon her. Finding purchase with each movement she quickly felt fingers wrap around the lip.

Hauling herself up and over she reached out finding her lover. Embracing him tightly, sending all her love through the physical and emotional bonds trying to share his pain.

She had no idea how long the screaming continued. Time seemed to slow as their spirits entwined.

Strong hands were trying to pry her away but she refused to let go. Releasing her hold only when she felt hands on her chest pushing against her. Eye's opening, she held a smiling Flynn at arm's length. The rock was very crowded now that Vaike and her mother joined them atop it. "I'm surprised it worked. I seriously thought it would be too much for you."

"It would've been if not for her" Flynn said before leaning in and kissing her. The kiss was not long or passionate like she fanaticised about all these months. Little more than a peck on the lips but it was perfect. The emotion it carried made her forget her next question, thankfully Vaike remembered.

◆

It was worse than he could imagine. Maybe there was too little elf in him. Maybe he was to corrupted, to tainted. Because whatever it was, it was tearing him apart. At a base level. The pain was intolerable.

Like being simultaneously burnt and frozen, bones were breaking as quickly as they mended. Like his skin was being peeled of just to regrow over the wound. He was being cut and pulled apart just to be sewn back together so it could happen again.

Yet somehow, he was aware of what was happening around him. Like his spirit was outside his body observing. Fighting. Loosing. He watched Vashti approach him with closed eyes. He had no clue why she scrunched her eyes shut but she persevered. So, he persevered also.

Chapter 20

THE PROMISE

"This was all a test for you my dear daughter." The queen said looking at the princess for the first time in a week. "I knew how you felt. What you felt for a mortal. A mortal with elven blood in his veins."

Realisation dawned on her children's faces as they grasped the magnitude of her words. "However, it is very minute, or was I'm not sure how that works now. I was expecting it to fail but Flynn chose to face the risk for the chance at a future with you."

"I thought the legend said they are reborn without scar or blemish but Flynn has them all" Vaike asked observing Flynn's empty eye socket. "I was thinking that too but no human has actually been granted this gift before so we have no actual reference point." "Well I am glad I wasn't."

"But why I thought you'd want your left eye back" the Queen asked puzzled. "Because" Flynn stated determinately. "The scars on my body are symbols of the life I've lived. They're medals of honour I gained while fighting for my family and with it. With them, this body carries the memories of all the people it holds dear."

"I completely understand brother" Vaike said helping Flynn to his feet. "Don't worry mother it's a warrior thing" he said in answer to her bemused look.

The Queen stood on the ground beside Vaike who helped her climb down. The former pirate, her daughter's lover stood atop the raised stone holding her hand. Breaking eye contact long enough to glance at her son who offered a quick nod in response.

"Vashti" he began. "I am a scoundrel, a liar, a murderer and thief. I have sired bastards and orphaned others. Massacred my way through cities just to fuck my way through the next. The blood on my hands is immense, it will never be washed away no matter how long I live and that is forever now.

Vashti. Still, I never dared hope, never dared to dream that I would get the chance to say this. To ask you this. But the pain, the suffering it was all worth it just to utter this one question. Vashti will you marry me?"

❧

The bed was soft and warm. He could feel the sun shining against his face. The symphony of birds chirping and singing greeted his ears. Sitting up awake he watched birds chase each other past the window, completely unperturbed by the growing winter outside the forest.

He was in an unfamiliar room but at least it wasn't a cell. Shaking off the shackles of sleep, Flynn struggled, trying to remember what happened. They started the ritual, but what happened. Did it work?

He wasn't dead judging by the throbbing at the back of his head. Reaching up to discover it bandaged along with his left eye. Throwing back the quilt he was wearing lightly woven pyjamas, defiantly not what he wore during the ritual.

The window faced west into the forest with a basin for washing beside it. A massive bed made from oak took up the majority of the room with a vanity and mirror against the opposite wall. Not wanting to see his reflexion Flynn looked elsewhere.

The dwellings design reminded him of Vashti's house but it could match any number of elven dwellings for all he knew.

Sitting on the edge of the mattress stretching, the earthly scent of cinnamon wafted through the door. His mouth began to water as the scent reached his nostrils, he was ravenous.

The wooden door to the room swung open effortlessly as Vashti entered carrying a tray of freshly baked pastries. Seeing her was like gasping down a lungful of air when you almost drowned. The rituals pain and success returned to him.

"Good your awake" she said glowing with happiness. "You slept all of yesterday so eat up." "What happened. And, where are we?" "Don't you remember anything?" Vashti asked looking sullen.

"I remember you embracing me, helping me through the transformation. I remember proposing to you after, and that's it. I don't remember your answer and what happened to my head?" Flynn asked reaching up to touch the bandages again.

"Well" Vashti began before grabbing a Cinnamon pastry and biting into it before continuing. "That's because I was so excited that I tried to hug you and jumped forward into you. Tackling you off the rock.

You hit your head on the ground so we brought you here till you woke up." Vashti said looking away during the retelling out of embarrassment. "That's hilarious" Flynn said laughing, stopping only when it made his head ache.

"So where is here anyway?" "My room" she said as a matter of fact, like it was obvious. "Now eat!" Flynn had more questions but Vashti made it clear she would answer no more until he'd eaten so he begrudging took a bite. It was delicious. Fluffy and crispy outside, the inside buttery and flaky. In apple, cherry, cheese and cinnamon she clearly went to a lot of effort.

"So, it was a yes then" he said reaching out with his free hand, placing it over hers. Eyes brimming with tears of joy she nodded before embracing him deeply again. Flynn just held her tight, pastries sprawled forgotten as he held the love of his life.

❧

A month since Ivan's execution and they gathered in the throne room. They were calling it a coronation. The crowning of a new king but it was merely to please the citizens calling for a leader. Baird was becoming more of a caretaker.

Not wanting the crown until having the chance to first speak with all the leaders of the east. He was planning on offering each of them their independence again. How it was before Olaf if they should desire. Otherwise they can stay on as his citizens, receiving the same rights and privileges as he has shown to the people of this city.

Word was sent two weeks ago after finally reaching an agreement. However, with winter now settling in they don't expect any summit until the fall.

Baird did agree to let this farce go ahead on the provision it was known that he was only acting as a caretaker for now.

This didn't stop the people from finding some gaudy old crown hidden away somewhere. The thing was bulky and encrusted with jewels. Needing braces that rested on the wearers shoulders just to support its weight. It was totally impractically and out of fashion by at least a century.

However, Baird still nodded along with the master of ceremonies. Reciting the oath agreed upon beforehand, deciding Olaf's own were distasteful. It took two people to lift the crown onto Baird's head, sagging under the sheer weight of gold. Kneeling to receive it left him unable to stand up.

"I told them. It was completely impractical" Garrett muttered. "I know but let them have their moment" Ailish replied. The two standing behind Baird, bored with the evening's proceedings.

❧

They wanted to spend all day in bed, all week even. Yet no sooner had Flynn woken then Vaike appeared at the door. The Queen already summoning the three of them. Commanding their audience immediately.

With muttered curses and procrastination, they dressed, Vaike hurrying them along through the door. Stomachs growling, they looked longingly at the pastries scattered around the bed. Many of which were now squashed. Sheets and clothes stained red with smeared cherry.

Flynn was transfixed by the beauty of the woman he loved. The woman who was soon to be his wife. He couldn't help it, giving her a cheeky squeeze on the arse as she opened the door. The first thing Vaike saw was his sister's rosy cheeks and her betrotheds wicked grin.

Telling them gruffly how there was no time for funny business they left. Flynn laughing over the phrase funny business the whole time they walked. Stopping only when they reached the stairs to the Queen's council.

The council wasn't present. Their thirteen seats removed. Replaced with a small table laden with fruits and delicacies, four chairs tucked underneath.

Standing beside them was the Queen. Wearing light brown robe's, the same as many elves wore. Relaxed, less poised and dignified. "Welcome. I wanted to have breakfast with my family." She greeted them not as the Queen, but as a mother.

She shooed Vaike away when he tried to pull out her chair preferring to do it herself. Indicating for the others to sit, Vaike on her right, Vashti on her left. Leaving Flynn to sit opposite her.

The eyes that sized him up were not the eyes of a ruler looking at a subject. It was the eyes of a mother. A mother wanting what's best for her children. It somehow unnerved Flynn more.

"Allow me to be the first to congratulate you two on your betrothal" she said smiling. "And congratulations to Vaike, soon to be king. Your task was successful. In spring the crown will be returned to your father's grave and you."

"Wait what. In spring. Return" Flynn had to turn his head to see Vaike, still adjusting to the blind spot on his left side.

"Ah yes you can enter the blow hole most of the year. With Spring being the safest and easiest time to do it, plus I have the key needed to open the external door. However, the northern convergence, when we can ask for Mithra's gift happens only once every ten years, so we had time constraints."

"Well why not send an entourage, or have sent someone while Flynn recovered. The task didn't entail sacrifice or prove his worth. That was done during our travels. Proved when he gave up an eye" Vaike asked slightly agitated.

"Because the task wasn't the crown. But it was for the both of you to complete." "What" exclaimed both men. Flynn calming when Vashti held his hand under the table, smiling contentedly.

"What was it I told you. A century ago on your one hundred and fiftieth birthday. When you first asked what it took to be a king?" Vashti found herself blushing again, as Flynn raised an eyebrow."

"You told me that when a king takes up his sceptre and raises it in the name of something. It could be for friend's, his people, glory, it could even be for justice. At the end of the day what makes it stand up is the strength he puts in his right hand."

"Well there you go." "There you go what? I don't get it." The queen just stared at her son, waiting for him to figure it out.

"Of course," gasped Vashti, figuring it out first. All these years you took it literally. Training, learning to lead men. Becoming the warrior that our father was. Trying to become the king he was. Making your right arm as strong as possible. But it's a metaphor isn't it?" She asked directing the last part to her mother.

Both her brother and lover stared at her with bemused expressions. Both too literal. The only metaphor either could even consider was it being fighting strength. Military might. No wonder they couldn't see it.

The queen nodded her head in agreement signalling her to continue. "The metaphor isn't about your right hand, rather who is your right hand."

"I'm not surprised you figured it out first" smiled the Queen. "Vaike has always been singularly focused." "That's a nice way to put narrow minded" jibbed Flynn laughing.

"Your one to talk" Vaike retorted. "Fighting, booze and women are all you think about." "True. But a mortal Remem.. Hmm I guess not anymore." "Exactly" replied Vaike. Now his turn to laugh.

"Yes Vaike, all along you needed to be searching for a second. A second who you could trust with yours and Vashti's lives. One who would do the impossible if you asked.

A second who would be willing to die for you and your kingdom. But most importantly one who won't follow blindly. Rather one with the wisdom to think for themselves, who has different opinions and the courage to tell you if your wrong."

"Many of the elves I have commanded and fought beside fit that bill." "Mostly" the queen added. "The best fitting ones were older. From a different time. A different era. You needed to find someone who'll help you make this new era your own."

"Is that what you meant mother before we left to find Baird, when you said ill complete my brother?"

"When you were born the Dreamweaver's came to me." The Queen began, giving an elaborate answer. "They told me you would meet a human whom you would fall for. A human who is your brother's other half. His complete opposite. A human who you would marry and in turn become Vaike's best friend. Vaike's brother.

I didn't know for certain it would happen during that journey. Or if it would in fact be Flynn. It could've been another human you met in a thousand years. However, I had a hunch and when Flynn tore out his own eye." Guilt flashed in those ancient eyes at this. "I was certain. But I couldn't risk it with his mortal lifespan. I had to gamble, think about the long term."

"I get it." Vaike said. "You had to put your people first. Flynn dying in thirty years would've crushed Vashti. She may never have recovered and I myself may never have found an equal." "Ah shucks you're not so bad yourself" Flynn interjected ruffling Vaike's hair.

"Even when you are an insufferable boob" Vaike sighed. "I love you too, you big lug" Flynn said mockingly. Knocking over the table as he jumped up to hug Vaike, planting a wet sloppy kiss on his cheek.

The queen was laughing. It was the most delightful and joyous sound in the world. Despite various stains spreading across her dress or the ruined breakfast she was happy.

❦

For the past week Vashti had stayed at the palace with the Queen. Leaving Flynn alone with Vaike. It was a week of preparation for the woman and a week of traditions for Flynn. He barely slept a wink all week.

Studying up on elven wedding traditions, wanting to make it perfect for Vashti was taxing while having to complete the traditional tasks of a bridegroom made it near impossible. Some tasks were easy thanks to his new immortal body growing stronger everyday giving him increased flexibility, agility and muscle mass. So, when challenged to hit flying targets with an arrow or wrestle multiple challengers and other feats of strength he breezed past.

Others were hard like having to pet a sleeping wolf or place a stone marked with your own name in a bear's lair. Tradition proving strength, ability, cunning and luck. Traditions that Vaike didn't tell him until after the bear gave up on chasing him were optional. Only three needed to be completed. Three selected by the bride upon accepting the betrothal.

Still a fourth one was mandatory, one that he took seriously. The one he struggled with the most. His Achretic.

The elven equivalent of vows, only each one is individual to the person. Some elves recite poems or speeches while others unveil sculptures or works of art. One elf he met even had it tattooed on his body.

Flynn always struggled with finding the right things to say, never being one to really express his feelings. More comfortable risking his heart than sharing it. His end result was an adaption of an old children's story, long buried at the back of his mind.

It was about a duck who grew up as an outcast. Shunned by its siblings, hated by its parents. Waking up to discover it was left behind come migration season he set out on its own. Meeting other animals some friendly, others not so much. It journeyed alone, skirting with death while discovering itself.

Eventually it found a duck who looked the same as himself. Just to learn he wasn't a duck after all, rather a glorious swan. It found a new flock, a new family and a mate.

Flynn also wanted to surprise Vashti and present it in elven, not the common tongue. Even though it was now the dominant language spoken here. Few elves bothered to even communicate entirely in elven anymore.

After the incident with the bear Flynn didn't want Vaike's tutelage. While he highly doubted that Vaike would sabotage his sister's wedding he couldn't be sure. After all, if the roles were reversed Flynn would take the opportunity for a joke if it presented itself.

Whyda agreed to help when Flynn asked. He proved to be an apt teacher, displaying a cunning intellect despite his position as Vaike's manservant.

Flynn decided this was the best way to describe his role. Cooking and cleaning up after the prince whenever Vashti wasn't there. Working at the palace whenever she was.

Vashti opened the door to her old room at the palace, marvelling at how nothing had changed since she moved out with Vaike a century ago. She always felt confined in the halls. Not physically since their entire house is three times the size of her room here.

Rather it was the pressure, the rules that suffocated her. Vaike was more than happy to move out too. Not that the palace bothered him just that their house was significantly closer to the practice grounds.

"It's exactly as I left it." "Not exactly dear, I'm told you left quite a mess." "I would hardly call an unmade bed a mess but why has nothing changed, it has been almost a century?" "It will likely stay that way for a few more" shrugged the Queen.

"Besides it's not like I am personally responsible for cleaning so unless you decide to move back in, the room awaits a new occupant." Her mother closed the door on her winking as she finished talking.

Chapter 21

THE WEDDING

Flynn stared intently into the mirror in his room, in Vashti's room. At Whyda's insistence he was shaved and shorn. Hair scrubbed till his scalp hurt. The four strands of coins remained. Vaike joining Flynn in his expostulations.

A fake eye was fitted into his empty socket. Metal orb cold against the exposed flesh. The workmanship was incredible, the eye looking even more realistic then his right eye. He found it unnerving as it stared blankly ahead. Destroying the eyelid when he ripped it from his skull made it impossible to blink or cover.

❧

Vashti was seated in her childhood chair, her own nervous features reflected back at her from the mirror above her dresser. Idly watching as a brush was run through her long silver hair.

It surprised her that her mother insisted on doing it herself, dismissing all staff she styled her daughters hair. It was tradition for the bride's mother to get her daughter ready for the ceremony but Vashti never expected it. As close as the pair were, not once had she ever brushed her hair or helped her pick out clothes. Always to busy, always needed elsewhere.

Picking up a wooden horse from her dresser Vashti fiddled with roughly carven figure. It was a gift from Vaike on their thirteenth birthday. She remembers how proud he was when he gave it to her.

Spending months teaching himself how to carve it after he saw how excited she was learning to ride.

The piece was out of place in the palace and something Vaike had probably forgotten about completely but to her it was sentimental. A reminder that someone was always there for you no matter what. She now had two people like that.

Looking up her mother had finished brushing and now braided her hair. Watching her fingers work, nimble despite their age she dared to finally ask the question she'd been brooding on all week.

"How did you know it wasn't a legend. That Ebsallom or Mithras would make an appearance during the northern convergence. I mean Flynn disfigured himself because of your game so how confident were you?"

"Well as I already said I wasn't expecting him to react that way" responded the Queen while continuing to work away. "And while I wasn't positive that he would survive, I knew for a fact that Mithras would grace us with his presence."

"But how because of some legend. You said it yourself, no human has been granted this gift." "Girl how many years have you spent exploring the forest?" "Hundreds!" "Exactly hundreds and before now, how many times had you encountered that clearing?" "Uh that was the first time."

"Not surprising since it only exists during the convergence." "Okay so Mithras presence is real. How did you know it wasn't him paying a visit to his acolytes?"

"Well how did you honestly think you and your brother were conceived centuries after your father's death?" 'Wait what! I thought you took a tonic to delay the pregnancy. Preventing us from growing until such a time that the kingdom was stable."

"Seriously girl" laughed the Queen walking around to look her daughter in the eyes. "Bbbut, that's what you told me as a girl." "Of course, I did. You were to young to comprehend the truth. Vaike sought out the truth a long time ago, I just assumed he shared it with you."

Sighing the Queen took a seat beside her, hair lying forgotten across her back. "Firstly, there is no such tonic that can pause a pregnancy. We can only cause miscarriage's which hasn't been done since the war.

Secondly. Whenever your father visited during the war we never lay together. He was always to busy with reports and discussing tactics. So, by the time he did come to bed he would fall asleep instantly.

After he died, I took over as ruler and kept the kingdom running as best I could. It wasn't easy. Everything was a wreck in the war's aftermath. I was that busy I never even got a chance to mourn his passing properly.

It was decades later when things started to run smoothly that it dawned on me. I had not only lost the love of my life but my children also. I began to spiral deeper into my grief. I began to forget our people before the convergence arrived.

Desperate I sought out the legend and found the rock. I was prepared to pray for hours, days if needed but their he was, your father. Exactly as I remembered him sprawled out on a blanket with a basket of food within reach. We only had the evening. Upon waking, the clearing and your father were gone.

I returned two more times before falling pregnant and a third time after you were born. He never showed the last time but I wasn't disappointed. I felt happy. I knew he was at peace, watching over his family.

You see daughter, Mithras knows what you desire. What you truly need and he will gift it to you if he thinks you are worthy."

The location was chosen by Vashti as per tradition. A spot in the forest that speaks to the bride. It could be a pleasant memory, the locations beauty even a particular way the sun shines down on it. Flynn didn't know why this particular spot, nor was he supposed to.

The ceremony itself was a small, private affair. Only family members attend with a single prelate presiding over it. Flynn stood naked above the waist except for a single gold coin resting over his heart. Bare feet and a wreath of wild flowers adorned his head.

Vaike had to near force it on him. Flynn doubting if it was a real tradition or not. Only Whyda confirming it in his bored voice had

Flynn stripping down. Baring their hearts and souls while baring their chests apparently.

Vaike stood facing Flynn of to his left, behind where Vashti is to stand when she arrives. The queen to take a place beside her son. Flynn didn't need to turn around, knowing full well behind him was empty. Having killed the closest thing he had to family a few months ago.

The prelate stood on Flynn's right. Dressed in a flowing robe of green cotton. Designed to blend into the forest, almost like he wasn't there. It was a family thing after all.

Flynn stood without moving for ten minutes. Then twenty, forty, nothing. His nose itched but he wouldn't scratch it, the fake eye irritated him but he didn't rub it. Feet ached but he wouldn't budge easing the discomfort. If he locked his knees he'd probably have collapsed by now. Only standing and watching. Waiting for his bride.

An hour of waiting and the queen entered opposite from where Vaike and Flynn did. Similarly attired to the last time Flynn saw her, not as a queen but as a mother. She walked straight to Vaike stopping beside him.

Flynn didn't watch this however, he only had eyes for one thing, Vashti. Slow elegant and graceful she seemed to glide towards him. Step, feet together pause, step, feet together pause.

Dressed in pure white fabric. Whiter than the cleanest pearl. A long skirt grazed the tips of grass beneath her bare feet. Two strips wound up from her hips, covering her breasts before wrapping around her neck to join at the back.

Silver hair plaited to the sides. Two on each side, matching Flynn's own four. The main body flowed behind her trailing in the breeze. Flowers encircled her head, a blossoming crown.

Flynn watched on shivering. Not cold despite the cool evening breeze caressing his bare chest. Not nerves either.

The sight of Vashti, her beauty caused his body to quake with excitement. Not primal instinct telling him to plant his seed. Not that he didn't have that exact desire. Rather it was the realisation that he had a life, a future with this perfect being. This goddess among men.

Flynn just stared, unable to talk, unable to move. Paralysed when Vashti stopped in front of him. So close he could smell the soap in her hair through the perfume of rosewood and strawberries. Taking his hands in hers the prelate spoke. It was muffled noise to Flynn, like people talking while you're starting to wake. Words without meaning, sound without source.

Hearing the words "I do" snapped him from his trance he instinctively blurted the same. Vashti's thin lips curling up at the corner in a cheeky grin as Flynn heard the prelate speaking. "And who stands witness to this man" ah only at this part Flynn thought. 'Oops, jumped the gun there. Still no one is here for me.'

"I do." The words sounded behind him. Flynn new that voice. He could see with his right eye he no longer stood with his mother. He knew who it was that spoke, yet still Flynn let go of Vashti's hand and turned.

Vaike stood behind him, as his family. Left eye watering, tears starting to form. Flynn turned to face Vashti again, not bothering to wipe his left eye. No need to, he can't see out of it anyway.

Vashti's eyes began to well up at the sight of Flynn's. His old eyes having forgotten how to cry but his new one matching perfectly with the heart of the new Flynn.

Eyes wet with tears, the prelate now addressed the pair. Flynn first, forcing the words through the lump in his throat. The first to take the risk, diving headfirst in giving the woman more time to reconsider her options while she listens to his Achretic.

It doesn't mean the woman can be slack with hers. It's obviously an insult and bad manners, but also signals the marriage is doomed to fail, so more pressure on the woman here. 'Probably a good thing Flynn thought as he prepared to take a huge risk'.

Last night he found himself sitting at a desk unable to sleep. He just started writing, getting everything off his chest. Finally drifting off to sleep before the ink had even dried on the final page.

Discarding his story, abandoning all his preparation, his practiced elven. Reaching the decision while he slept to go with the raw emotion of the previous night. If he doesn't bare his soul on his wedding day, when will he?

"Looking back upon this path I have journeyed upon I am unable to believe what my eyes see. From the empty shell I was, existing on hate and lust to the man I have become today.

Vashti. I still recall the first time I saw you like it was yesterday. From across the room I saw the face of my deepest, my most unknown desire. I still feel like your something right out of my dream's.

Now I just stand here lost, frozen. Unable to find the words to show you my love. I try and try but no matter how I search they don't come to me. They just stay locked up in my head.

I have been running my whole life. Racing with one foot upon whatever path I walked. Closed of from the world, scared to let anyone in, terrified of them leaving me.

But like a moth drawn towards the flame you pulled me in. You pulled, you persisted and your fire burned away all of the fear that I held deep inside off my heart.

Despite everything I am. Despite everything I've done you still decided to stay. You dared to look inside and see me for what, for who I am. Dared to find a spark, a small spark you grew into a fire. A fire you didn't let fade away.

Vashti, I vow until the day this body fades away to never stop loving you. To never stop fighting for you and to never give up on you. I can't promise that you will never cry, only that I will do whatever I can to never be the cause of those tears.

Vashti… I love you."

Reciting from memory as per tradition Flynn stared deeply into Vashti's eyes. Fingers entwined as so too did their souls, their lives.

Pausing often, fighting to keep his voice under control. Breaking from emotion, choking back tears the Achretic took longer than Flynn expected.

They held each other's gaze for an eternity. Time stood still. The prelate actually having to grab their shoulders to make himself heard. Who knows how many times he asked Vashti the same question?

After a painfully long pause Vashti answered "I do", not reconsidering judging by her grin merely wanting to make Flynn suffer a bit.

Vashti wrote a song for her Achretic. Unlike the slurred, rowdy, tone deaf voices Flynn was used to she sounded like an angel.

She sang of an internal struggle between oneself, of feeling incomplete. She spun a web of loss, love and sacrifice. Wrapping up with futures of joy, pride and comfort.

Concluding by taking the lead and wrapping her arms around Flynn's neck. Pulling him inwards they kissed deeply, unable to wait for the prelate to instruct them. Not that it mattered they were wed. It was done.

The distinct sound of a twig snapping startled everyone, Vashti and Flynn breaking apart, kiss forgotten. A white buck strode into the clearing, stopping a few paces from the Queen. Antlers four feet long protruded from his head. The ultimate trophy for a game hunter, the hunting of cowards. Other than food you shouldn't hunt something that can't hunt back.

The buck bent its front leg kneeling down. The Queen, prelate and Vaike all bowed likewise leaving Vashti and Flynn standing alone as a solitary figure. Wrapping her arms around his neck Flynn took the lead this time. Kissing Vashti on her rosy red lips.

By the time they broke apart the buck was gone along with the prelate, leaving the family alone.

❧

Flynn was awestruck stopping at the base of the ten thousand steps. They had only been gone a few hours yet the transformation was incredible. Lanterns of various colours, red, blue, green, yellow hung from ropes stretching between boughs of great trees. Decorations that sparkled like stars as the light danced across them coating the branches all around the clearing below the city.

Elves danced and sung in a symphony of joyous gaiety. More elves then he had ever seen before, all coming together to celebrate his marriage. Vaike had told him weddings were a cause for celebration amongst their people since they were so rare. Seconded only to the birth of children. Flynn never imagined this. The ceremony was a private affair but the celebration was an open invitation.

A celebration that would put mortal kings to shame. Bankrupting their kingdoms in an attempt to replicate. Fire jugglers and eaters entertained the crowd while actors graced a stage opposite them. Wearing masks and costumes all masterfully crafted and dazzling to behold.

Food and sweets filled hands as elves bounced around enjoying the festivities. Every male elf that sauntered past reached out, touching Flynn's exposed shoulders and chest. The skipping females doing likewise to his wife.

A tradition. It was for good luck and fertility Vaike explained when he asked. Unable to ask Vashti who strode twenty paces away escorted by her mother. Another tradition apparently. They are to be re-joined at the feast but for now, they are reminded that they are joined with everyone. All part of the same race, the same city, the same extended family.

Flynn grit his teeth and bared with it, as hand after hand touched his bare skin. Never being the most intimate person, even after sex he preferred to be left alone and not cuddle, it made him feel uncomfortable. For Vashti however the discomfort was worth it.

The feast table was impossible, no other word for it. Maybe two hundred metres long as far as Flynn could tell laden with so much food the wood groaned under its weight. Duck, fowl, pig, venison, fish, mutton, beef. Nuts, fruits, vegetables and fungi. Baked, roasted, glazed. Seasoned, stewed or smoked. They had everything cooked in every way you could possibly imagine.

Barrels stacked three high, full of wine encircled the table. Groups of six barrels to every fifty elves. Silver plates pushed dangerously close to the tables edge, teetering on the brink goblets balanced precariously in their centres.

Long wooden benches ran the length of the table down both sides. Broken only by two high backed seats on the left side. Plain timber chairs polished and worn smooth on the seat with flowers interlacing the backrests.

According to Vaike the seats were centred underneath his and Vashti's house, now also Flynn's house. Looking up it was impossible to tell, too far to see anything despite the overhead branches.

Flynn stood behind the right chair hand draped over the back waiting for Vashti to join him. Only a few paces behind she promptly took up residence beside him while Vaike and the queen sat beside them, Vaike on his right.

All other seats were filled with elves standing behind the benches waiting for the feast to begin. "It has been far too long since we last celebrated like this. To long since we last had anything to be joyous about. We had grown complacent in our own existence. That is also my fault as your Queen." Despite the vast number of guests there was utter silence as the Queen addressed them.

"But today, today I am a mother celebrating her daughter's wedding. I celebrate the growth in my family and look forward to the promise of it growing more." Vashti's cheeks reddened at the implied thought.

"I also celebrate as a Queen. A Queen who can see the direction her people, her kingdom is heading and it is a bright future. A promising future.

For this wedding not only joins two cultures. Two people. It births a dynasty, a future. One where Vaike is no longer your Prince General. But one where Vaike is your Prince Consort and Flynn as his, as your new Prince General."

Vashti elbowed Flynn in the ribs as he snorted trying to silence his laughter. Despite the honorific being given him.

"But let's not forget whose day it is so I invite you all in toasting the happy couple. To Flynn and Vashti." Shouts of Flynn and Vashti echoed around them as everyone toasted.

Plates were piled high with food as the wine began to flow freely. Elves talked, laughed and drank. Songs and music flowed around them while some decided to dance. Between mouthfuls of honey glazed ham Flynn turned to Vaike.

"So why are you the Prince Consort, was something lost in translation?" Flynn asked Vaike, struggling not to laugh as he asked it.

"Because it's a transitional phase. One where I work side by side with the Queen as she slowly hands the reigns over to me. At which time I'll be named King."

"I figured that but a consort to humans is someone who is married to a reigning monarch." "Okay, that is definitely lost in translation then" chuckled Vaike.

The revelry continued as people broke up into groups. Tables stayed laden with food as elves came and went whenever hunger drove them. Apparently, the festivities could run on for days.

Some Dusk watch soldiers sat to the side partaking in drinking games. A game completely foreign to Flynn but he knows a drinking game when he sees one. Looking around to see Vashti smiling talking with a group of females Flynn sat down joining them.

The game looked simple enough but it was actually incredible complicated. They called it Barka, 'Troll'. A hat, two dice and a mat five inches squared were all you needed to play.

The troll wore the hat and they took turns in rolling the dice on the mat. If a die fell off the mat the roller missed his turn and became the new troll. If they both stay on the mat, the total rolled detailed what happens. A three or total of makes the troll drink. Seven and the person to the left of the roller drinks, while eleven and it is the person to the right drinking. A ten resulted in everyone drinking.

That was the easy part. It got harder when you incorporate the doubles. Whenever a double was rolled you can make up a new rule and roll again. The only rule here was it can only target the troll or everyone, you can't pick on a single person. Three doubles in a row also skips the third one and makes you the new troll.

Because it was his first-time playing Flynn was automatically made the troll. Another convenient rule.

Rules were already in place where the troll had to spin around and grunt before each drink. Something Flynn repeatedly forgot to do which caused a penalty of another drink. They quickly added up.

The troll passed hands several times. Flynn getting it the most when Vashti touched his shoulder from behind. Unfortunate timing as he had just shouted out that he loves cock. An amusing rule he added earlier that the soldiers found hilarious too.

Finishing his drink, he excused himself from the game. Walking away from the celebration, hand in hand with Vashti. Vaike falling into step behind.

They walked for ten minutes away from the revelry to a little cottage amidst the trees. An unhabituated cottage that served but one purpose. Consummation of marriage.

The cottage was small and clean. A dividing wall split the cottage in half. A large bed and nightstand occupying half. A pitcher of water and platter of fruit and berries sitting atop it. A tub full of hot water occupied the remaining space. The air in that portion was thick with steam.

Stepping through the threshold Vaike pulled the door shut behind them. Through the little window Flynn saw him standing sentry outside the now locked door.

"Umm.?" "Oh that. That's another tradition." Vashti said noticing where he looked. The brother or best friend of the groom, whoever is best suited for the job really.

He stands guard against the bride's family or admirers. Really anyone who might attempt to break up the marriage."

"Does it happen often then?" "Not since we were made immortal, no. Yet the tradition remains."

"We can send him away if it makes you feel uncomfortable?" "I'm fine if you are. Beside he'll be more uncomfortable with it then I am." Flynn laughed before nibbling on the pale skin of his wives' neck.

Blushing she dragged him to the bed silk sheets greeting their exposed flesh they fell entwined.

❧

Vashti lay on her side. Silk sheets cool against her goose bump riddled flesh. Watching as Flynn's chest steadily rose and fell as he slept. Exhausted after their love making, lasting through the night until morning. Vaike standing guard through it all, unable to leave until the newlyweds do.

It was her first time and Flynn was very gently, easing into it. The first time was slow, with Flynn kissing her slowly working his way down. Caressing her breasts, lightly touching her skin. Before stating he was going to taste her.

Taste her he did, bringing her to orgasm twice with his tongue. With her legs on his shoulder as he knelt on the floor. Pulling her hands away the second time as she tried to push his head away.

As spasms wracked her body from the sensation, he unbuckled his pants. She remembered seeing his naked form on the rose or when she cared for his injuries after fighting Olaf, but she never saw his manhood rise. Knowing and seeing were two different things with how big it could get. Noticing what drew her eye Flynn told her it was well above average for a human. As for an elf he had no clue.

Still it looked like it would hurt and hurt it did. Despite Flynn inserting it slowly, stopping to ask if she was okay. It hurt. Telling him she was fine he continued, no longer the euphoric feeling between her legs.

Hyman ripping blood began to mix into their love making. She had heard of men being drunk and pounding away for hours unable to finish. Even being gentle she wasn't sure if she could take it that long.

Both thankfully and disappointingly it was over quickly with Flynn finding release. Pulling out he wrapped his arms tightly around her. His chest pressed firmly against her back, she felt safe and secure.

She joked about how quick he was to kneel before her, his reply piercing through to her heart. Stating he will kneel only for his wife, his Queen. No other person holds his allegiance. He bows for no one else.

Feeling dirty, her skin slick with sweat and blood drying on her thighs Vashti lifted Flynn's arm of her and headed to the bath. Flynn watched her walk, an idiotic grin on her face, similar to a boy seeing his first boob.

The warm water was soothing the second her foot broke the surface. Sitting the water came up to her shoulders, a hint of rose greeted her nose. Dunking her head under the water she scrubbed at her hair, entangled with leaves and flower petals.

Resurfacing, hands wiping the water from her face she savoured the moment. Today had been a big day, a big moment. But she was happy. Eyes opening, she saw Flynn leaning against the divider watching her. Still naked radiating absolute confidence. Scars appearing more pronounced against his flesh as he stared at her completely in awe.

After asking if she minded, he joined her in the tub. Sighing as the warm water eased the muscles in his legs. She was apprehensive not knowing what to expect, everything tonight being a new experience.

However, if she had to guess it wouldn't have been this. Flynn grabbing a sponge and proceeded to wash her back. Not hard, just a nice consistent pressure he scrubbed against her naked flesh. He then washed her hair, digging out leaves and massaging her scalp.

She felt it when he was ready for her again, his manhood digging in her back. She didn't even return the favour and wash his back, by this time wanting to feel Flynn again she jumped on him. Water splashed out over the rim of the tub flooding the stone floor.

Unperturbed she kissed Flynn deeply hand reaching down gripping his wood. Flynn lifted her up under the arms carrying her from the tub, tongue twirling inside her mouth while he stood. He slipped on the wet floor crashing back first into the wall.

His grip loosened on impact but he never dropped her. He just laughed while he carried her back to the bed. Inexperienced though she may be, Vashti took charge telling Flynn what she wanted. Flynn did everything she wanted spectacularly and while she tried some things that she knew probably didn't feel the best he never scolded or yelled. Directing occasionally but letting her lead. As painful and awkward as the first time was the second was amazing.

They went three more times finishing up not long after the sun shone through the window. Shining past the flushed ears of Vaike. Embarrassed after hearing everything that happened during the night. The third time Vashti decided to taste Flynn, taking him in her mouth.

His moans of pleasure and hands tight in her hair telling her how thoroughly he enjoyed it. The next two times growing even more incredible as she let go of any control letting Flynn run with it. He took her against the walls, on the floor, standing and some strange yet enjoyable things with fruit. Even briefly in the tub in various positions she never would've thought of in a thousand years.

She idly traced a scar along his muscled abdomen that stopped just above his groin. She blushed thinking how grateful she was that no cuts reached that low. Even his thighs displayed only a few shallow cuts. He obviously went to a lot more effort to protect his jewels then his vital organs.

Flynn stirred as she touched the ugly star shaped scar on his left thigh. The only visible remains from his fight with Olaf. Smiling he greeted her as his wife. Their first morning together.

Asking if she woke him for another round. Apologising, she said as much as she would enjoy that, they should probably put Vaike out his misery. Flynn wasn't to upset by that, explaining that he had never gone more than three times in a night, with two being more frequent the last few years.

She buried her face in the pillow embarrassed as he told her she was amazing, the best he had ever had. Not just the most perfect body, or most beautiful woman. But the connection. The fact he loves her made it special. Makes it actually mean something more than a physical release. Lifting her face from the pillow she stared deeply into Flynn's eyes, left eye staring blankly back. Placing a hand on his cheek she told him it was everything she had hoped for before leaning in to kiss him. Enough to arouse him before pulling away, leaving him wanting more.

❦

She was a fast learner Flynn thought as she broke away. That kiss caused his heat to rise as he wanted to take her again. She just smiled knowing exactly what he wanted before dropping a grape into her mouth.

"So" she began. "Vaike tells me you prepared a different Achretic." "Did he now" Flynn groaned blowing a raspberry on Vashti's stomach. Laughing she slapped the top of his head. "Come on, did you?"

"Yes" he sighed. "I had prepared a speech based on a children's story that matched my life. I even learnt the whole thing in elvish. The pronunciation and accent of which would probably have been an affront to your ears."

"What made you change it?" "Honestly. I choose the story because I struggled to find the right words. But I couldn't sleep the night before and just started writing. The words, they just flowed. Even once I looked at the words on paper I was torn about changing.

I have never been very expressive, preferring to keep my emotions in check. But I thought of you, and I thought if not now than when." "Well it was perfect, I'm glad you did" the smile telling Flynn she truly meant it.

Chapter 22

THE UNWISHED DREAM

They lay in bed talking late into the morning. No deep conversations or discussions about the future. No flirting or hidden agendas, just two people enjoying the others company. The bath water was still warm by some magic of the elves but it was by no means clean after last night. Still it was better than walking around reeking of sex. Splashing water on themselves they quickly bathed and dressed in their clothes from the previous day.

Flynn now had cuts on his back from Vashti's nails. Her own hair now a tangled mass worn to cover the marks Flynn left on her neck. Thankfully her dress covered the other marks that weren't in polite places.

Vaike still stood guard outside the cottage. He turned at the sound of the door opening, fixing his tired gaze upon them. Empty plates and cups lay nearby. Obviously having eaten just not sleeping made him a little irritable as he greeted them.

He made no comment on the events of the previous night. Simply trailing behind the couple as they made their way back to the feast.

Flynn laughed as they approached the festivities that were still in full swing. Elves lay passed out sleeping on the grass while others danced around them. Some slept in chairs while their drunk neighbours continued their conversation oblivious to their loud snoring.

Some were energetic and wide awake while others tottered around, on the verge of collapsing. Some fashioned breakfast while others ate dessert nearby.

Spilled drinks and food littered a section where several elves sat bloody and bruised after a good brawl. All now laughing like good friends who hadn't just exchanged fists.

"It is exactly like a human feast" Flynn exclaimed. "Not quite" Vaike spoke from behind. "We have plenty of debauchery but without the lewdness."

"Oh, I don't know" Flynn said turning to face Vaike, his one good eye drilling him. "There was plenty of lewdness last night." Flynn never would've guessed that someone's ears could turn that red. Glowing like bright cherries Vaike was left speechless.

"Stop it" Vashti whispered bashfully. Her own face burning with embarrassment. "Really you seemed to enjoy it last night" Flynn laughed sticking his tongue out. Vaike walked past not wanting to be privy to the conversation, Vashti buried her face in her own hands. Not covering the red as it spread to the tips of her ears.

"Come on let's go get some food" Flynn said pinching her ass. She yelped in delight, playfully slapping Flynn's arm. Embarrassment gone, replaced with a flushed face of excitement.

The attention of the previous night was gone. Drifting through the throng unnoticed, Flynn preferring the anonymity. Vashti also seemed to enjoy it walking side by side, arms linked. Finding a secluded spot at the table took them to the far end. Most elves seemed to have stayed to enjoy the festivities, only the council and a few elders having already left.

The table was still laden heavily with food from yesterday. Stomach growling as Flynn eyed the food before them. "I didn't realise how hungry I was" he said placing a hand over his bare stomach. "Well you did expend a lot of energy last night" Vashti answered winking. Her turn to make Flynn's face burn. He couldn't remember the last time that happened.

With no snarky retort coming to mind Flynn bit into a roasted chicken leg. Despite being cold it was delicious. Stealing a glance at his wife, Vashti grinned at him well aware she had scored a point.

They ate, drank, danced and enjoyed the festivities. Vaike finding them during a comedic performance that Flynn didn't really understand but Vashti laughed loudly over. Reference humour to something that happened before his mother was even born so it was completely lost on him. Still the skill of the actors and writers wasn't missed by him. Vaike came to wish them well, saying he was off home to sleep.

"I hope you have realised how much fun you can have in a bed. Or out of one." Flynn said not missing the opportunity to mess with his brother and getting in the last word as Vaike left.

❦

Vashti blinked, eyes adjusting to the light. The forest lighting up as the sun rose somewhere outside the canopy. Several others rubbed at their own eyes or shielded them against the sudden glare.

The smoke from the previous night keeping everyone who partook partying through the darkness. Flynn's own eyes were still bloodshot, never having partaken before. A special mix of Kantermian berries, toxic mushrooms and a few other herbs. The smoke stimulates and causes hallucinations resulting in interesting scenarios.

In fact, her first experience was something she would rather forget. Waking up two days later wearing a pair of male undergarments as a crown while holding court with some dead ducks. The undergarments she was convinced belonged to her brother.

The open area made the smoke less potent but it still packed a wallop. Having been ten odd years since she last partook. Only coming to her senses after splashing some cold water onto her face from a bowl laid out for that very reason. Looking at Flynn only to rub her eyes again unable to believe what she saw.

Flynn really had fun with the smoke. Wearing nothing but some undergarments and a hat stolen from an actor's costume perched on his head. He wielded a branch like a staff and ran around casting spells on others. Some giggled and played along still under the effects while the clear-thinking ones winced, recognising their new Prince General.

Flynn had no clue where his pants were, nor did he show much interest in finding them. Continuing on with whatever game it was he played, even with the smokes effect wearing off.

Vashti sighed defeated. She knew what he was like but an eternity just seemed daunting with this level of immaturity. However, by their standards he was little more than a child. An unheard-of age for elves to marry. 'Did they use human or elven standards to measure him by now?' she mused silently.

By lunch time Vashti was exhausted. Head buzzing, eyes itchy and limbs heavy she needed sleep. Flynn was still going strong already drinking again with a few guardsmen.

He came over noticing her trying to stifle a yawn. Asking if she was tired and wanted to go home. She didn't want to spoil his fun but Flynn wouldn't take no for an answer. Noticing how tired she was they left without a word. Slipping away unnoticed from the still raging party.

❦

He still has a lot to learn Flynn scowled, berating himself. Vashti was beyond exhausted and for what? Just so he could party. It was different out on the road. You did what you must but here. Here, he needed to be more thoughtful towards her.

She held his hand as they stood silently on the travelator. It was surprisingly quick, taking about ten minutes to reach the main level of the city.

Vashti leant against him, sleeping soundlessly as the platform jolted to a stop. Staggering to stay upright as he caught her, managing to somehow sleep through the disturbance.

She stirred enough to be dragged along by the hand. The laboured staggering steps of a drunk man looked almost comical from his wife's delicate frame.

Sleep won out as their front door came into view. Scooping her up in his arms, Flynn carried her the last few steps. Not wanting to put Vashti down who now drooled on his shoulder, her arms wrapped tightly around his neck. Flynn knocked on the door, kicking it with his front foot. Vaike must've been out since no answer came.

The door knob, such a simple mechanism. So easy to manipulate a child could do it. Yet here he was struggling to open a door while carrying a sleeping woman.

After much frustration and a few choice phrases that would've bothered the neighbours if they were home the door swung open. Flynn carried Vashti across the threshold and up the stairs to her room. Their room.

Vaike silently sat beside his mother as she oversaw the council. He knew ruling could be tedious but this was insane. A wedding festival was in full swing on the forest floor and he was stuck here listening to reports on levels of rainfall and expected forest growth as a result.

It wasn't even something interesting like how the dark would spread or grow bolden to claim the new area. Although that was ten years plus before trees occupied the supposed area. Plenty of time for that report Vaike sighed. Earning a frown from his mother.

The reports and discussion continued in a similar fashion. Finally, the council finished for the day as the light began to wane. Arriving at his front door after the lanterns hanging from branches and houses were lit.

The door was scuffed with boot prints but not broken. Not giving it a second thought, he strolled inside, mouth beginning to water at the scent that greeted him.

Whyda had outdone himself, even with the feast still fresh in his mind. Although he has been preparing his meals for over a century so he does know what he likes. Even after second helpings Vaike found room for dessert. Freshly baked apple pie laced with cinnamon.

Feeling like the buttons on his pants were about to burst Vaike headed to bed. Needing a lot of rest for another day of painfully boring reports.

Vashti's door was ajar giving him pause in the corridor. His sister was passed out sleeping, head resting on Flynn's chest, left arm draped over his torso in a tight embrace. Flynn lovingly stroked her hair. Making eye contact Flynn nodded. Vaike returned the greeting as he pulled the door shut.

Vaike spotted Flynn early the next morning as he made his way to the council room. Taking the shortest route, he passed by the clear platform used as a training area. A hundred metres squared it was the largest area on the upper floors. Straw targets were set up on the far side so any stray shots travelled safely away from the city.

Flynn was completely alone, having the full space to himself. Deep in training he swung a weighted iron rod around as sweat soaked through his shirt. Cursing loudly as the rod slipped from his grip bouncing across the floor.

Picking up the rod he returned to his forms as Vaike lost sight, disappearing amongst the buildings.

⟡

The festivities carried on for the next week. Shrinking each day as fewer elves continued to participate in the revelry. The upper levels gradually returning to the norm with the last stragglers quitting on day ten. The old Flynn would've stayed to the last but the new him has been out training.

Stronger and faster he almost lost his sword the first time he unsheathed it. Sliding free faster than he expected it to it shot from his hand landing feet from the edge of the training area. If he was carful it was fine but after two more close calls he gave up.

Not wanting to lose his swords he needed to develop finer control. He now swung a heavy iron rod used to build muscle and endurance. Arms burned and shook as he swung the rod around. No grip on the cold steel, the rod slick with his sweat.

Each day he woke up and kissed Vashti's forehead. Choosing to sleep in most days he returned from training to freshly baked goods. She enjoyed playing housekeeper, cooking and cleaning for both him and Vaike.

Still the warrior princess however, she would join him for an hour or so most days. Focusing on technique she failed to work up much of a sweat. Although she did plenty of that each night. Flynn was eating three helpings each evening just to maintain muscle mass he was working that hard.

A week after his wedding he heard heavy breathing as someone trained hard. Beating him here this morning he cleared the buildings finding Vaike working out. He was shirtless running laps. He waved Flynn over, signalling to join him. "Fucking hate running" Flynn grumbled pulling of his tunic.

Not that he was slow or bad at running, it was just you couldn't run on a ship. Plus, there were far more enjoyable ways to build up endurance he grinned.

They ran side by side in silence for an hour. Vaike doubled over hands on knees when they finished. Flynn's own breathing ragged, the pace they ran at was something he couldn't manage a month ago.

They continued this routine each morning for the next week. Flynn waking up earlier each morning trying to beat Vaike there. Vaike was always there first. Already running. All it achieved was them running longer and longer. The last morning Flynn thought he was going to throw up, his lungs burnt and he tasted the coppery tang of blood in his mouth.

Coughing he waited for Vaike to leave. Deciding he was going to skip training the rest of the day. Running for over two hours was enough. His legs wobbled just trying to support his weight. Pain shot through his right side from a stitch. If he had eaten any breakfast it would be on the ground by now.

But Vaike didn't leave. He just watched on with an amused expression. "I don't have any meetings for a while. What do you say to a little sparring?" Vaike asked. Knowing full well that Flynn had too much pride to say no.

They used wooden swords, not wanting to injure or kill the other with the weight of the iron rods. Flynn was grateful for the excuse, knowing he was too tired to keep up with the prince.

It felt like training with Edward, with Iron fist a decade ago. By the time they finished his body was covered in bruises and welts. Vaike it seemed was almost as exhausted as he was, so their skill and speed were on par but he kept getting struck. Struggling to land even a handful of blows he performed better as a human, or mortal. He was still confused how that worked out.

Flynn was confident Vaike didn't pick up on the weak point, either that or he was showing pity on him. Flynn assumed it was the former, Vaike knowing full well how much being showed pity would infuriate him. It was only a matter of time then until Vaike focused attacks on his left side.

No longer able to react as fast on that side left him vulnerable. He kept having to turn his head which just shifted the blind spot onto his right side.

"We should try doing this every day." Vaike said draining his water skin. "It will help you get used to your body better." 'It seems he didn't pick up on it. Or maybe that was what he referred too' Flynn thought. "Good idea" he answered unable to think of anything better to say.

❧

For three months he trained everyday with Flynn. His mother granting him the time after he explained it to her. Only running every few days. they would cross blades for hours.

It was destroying him to watch the struggle his brother was going through, as his very identity was being torn apart. He struggled with the loss of strength. Not physical strength. Rather his fighting prowess.

Vaike quickly identified how weak his blind side was and how to exploit it. The problem wasn't the loss of an eye it was how it affected his fighting style. Relying on reflexes and natural instinct he needed perfect vision.

The blindside forced him to fight differently which wasn't working. Either muscle memory prevented it or a skill that Flynn simple couldn't grasp, it was impossible for him to adapt. Three hits on the left and he over compensates and gets hit on the right.

Acrobatic movements now left them entangled, as he would trip over Vaike or crash into him. Not seeing his own movements in time. Once equals now Flynn struggles to strike him a handful of times.

He threw tantrums more akin to a spoilt child then a seasoned veteran. Weapons thrown, directionless cursing and screaming.

Vaike tried to subtly hold back once. Just enough for Flynn to start figuring it out. Gaining confidence. Flynn realised immediately, punching him in the face. Rubbing his jaw, he just watched as Flynn strolled away refusing to train for the rest of the day.

Today Vaike changed it up. No sparing they ran through the woods. Vaike planned to run all day. Planned to run until their legs gave out. Run until they coughed up their lungs and clutched at their sides. Until the only thoughts they had were breathing and the next step.

He knew Flynn would get it eventually. He had nothing but time, but today. Today was purely mental. Forgetting the last few months and starting anew.

Sweat rolled down their backs and wet hair clung to their faces. Eyes burned from the salty sweat not stopping to dry their faces. Shallow cuts and scratches covered their bodies from twigs and branches as they broke from the path. Forging ahead without direction through the brush.

Stars began to look down upon them as they returned to the Eastern entrance. Shivering as the cool evening air caressed their damp clothes. Neither man with the strength left to make the climb they rode on the travelator in silence. Seated Flynn was alone with his thoughts.

A palace attendant waited for them on the landing. Approaching before the platform had even come to a halt. The Queen summoned them at their earliest convenience to dine with her that evening. The polite way of saying clean yourself up, get presentable and get your arse over here.

Flynn groaned and Vaike agreed with the sentiment. The last thing he wanted to do was attend a formal meal after that run. His breathing was still ragged making it hard to speak. Hunger gnawed at him, having eaten nothing since breakfast and his legs still wobbled with each step. However, both men knew better than to refuse.

❧

Flynn stood observing his reflection in the mirror. Vashti already at the palace having laid out clothes for him she left while he bathed. A purple tunic laced with gold thread woven with frills around the collar and cuffs. Fluffed out sleeves on the upper arm made it look like he had deformed biceps. Worst of all was the cape. A lighter shade of purple that stopped at his lower back. 'What sort of fashion was this?' Flynn grumbled pulling on the matching pants.

He fiddled with the fake eye, turning it over in his hand. The thing felt wrong and was uncomfortable to wear. Despite being the perfect fit. It was still cold and hard, nothing like a real eye.

He knew Vashti preferred to look at him with it in so he put up with the discomfort for her. While training, he preferred to wear a leather eye patch similar to those worn by his pirate brethren.

Whenever he bathed, he would take it out to wash the empty socket. A strange sensation that, washing the inside of your head essentially. It needed to be done to prevent infections or abrasions, learning early on to use warm water as hot or cold water would burn the thin skin or cause his nose and skull to ache.

Sighing he plopped the eye in, gritting his teeth against the cold. The pupil was off centre and with no eyelid he was forced to use his fingers to adjust it.

Looking in the mirror with two eyes staring blankly back he now brushed some lint of his lapel before adjusting his collar. 'Could probably use a shave' he thought leaning in closer to the reflective glass.

A strange notion given elves don't grow facial hair. His own growth stunted since the ritual. Unsure if it will ever stop growing or just continue slowly, they had no clue. As such Flynn continued to shave once every month or so. Just enough to remain respectable.

A rap on the wooden door was followed by Vaike's muffled voice through the wall telling him to hurry up. 'Well next time then.'

"Please tell me that's not how I look" Flynn appealed opening the door to see Vaike. Wearing an identical outfit other than the colour. While Flynn's was purple, Vaike wore one of deep burgundy red.

"Afraid to say in that colour you're probably worse." "Fuck, I knew it. Come on then before I cut out my other eye" joked Flynn. He could feel Vaike watching him closely the whole way to the palace, probably making sure he was joking.

Chapter 23

THE FUTURE THROUGH NEW EYES

Vashti had to stifle a laugh as she watched her husband enter the formal hall. More comfortable in stained, loose fitting clothing rather than the tight formal wear of their court. He walked with stiff legs like his pants were too tight and he kept digging at his backside whenever he thought no one was looking.

Not that she enjoyed her formal dress much either. It was all layers and ruffles she couldn't even get dressed alone. It took two handmaidens to help her struggle into it. No corset thankfully as you couldn't see her figure anyway but she had to be careful what she drank. Even needing assistance when using the bathroom.

Flynn walked around the table situated in the hall to stand beside her. Council members stared at him. Scorn clearly written on a few faces, Andreas's face most of all. Flynn's promotion to his superior was a huge blow to his own ego. Sure, he didn't know their customs but neither did any off them at first.

Opening his mouth obviously about to pick a fight. She knew how frustrated and full of anger her husband was at the moment, no matter how hard he tried to hide it from her. Stamping down hard on his foot before he had a chance to do more harm, she silenced him. The wince on his face as she did told her she broke some bones.

Grabbing hold of his right hand in her left, not soothing or apologetically but to steer him. Guiding Flynn from her left to her right. At formal functions he now sits opposite Vaike, with the Queen seated at the head on his right side. When Vaike takes the crown Flynn will sit were he does now. The king's right hand. Her spot is beside her husband not between them.

She probably should've filled Flynn in on this detail. It having completely slipped her mind each night as she looked forward to their lovemaking. Despite his own frustrations he never took it out on her. Each night as loving and gentle as the first. Bitting down on her lip to stop her cheeks from reddening, she tried to think of anything else.

The two princes were the last to arrive with the council members and a few elders already here when she arrived. Twenty immortals stood around a table, ten to each side waiting on a single person. The Queen.

The Queen did not need her arrival announced in order to have the attention of the entire room. Her mere presence demanded attention as she took her time to cross the room. While her children all wore large bulky clothing, the Queen was garbed in a long satin dress that clung to her body.

Wrapping tightly around her curves and amplifying her assets. A few faces betrayed the desire of their hosts. Never getting used to seeing her dressed like this regardless how many times they saw it over the centuries.

Flynn was entirely in complete control of his own libido, that or he was completely bored. Maybe both as he too stood patiently, weight shifted favouring his left side. She'll have to make it up to him later tonight Vashti thought cheekily.

His right foot was a dull throb, lost amongst the numbness in his legs. Pain and hunger forgotten he only wanted sleep. Blacking out for moments while he stood waiting for the Queen to arrive. More than once he startled himself awake as he began to fall forward.

Several council members scorned him. Already resented for his promotion above them despite being an infant in their eyes. Now he was disrespecting their formal occasions. He was too tired to even give a shit. Probably a good thing or he probably would've jumped across the table and started swinging.

Regardless how old they are he can't handle disrespect from scholars or aristocrats. Someone who has never done an honest day's work, or at least a hard day's since piracy wasn't exactly honest.

The Queen finally arrived and casually strolled across the hall. Taking her time as she held the entire attention of the room. Flynn's legs were starting to shake, struggling to keep upright. Finally reaching the head of the table the Queen stood behind her chair, hands resting together atop the backrest.

Electing to address those gathered rather than sit. Nothing remarkable just a polite greeting and welcoming to everyone present. Nothing mentioned or hinting at the reason for the gathering. On completion she clapped signalling the attendants to begin serving the meals.

Stealing a glance across from him, Flynn saw Vaike's face turning red as he too struggled with standing. Minus the broken foot he was as sore as Flynn. The last plate clattered on the table, clicking against the cutlery placed beside it. The Queens chair was pulled out for her and pushed back underneath as she sat.

Flynn dropped into his chair, legs giving out in time with Vaike. Both men seated before the others even made a move. The corner of the Queens mouth turning up slightly in a knowing smile. The savory taste of dinner escaped Flynn. Eating tonight purely for sustenance, for need he ravishly devoured the plate of food. Ignoring the wine until he had consumed his second helping.

Vaike showed more decorum while stuffing his mouth. An art Flynn truly marvelled at. Eating like a pig but looking dignified. A few disgusted looks were directed his way as he wiped his mouth with the back of his sleeve. Forgetting how expensive his clothes were.

After the final morsel was consumed the Queen spoke. Telling them about a summit of all the Eastern leaders to be held next month in Voldengird. The new caretaker Baird, was holding the audience before his coronation.

He sought approval from all leaders before they become his subjects. Alternatively, he is granting independence to any nation that desires it. The Queen will not be attending it personally, rather Vaike will go in her stead, his first official duty as Prince Consort. Flynn and Vashti will accompany him as they to have a good rapport with the young King.

With that news she clapped her hands again summoning attendants to clear the setting. Once dispersed chairs scrapped against the floor as everyone stood waiting to be dismissed. With a lazy flick of the wrist not even bothering to stand she waved everyone out.

As he reached the door about to leave the hall, she called to him, asking him to remain behind. With a puzzled look Vashti kissed him on the cheek saying that she'll wait outside. Nodding Flynn turned and walked back to the Queen.

He stood silently as she looked him over, judging him. "Sit, please." Flynn sat in the offered chair, unsure what to say.

"No need to look so worried I'm not going to eat you" she said flashing her pearl white teeth. "I haven't exactly come out to great after our conversations," "True you have come out a little worse for wear. In the short term anyway." Regret passed across her face as she looked at his fake eye. Staring back lifeless and empty.

"So, I wanted to ask you how you were doing?" "I'm doing fine. I'm stronger and faster than before and I'm married to an amazing woman." "Hmm. I truly wish I could believe you. Now. Tell me, how are you really doing?" She demanded of him.

"Honestly" Flynn said sighing. "Not well. You bestowed this huge honour upon me, this great responsibility. One I am most certainly not worthy of, not worthy of this trust bestowed upon me. Not worthy to be Vaike's right hand." Flynn said left eye welling up in tears, throat constricting struggling to speak as he poured his frustration, fear and anger out.

"I can't fight by his side anymore. I can't fight for him. Shit, I can't even defend Vashti. How am I meant to be his general if I can't stand on the front line? Even if I manage a new fighting style, I'll never be your sons equal. Losing my eye is akin to losing a hand. I'm useless."

"You're not useless" the Queen said holding his head in a motherly embrace. Flynn's tears flowed freely from his left eye as she held him.

As the tears slowed, she held his face in her hands looking into his good eye. "You too are my son, don't forget that." Kissing his forehead, Flynn was reminded of long forgotten memories. Memories of happy times when his own mother was still alive.

"And as my son I have a gift for you." "I don't need anything" he protested. Completely satisfied with the gift of a loving mother. "Oh nonsense, how many gifts do you think the other two have gotten over the years. Besides think of it as a belated wedding gift."

The Queen pulled from her pocket a green satin pouch. Small, it fit neatly in the palm of her hand. Taking the pouch from her it felt light. A small solid object nestled inside, the size of a pearl.

Overturning the pouch an eye fell out, grey iris staring back into his own. "Go on try it out." Not about to refuse the Queen, Flynn popped his old eye out placing it on the table. Bracing for the shock Flynn fitted the new eye. It actually was pleasant. Not as cold and a better fit. Made out of different material perhaps.

"How does it look?" The Queen asked handing him a mirror. The eye wasn't crafted as masterfully as his old one. The grey not as perfect looking slightly warped in the iris, little imperfections that made it look more real.

"It looks more real." "Anything else?" a grin spreading across her face as she asked. "Well it fits better. I don't have the constant urge to rub it and, and." Speechless as Flynn realised, he was looking through that eye.

"I can see" he shouted, voice echoing around the sealed room. "I. I don't know what to say?" "How about thank you." "Yes of course. Thank you. Thank you, a million times over." "You don't need to go that crazy. This wasn't just a gift for you, but it was a gift for Vaike and Vashti as well."

"In giving you your sight, I can give them both you. The you they both love." "I get it" Flynn said. "I was losing my identity and in turn they were losing me." The Queen nodding in confirmation. "But how is this even possible. I thought you couldn't restore my sight?"

"We couldn't heal your sight your original eye was to damaged, a distinct difference. Plus, I figured if you survived the trial you would come back with it. But once I realised that didn't happen." A guilty look spread across her face again. "I had my spell weavers work on it. It's not your real sight only an artificial construct. If you lose the eye you lose your sight again. It should also stay centred on its own. No need to be constantly adjusting it." "So just like a normal eye then" "Yes I suppose your right" She chuckled.

"Now get out of here. I think I've deprived my daughter of your company for long enough." Flynn left without another word, practically running for the door. Smiling ear to ear.

Flynn nearly ran from the palace. Full of more energy and excitement than she'd seen in months. Taking her hand in his without a word, he steered her away. Not in the direction of their house. Stopping instead before a rope bridge branching across the gap to her hidden landing. A place they hadn't been to visit since he returned and lost his eye.

Not waiting to see if she followed, Flynn traversed across the bridge as it swayed and rolled underneath his weight. Vashti followed a few steps behind. Tripping over in her eagerness to see what they were doing out here. Hands gripping tightly, catching herself before she could fall the forty feet to the level below.

Proceeding with care, she crossed the second half slowly. Flynn stood waiting, holding the first rope ladder out to her as she caught up.

"There is a reason I prefer pants to dresses" she said as he motioned for her to go first. "It's nothing I haven't seen before" he replied winking, catching on to her meaning.

"It is still undignified for a lady." "You just want to check out my arse, don't you? Not that I can blame you." Before she could respond he swung a foot onto the first rung and disappeared. Not waiting around, he quickly rounded the tree reaching the second ladder. Amazingly an even faster climber then before.

Pulling herself over the last rung onto the landing she found him seated on the bench watching the horizon. Soundlessly she sat beside him, placing her hand on his own. "Beautiful"

"Yes" she responded. Staring out at the dark ocean stretching into the night sky. "Still it pales in comparison to sailing upon it." "That's not what I meant." Turning she looked into Flynn's eyes.

"You are even more beautiful at night under the moon. It makes your hair glow." "Stop it" she said with a flustered voice, covering Flynn's good eye to hide her embarrassment. That wicked smile that said he was up to no good crept across his face.

"I love that bashful look of yours. It's really cute." "Now you're just teasing me" she pouted. "I'm not, I really mean it. I love everything about you right down to the way you purse your lips when you pout." "Wait, how did you know I was pouting?" she asked pulling her hand away from his face.

"I can see." "I know that I uncovered your eye." "No, I can see look. Hold up some fingers and ill guess the number" Flynn replied covering his own eye. She examined his hand making sure he couldn't see around it. Sceptical of him as he chuckled at her paranoia. She assumed this was some joke he was playing with her. Satisfied she held up three fingers.

"Three. One, one, five, none." She stared at her closed fist. Five from five he had to be telling the truth, but how?

Looking into her beloveds face she didn't care why. Seeing that bright smile she knew he was back. She knew the man she loved was no longer lost but hers again. Jumping forward she tackled him off the bench. Rolling on the landing they passionately kissed. Oblivious as they rolled precariously close to the edge.

She lay there panting out of breath shivering, the evening air cold against the skin, her naked flesh riddled in bumps. In response Flynn cuddled up tightly to her, offering her his own body warmth while draping the remnants of her dress over them as a blanket.

They had just experienced the most passionate session of lovemaking in a while, if not ever. Lost in the throes of passion she lost any inhibition she had about being outside, even in a secluded space. Flynn didn't have any, tearing her dress to shreds getting it off her as they both became engulfed by their desire.

The risk of getting caught, the excitement, it added to the ecstasy. Her loins still ached with desire, wanting Flynn to fill her again. But she had best let him sleep. He was exhausted already and he still needed to run back home soon to get them both a change of clothes. Caught up in the moment, driven by primal instinct he tossed his own pants off the edge.

Plus, she thought, cheeks reddening. She still had to make it up to him for his broken foot. Something that she forgot about last night. Regaining his vision and their love making drove it from her mind.

❧

Yesterday he woke happy. Not because he was naked under the stars with the most beautiful woman he could imagine. Nor because his sight was returned in his left eye. No, he was happy because he was in love. He was loved and they were both stronger than ever.

Unbreakable. Today he woke early ready to leave the forest. Heading north to the runts summit.

Well not really ready he thought, heat rising in his face. Vashti greeted him this morning, from her knees. Keeping him from getting dressed while she pleased him with her mouth. His own fingers interlaced in her hair as he moaned in pleasure. Her own green eyes locking with his as he finished. Vashti swallowing every drop without breaking eye contact.

Seated in the saddle they waited for the Queen to see them off. Rubbing his right foot, Flynn tryed to ease the discomfort. Only a minor break thankfully. Made worse by his forced naked sprint through the streets home and back.

A few early risers saw him streak past. He was fairly confident no one recognised him, putting on an extra burst of speed whenever he saw someone. Plus, it was still dark. Then there was the ten thousand steps. Those fucking steps. Vaike wasn't aware of his injury and Flynn wanted to keep it that way so he endured the long trek down. Much to his wives' displeasure.

It doesn't matter anyway. If he can manage the stairs and run, he can fight. As unlikely as that was with an escort present. Even desperate bandits won't attack a company of elves and the goblins have been driven back for a while.

Besides with the escort it will take the best part of a month to reach the capitol, giving him plenty of time to heal.

A sparrow fluttered down from up high coming to land on Vaike's shoulder. "We've been waiting for over an hour and she can't even be fucked coming down here herself." Cursed Flynn. Aching foot making him irritable.

"I'm sure something important came up" Vashti replied defending her mother. Her own voice betraying her own frustration at the situation. How often had this happened to her during her life. An absent mother putting her duties first.

It was sad how much the twins seemed used to it as he rode over, the sparrow now fluttering away amidst the trees.

"Something urgent came up that the Queen must attend too. She wishes us well and safe travels." "Of course, she does" Flynn muttered loud enough for those closest to hear.

While the soldiers escorting them were loyal to the Queen, she handpicked many of the younger elves to accompany them. Those who came up under Vaike, fighting alongside him. More loyal to the Prince then herself. Apparently, they need to start building a rapport with Flynn as he will be leading them soon. As such Flynn didn't feel the need to hold his tongue around them.

Something he learnt commanding a ship. You want to surround yourself with those who trust and believe in you, not necessarily always the best fighters. A man who trust's you completely will gladly storm hell with a smile on his face. Gladly risk his life and even die for his belief in you. The quickest way to find these men is be yourself.

If you walk on eggshells worried about offending people you won't get anywhere. Those who follow you will leave when the shit hits the ceiling, when your true self comes to the surface.

While a few soldiers grimaced at the disrespect shown to their leader, understanding and agreeance shone on even more faces. Vaike even glanced down briefly agreeing with the sentiment.

Chapter 24

THE NEW KING

Lush grass swept across the land. Winter giving way to spring, the only time the human lands resembled anything like the elves home.

Each blade of grass sprang back up at attendance after the horses trampled it underfoot. Daffodils and other flowers broke up the sea of green. Adding their own colours blending together like a child's painting.

Their escort rode on in gruff silence. Setting the pace and deciding on the course, they had no say regardless of the fact they outranked them all.

They slept deeply each night. Not needing to keep watch, that was their escorts job. Vashti unfurling her bedroll each night beside his own. Falling asleep each night with his arms around her. While Flynn breathed her scent in deeply as her silver hair tickled his face.

Flynn would nibble her earlobe once the darkness engulfed them. He could feel her heart flutter as her desire for him grew. His hands would trace the outlines of her curves as his manhood would rise. Digging into her back she would wrap her legs around one of his. Stroking his foot with her own.

As much as the close proximity to others didn't bother him, he knew it bothered Vashti so he wouldn't do anything for a few long, painful weeks.

Still he could tease Vashti each night. Remind her what she was missing. Judging by the flustered looks she would shoot his way during the day she was desiring him as much as he wanted her.

The scars of marching armies still marred the land. The winters snow not enough to conceal the signs. Blackened timbers of burnt homes and farms. Dead stumps of fallen trees, required to build siege engines. Fields empty, bare of crops with no farmers around to tend to them, either killed or driven out. It was only a small campaign but it will be years before the land recovers.

Three and a half weeks of slow tedious riding came to an end. Voldengird, the human's northern capitol shone in the distance.

A bustle of activity surrounded them as they approached the walls. Workers hurried about carrying timbers and tools. Carts wheeled in shaped stone blocks. Shouted orders and the pounding of hammers encroached them.

"Fuck me I am impressed" Flynn said whistling as they rode past the yawning hole in the wall. "It is defiantly one way to take the city" Vaike responded. He too in awe by the destruction. "What can cause destruction like that?" Vashti asked. Concern on her face.

"No weapon I have ever heard of" Vaike answered. "However, humans are probably as industrious as goblins when it comes to methods of killing one another." "That may be" responded Flynn. "But I have never heard of a weapon capable of doing this.

The destruction carried inside the city. Freshly constructed houses stood proud beside the skeletal frames of those being built.

The cities gates stood open, soldiers standing guard, armed and alert. Protecting the gates while a breach existed seemed comical. They were waved through without any resistance, they were after all expected at the palace.

❦

Dignitaries and lords had been arriving for the past fortnight. Formerly empty rooms were now full with guests as the castle bustled with activity. Servants darted around carrying food trays to those who chose not to dine in the hall. Fresh linen and laundry were carted around by the armful.

Still Ailish waited for the visitors she most desired to see. The summit was due to start today and still Vashti hadn't arrived. She missed their chats. Being surrounded by men made her realise how much she missed female companionship.

Even Garrett had been absent the last two weeks. Holding meetings with Baird and dignitaries before the summit. Answering questions and getting a feel for which way they planned on swinging.

Her war chief, Jorgenson arrived reeking of mead and sweat. Covered in pelts of bears and wolves despite the warmth. In the mountains her people were split into seven tribes all governed by their own chief. The war chief is whom the six others swear fealty too. A title chosen through combat and feats of strength.

Her own father was the younger brother of the Chief. Killed defending the chief when the Vampires attacked.

Jorgenson did not recognise her. It was curiosity and her looks that drew his attention at first. Inviting her to join him for drinks and talks not long after being shown to his room. Acquiescing his proposal, she sat in the gazebo deep in the castle gardens.

Jorgenson wasn't looking for another wife or companionship, his own wife travelling with him. He just sought to converse with someone from another tribe. Growing bored with the same faces over the past few years.

The conversation grew sombre when he asked why she left the mountains. She told him about the massacre of her tribe and setting out to seek vengeance.

He had heard of the destroyed village from a few survivors who fled to nearby tribes. The news of the Vampires was new. All his reports varied from neighbouring villages to phantoms. Olaf was blamed with a few reporting goblin attacks.

Fifty survivors all reporting different things. He visited the village personally but found nothing but smouldering ruins and corpses picked clean.

Jorgenson asked if she was successful. If her family was avenged. She proudly informed him yes, thanks to her friends. She was no match for them alone.

❧

The tables in the hall had been removed to clear away enough space for the summit. Fourteen chairs encircled the clear floor. Everyone seated as an equal, looking each other in the eyes. Each leader would sit with a single advisor to their right. All other lords and guests were to stand behind them.

Fourteen chairs for the seven factions. The seven territories of the east. The northern land with Voldengird as the capitol, Baird's land. Bordered by the Elves and the mountain folk. The latter being a war chief overseeing all the other chiefs.

Lord Cordonn, housed at Crow's Perch governed the centre. With the leader of Koyake representing the west.

Foden's cousin, Aeedon the new ruler of the desert tribes sat beside the delegates from Beildronna, the southern kingdoms.

Five guards from each faction lined the walls. Eyeing each other off, sizing up potential threats. Some encased in heavy plated armour, sweating in the heat. While the nomad guards wore light cloth robes better suited for the weather.

Baird had no idea how most people would be voting, or who they would follow. He knew Aeedon and Jorgenson intended to remain independent. No surprise since Olaf never managed to subjugate them. He was clueless on the other major territories.

Two seats to Baird's right sat empty, the twins whom were yet to arrive. He knew they weren't far off. Seeking fresh air before the council Baird stood on his balcony. Gazing out over the city he saw a group of riders approaching the walls. Too far away to make out their banner. Nothing more than dust clouding behind small shapes.

Shapes that came from the south west, riding across fields not bothering to follow the roads. With everyone else here it had to be them.

Impatience growing on the lords faces Baird started. The guards had orders to grant them admittance and his friends were already aware of the first part anyway.

"Greetings my lords and ladies. Welcome to Voldengird. The Jewel of the north." A Few sneers at that. No surprises there, it was a new name. Baird was trying to start anew. Forgetting about the death and blood associated with these stone walls.

"I have met with most of you and you all had the same question. Who am I? Where did I come from? Well I didn't want to repeat myself, so before discussions begin, I'll tell you.

It all began over a year ago, after a goblin raid wiped out my village." Baird retold his adventures. No embellishment, no lies. Being completely honest save for omitting sensitive details involving the elves and Flynn's crimes. Happy to admit his own shortcomings, his growth and the aid of his friends.

◆

Every head in the room turned as the doors swung open without announcement. Even the soldiers that stood guard couldn't help but to betray themselves.

Three people stood framed in the doorway. Ailish smiled, trust them to make an entrance. The whole hall went deathly quiet as everyone noticed the pointed ears. The angled faces of elves. Every pair of eyes followed them as they strolled towards the empty seats, swords still hanging from their sides.

Baird was the first to speak, breaking the suffocating silence. "My Lords please allow me to introduce Prince Vaike and Princess Vashti."

Vaike took the seat beside Garrett. Sitting more upright and dignified then every other ruler present. Ailish was surprised to see Flynn not Vashti take the empty seat beside him.

While Vaike displayed grace and poise Flynn was the exact opposite. Slouching down in his chair, legs outstretched. Sitting before the leaders of the west and he shows them all disrespect. Like they weren't worthy of his time.

There was something different about the three of them. Ailish couldn't quite put her finger on it, and what was this. Were Flynn and Vaike now friends. She couldn't believe it. Flynn caught her gaze and she almost retched.

Even from across the hall she could see that disfigured face. Eyelid destroyed, he stared ahead unblinking. It was unnerving as one eye stared ahead, not following the other one as his gaze drifted around the room.

"Now, where was I?" asked Baird. "Ah yes, we were about to clash with Olaf's army." "What the hell is this" demanded Lord Cordonn. "We all agreed. No weapons!" "My lord we kept our swords because we brought no guards in." Vaike answered in a neutral voice.

"And what the hell are you people even doing here?" Cordonn didn't even bother to hide his disgust and hate as he spoke.

"We were invited" Flynn answered over the top of Vaike. Without our help Olaf would still be sitting here. You would still be kissing his boots, hoping he let you live. So why don't you just be a good little boy and shut up."

"How dare you speak to me like that. I am the ruler of Crows perch. I control the heart of Eastern Thaldesa and I command your respect." "No. You demand my attention."

"King Baird, is this the of level company you choose to keep?" Cordonn screamed, turning his attention to the young ruler. "Yes. Without those two in particular I wouldn't be sitting here. As I was about to explain, Flynn himself duelled and killed Olaf. So please, by all means continue to antagonise him. See how that goes" grinned Baird. Losing patience with Cordonn too, it seems.

"You sit there acting all smug. Thinking you've won. That we'll all bend the knee to you just because the elves are with you. But I know the truth you little bastard. Why don't you tell us the truth, tell us all why you really visited my city? How it wasn't to recuperate and resupply but rather to assassinate my guest. My friend.

Admit it, you were working for Olaf all along. Just biding your time waiting for your chance to overthrow him." Several other leaders stirred with unease at the accusations.

"Well I was going to bring it up later but fine we might as well get it out of the way." Baird responded with more authority then Ailish had ever heard him use before.

"Yes, it is true we murdered a visitor of yours in Crows Perch. A visitor who also happened to be a Dalthenian spy. Working for Maroxis and paying you off. You were promised the governorship of the East. Answering only to Maroxis himself."

Cordonn's face paled as Baird revealed the extent of his information. To his credit he recovered quickly. "I don't know where you got this fantasy about Maroxis from. Yes, he was an agent working for the Dalthenian. But it was to overthrow Olaf, granting us independence from him. All it would cost us was Voldengird."

An obvious lie Ailish thought, but one that a few leaders bought. "Believe what you want to believe" smiled Baird. "But you have one of two choices.

Firstly, like everyone else here you can govern yourself, becoming an independent state. Or you can choose to remain a subjugated territory under my crown. Doing so and your betrayal will be forgiven. You will not be tried for treason but you will abdicate your title."

"What kind of choice is that" laughed Cordonn. "I King Cordonn will not bend the knee. I never intended to bend the knee. I just came here to confirm my suspicions. Find out if you really are responsible for my friend's death.

Your army is weakened, your walls even more so. So how about I give you two choices. Bend the knee to me or my army will return killing you all."

"Allow me to save you some time" Flynn said. Arms crossed as he slouched even deeper into his chair. "The runt isn't responsible for killing your friend, I am."

"Well how about I give you a third option then" Cordonn said to Baird. King to King. "Hand over Flynn and I will call it even. We can go our separate ways and I won't invade."

"I am afraid I can't do that. For you see Flynn is not a citizen of mine. I have no authority over him as he doesn't call any of my territories home."

"Fine have it your way" Cordonn scowled. I will be seeing you in a few months and drag him out myself."

"I wouldn't advise that" Vaike cut in. Speaking for the first time in a while. "You see Flynn isn't a citizen of Baird's lands, because he is under the protection of my mother. If you raise a finger in anger towards Baird looking for him you will be fighting two armies."

'What the hell has happened in the months they've been separated' Ailish wondered.

"Not just two." Jorgenson spoke in his deep scratchy voice. Wearing the pelts of a white bear and a wolf's head draped over his own.

"We owe Flynn for avenging our people so we will stand by him."

"As will we." Aeedon declared rising to his feet.

"Fine then we will fight you all and if you elves want to interfere in human business so be it. Ill burn down your forest on my way here" Cordonn screamed a he marched from the hall. A line of nobles and soldiers trailing behind.

"Good luck with that. I'll be sitting in your throne before you make it a hundred yards beyond the tree line" Flynn laughed as he left.

"If any of your Lords have no faith in their King your welcome to stay. Swear fealty to me and you will retain all lands and titles. A few border lords halted as their fellows strolled past. Most either in no position to defect, doing so will have them surrounded by hostiles, that or they did actually believe in their new king.

"Well now that's over we might as well get to business then."

⚔

'This may not turn out to be a boring trip after all' grinned Flynn. 'Already a regicide, so killing a second matters little. In fact, if they were allowed weapons he probably would have already. It doesn't bode well to kill an unarmed monarch after all'

Four seats now stood empty with a large portion of nobles having left also. The ruler of Beildroma leaving shortly after King Cordonn. Already having bent the knee and allied with him. Fortifying the south against Baird.

The desert nomads and mountain tribes will remain independent. They did agree to establish trade and diplomatic relations along with the aid of troops.

The old greying leader of Koyake, Bortun spoke of the prosperity they enjoyed under Olaf. Now with Cordonn on one side and the Dalthenian's on the other they needed the help.

Bending the knee, he declared his fealty to Baird. Remaining governor of the west. One out of five, better then what he expected.

Talks then turned to promises of resources to repair the fortress at the Blood cliffs. Along with everyone promising troops to establish a garrison. The fortresses importance forgotten while they warred amongst themselves.

Pointless topics that held no impact to the elven domain. Talk's dragged out, driving Flynn crazy as his mind was elsewhere.

Vashti the little devil leant over as Bortun knelt, whispering in his ear so softly even Vaike couldn't have heard. Her breath ticking his neck as he heard the words that continued to circle around his head. "I want you inside me."

Chapter 25

THE REUNION

Baird was exhausted as the last of the nobles exited the great hall. Slumping down in his chair as the heavy ornamental doors boomed shut. Leaving the six friends alone for the first time in months.

Vashti and Ailish already embraced like sisters. The girls rushing across the polished marble floor the moment they were alone. Talking rapidly and over the top of each other Baird couldn't make out a word that was said. The girls seemed to understand what the other said for they broke apart promising to catch up later.

After a last hug the girls sat down in now empty seats. Ailish beside Garrett who had just moved to sit on his left, Vashti lowered herself into the cushioned seat beside Flynn.

"Before we catch up" Vaike said, taking control of the conversation. "I just wanted to say how impressed I am with how you have handled things. Not just today but up too this point."

"I don't deserve the praise. It just sort of comes to me." "Hmmm, so you are still having the dreams then?" mused Vaike. "Yes, I suppose. They are less visual, but I wake up with ideas and solutions to problems that were beyond me the day before."

"Well Ithiel was a brilliant ruler. Just continue to trust and follow any guidance you receive." "I intend to" chuckled Baird.

"Well I can see there is a lot to catch up on" Vaike said glancing at Garretts stump. A subtle twitch of the eyes that everyone noticed. "Yeah no shit" Flynn responded. "You need to be careful with whom you fist you know. They are liable to react poorly."

"It was in battle" Garrett snipped back. The loss of his hand was still a sore subject for him. "Your one to talk by the way. Did you slip while trimming your hair?"

"What this?" Flynn asked pointing at his left eye. "This was self-inflicted." How had he not realised it. The flesh around the eye was scarred and shrivelled. The eye didn't blink Flynn just continually winked every few seconds.

"Why would you cut out your own eye?" Ailish asked, sounding genuinely concerned for her lunatic friend. "Because I could" Flynn shrugged. While the twins didn't flinch the jaws of the other three dropped. Mouths agape.

"Good to see you haven't changed" smiled Garrett. His good mood returning. "Why would I, I'm awesome." Everyone groaned as Flynn grinned broadly.

"So seriously. How did it happen?" Ailish asked. "I'll fill you in later, for now I need to take a piss." With that he stood and walked from the hall. "Vaike asked him what happened after they went their separate ways so Baird recounted the story.

After a while Flynn still hadn't returned. Assuming he had gotten lost Vashti left to search for him. Declaring Ailish will tell her anything important that she missed.

❧

Flynn leant against the wall, idly picking non-existent fluff from his coat. "I was beginning to think you were tormenting me. I was about to head back in."

Vashti raced across the polished floor, foot snagging the edge of an expensive rug in her haste. Without speaking she grabbed Flynn's hand, dragging him around the corner. Opening door after door down the corridor without letting go of Flynn's hand. Hands clasped like he would disappear if she let go.

Servants and other occupants looked up as doors opened then slammed in their face. No apologetic words for the interruption or mistake. Blank, confused faces staring at the bizarre scene.

Towards the end of the hall she found what she sought, sort of. An empty, private room. Well room was a stretch. It was more a cupboard, full of mops and buckets.

Still she was desperate, her desire was so strong she was ready to pounce on Flynn like an animal during the summit.

Without giving Flynn the chance for a sarcastic comment she shoved him into the confined space. Wooden broom handles fell on them both as she stepped in after, pulling the lockless door shut behind them.

She couldn't see her hand in front of her face. Falling into complete darkness as the door closed. Their close proximity in the rooms tight space made it irrelevant. Flynn didn't hesitate, leaning in and kissing her ear. She found his cheek, her nose pocking his eye in the movement. Good thing it was his left eye.

Eventually he grabbed her chin. With that as a reference he soon kissed her passionately. His tongue twirled around her mouth, driving her crazy with desire as she moistened.

Fumbling with his belt in the dark she eventually gave up focusing on her own waist band as Flynn unfastened his belt.

It was short and needed, not enough to sate either of their desires but enough to stop the pot boiling over. It had been over three weeks since she last felt him fill her.

Blushing and laughing they crashed from the cupboard. Flynn finding the handle while they tried to dress. Flynn fell on her, covering her decency from any bystanders. Thankfully there were none since Flynn's pants were still tangled around his feet.

Vashti smiled looking down at the half-naked idiot she married. The idiot who tripped over his pants as he tried to get off of her, falling flat on his face.

They walked back to the great hall and their friends. Her hair was a mess no matter how much she combed it with her fingers. Both their faces were flushed and she kept readjusting her clothes. They just didn't sit quite right after Flynn stretched them.

❦

'You can't be serious' Vaike thought in disbelief. They couldn't wait until they were alone to jump each other. What's worse now they haven't even tried to hide it. Flushed faces, hair a mess and Flynn's belt was still unlashed.

Yep as he thought both Garrett and Ailish watched them walk back to their seats with eyebrows raised. Only Baird seemed oblivious to their bathroom trip.

❧

'Well well well. I guess it finally happened' Ailish realised, not that it was a surprise. She was actually more surprised that it took this long. She expected Vashti to return from their month at sea with stories of passion and lust. Not the boring, unbelievable tales of Flynn being the perfect gentleman.'

Once Vashti had sunk back into her seat, she glanced briefly at the others faces. All completely aware what they snuck of to do. Except Baird who continued with his recount of the last few weeks.

Vashti looked at her last, eyes meeting Ailish couldn't help herself. She winked, grinning as Vashti glanced at her feet, cheeks blossoming red.

❧

Flynn slouched down in his chair, hands resting on the back of his head. The others all knew, not that he cared. He wasn't exactly being subtle.

The runt still continued with his recounting of events. All pointless crap for him to hear anyway. Other then what destroyed the walls but he can just ask Vaike about that later.

Other than hearing that Ivan was executed nothing even registered to Flynn. Vaike was the diplomat, him the General. So, unless it was of strategic or military value, he held no value in the report.

For those report's he'll be better speaking with Garrett and Ailish, or perhaps Baird's general whomever that was.

"And that brings us to now. So, what happened with you guys when we split?" "Fuck were doing this now. I'm going to need a drink."

"Of course," replied Baird. Walking towards a small door at the back. He spoke a few words through the door before closing it on whoever he spoke with.

"They'll bring some food also." Hmm Flynn had to admit the runt definitely seemed to show more authority. Not that it was very hard one is more than zero after all.

They sat in silence waiting on the refreshments. They didn't have to wait long, in minutes several servants entered carrying platers of fruits and freshly baked pastries. Flynn ignored these going straight for a pitcher of ale, refusing the offered goblet. Preferring to drink straight from the clay jug.

"After you left in pursuit of Ivan the three of us returned home. We spent a month there while Flynn continued to heal after his fight with Olaf."

Vaike spoke while Flynn half listened. It was all stuff he already knew but with a wet throat and warm belly it was tolerable.

Vaike gave them a watered-down version of their discovery at the Blood cliffs. Even watered down the humans paled at the envisioned horrors.

Flynn was on his second pitcher when Vaike stopped talking to stare at him. He knew why, they had just returned with the crown and Vaike was wordlessly asking how he should proceed.

He mentioned why he left in search of the crown but only said my help was only given so I could stay. Something that was not worth an eye.

Four other sets of eyes fixed their gaze on him as he drunk deeply from the jug, draining half of it.

Smacking his lips together before speaking savouring the taste, it was actually good ale. "Might as well tell them the truth they'll find out anyway. Besides it's not like I cared about their opinions beforehand. Why would I now. They'll all be dead long before me."

"The way you drink I highly doubt that" joked Garrett. Flynn just raised the jug in toast before draining its contents.

"My mother tested Flynn, appearing to betray us in the process" Vaike continued. 'Shit' Flynn thought as he reached for the third pitcher much to his wives' obvious displeasure. 'Now I really do need a piss.'

Vaike gave a compendious account of the rebirthing ceremony up till now. Wasn't really much to tell anyway. A wedding and feast, a tumultuous struggle of oneself that Vaike didn't even mention and Vaike becoming Prince consort.

Shock from Flynn's gift of immortality turned to happiness at his and Vashti's marriage. The revelation of Vaike's and his own promotion overshadowed for now.

It was late in the evening when they finished. Baird promptly summoned servants to show them to their rooms after giving instructions to change it from three to two.

Flynn adding his own amendment that they needed adjoining rooms. It was his job to watch Vaike's back.

Their room was massive, double what theirs back home was. The bed and mattress large enough for five people to sleep in. Vashti just punched his arm when he jokingly said they could invite more people. A second punch landed when he declared that wasn't a no.

Two doors opened onto an adjoining balcony. Giving them access into Vaike's room. A second door opened into a private bath. Steam flooded the room making the air thick. Picking Vashti up and carrying her over his shoulder Flynn stepped into the hot water. Tired and sore muscles were soothed by the hot water. Vashti kicked and laughed as she was plunged into the water, both still fully clothed.

The servant who showed them to their room stood stunned. Unsure how to respond she backed out slowly, closing the door behind her.

⤚

Their clothes lay on the floor in a wet heap. Clumped together when the young servant girl returned. No more than fifteen, shocked by Flynn's display and probably her own. Calling her through the closed doors she bashfully entered the room staring at her feet.

The water had cooled clearing the air so everything was clear as they soaked in the water. Darkened from the weeks of dirt and travel grime washed from their bodies. Without looking up she carried the clothes from the room. A water trail following her across the floor.

Deciding dirty warm water was not relaxing to soak in Vashti stepped out the tub. A slap echoed around the tiled room as Flynn's hand clapped against her arse. She expected it and enjoyed it truthfully.

They forgot to ask the girl for some fresh towels, the ones laid out fell victim to Flynn's shenanigans. Rather than wait, Vashti strolled into the bedroom expecting to find some in one of the rooms various drawers.

A gentle breeze blew in through the open balcony doors. Vashti shivered, the light breeze cold against her wet skin. Prioritising drying over closing the door especially as she was naked, Vashti dug through the drawers.

Heavy and sturdy, the shelves slid easily on their oiled tracks. One after another Vashti opened and closed all the shelves, all empty waiting for clothes to fill them. Frustrated she slammed the last drawer closed, rattling the bottles and jars sitting atop it.

Sighing Vashti turned hands on hips, unsure where to look next. Startled, her heart missed a beat. The room was no longer empty. The young serving girl stood in the open door, fresh towels clutched in her arms. Mouth wide open staring ahead, frozen.

Blushing, she cast her gaze downwards realising she was staring. Apologising profusely, she walked forward holding a towel in outstretched arms.

The girls foot caught the rug at the foot of the bed. Rushing forward Vashti caught her as she stumbled forward. She could feel her own face flush as the girl's face fell between her breasts. She again apologised for being clumsy and causing her grief. Telling her it was no drama and nothing to worry herself about the girl opened her eyes.

Seeing exactly what her face pressed against she jumped back knocking over the table beside the bed. Deep crimson pooled across the floor, the wine jug atop the table shattering on the stone floor. Dropping to her knees, all awkwardness forgotten she set to wiping up the spill.

Kneeling down beside her Vashti helped using the only thing available, the fresh towels. Silencing the girl's objections and claims that it was her job.

Floor cleaned, they stood looking at two towels now stained red and smelling of wine. Still naked, Vashti shivered as the air cooled with the darkening sky. The girl blushed, remembering she stood beside a naked woman and rushed out onto the balcony. Returning almost immediately with a robe made entirely of silk. It was better than nothing and sent tingles all over her body as it caressed her bare flesh.

The girl said she would get some dry clothes and be back. Vashti would have none of that. She grew tired of being surrounded by men. Especially soldiers who seemed intent on proving their masculinity by seeing who could do the dumbest thing. Her husband was no exception often proving the victor, much to her chagrin. Some female company sounded ideal, even with a child.

Stating it was her duty to serve she stayed behind and talked. Not impressed with the reason but the result was what she desired. Sitting on the soft mattress they talked. Vashti and Mernda, elf and human, princess and servant.

Vashti asked what Mernda wanted out of life. The response surprised her. The girl wanted to get out and travel. See the world, party, get drunk, make bad decisions. Not stuck here serving those that do. But that was impossible, both her parents served in the castle. She had no other skills or prospects. She had resigned herself to a paltry existence.

While they conversed, Flynn grew bored of sitting in cold water. Walking into the bedroom unabashed and unbothered by his nakedness. He laughed when he learnt the towels were ruined and there weren't any dry one's spare. His good humour was quickly soured once he learnt what they had spilled.

Without bothering to dry off he dressed in some clothes Mernda had brought in for them. Shirt sticking to his wet torso Flynn left in search of food and drink.

Watching her husband leave Vashti realised Mernda didn't avert her gaze or blush when Flynn was around. Curiously she pondered, 'was she used as a bed warmer by some of the more repulsive nobles or residents.' It was definitely a possibility. Even she could tell she was an attractive girl.

Long coppery red hair that spilled around her shoulders. Freckles dotted her face covering her nose in an adorably cute fashion and her eyes. Eyes that you could get lost in, deep blue eyes that reflected the ocean.

"Uh my lady?" Shaking her head Vashti realised she did get lost in her blue eyes. "Sorry I spaced out there." Wait Mernda was blushing again.

It dawned on Vashti, understanding everything. "Mernda. You like women, don't you?" "What no. Yes. I mean" caught off guard Mernda stuttered, unable to form a coherent thought.

Vashti leant in and kissed her lips. Mernda was startled and pulled away at first before leaning into it. Returning Vashti's kiss.

'It wasn't something she had ever thought about before now. Maybe Flynn was rubbing off on her who knows but the kiss felt good.'

It was clear Mernda was as experienced as she herself was with women. She was however the experienced one in bed, taking charge untying Mernda's blouse. Vashti wasn't concerned. Flynn wouldn't care, hell he would be thrilled.

Chapter 26

THE FAREWELL

Flynn stretched, waking as the sun crept across the room. Throwing back what little covers he slept under he glanced at his wife. Still sound asleep, arms wrapped around another women.

He was surprised to find the two of them going at it when he returned with more wine last night. Vashti tasting the young girl like he has done to her several times over. Vashti was not shocked to see him. Just waving him over Flynn tore his clothes off, joining in.

He then spent most of the night lying by himself watching the two enjoy each other. Vashti made sure he finished but of the three, he definitely had the least fun. Still he never expected it from his wife.

Walking onto the balcony, blinking back tears as he gazed eastward. The sun starting its journey across the sky telling him it was still early morning.

"I hope this doesn't become a regular occurrence." Startled, Flynn turned to find Vaike sitting just inside his door. Watching the sunrise while drinking tea. An empty plate sat on the table beside him, breakfast presumably.

"What doesn't?" Flynn asked. Knowing it wasn't his sister and himself keeping the Prince awake with their nightly activities. That was already established. Was he talking about corrupting his sister. Did he know about the maid who spent the night?

"What do you mean what? Have you spent that much time naked recently you forget to wear clothes?"

'Oh, that was what he referred too' Flynn thought. Fairly obvious if he was to admit it. Thinking quickly Flynn pointed out his clothes pegged up beside Vashti's. "Well I need clothes to be able to wear them."

"What about the pair Baird sent up, I got mine? No wait I don't want to know" Vaike finished guessing what happened to that pair.

"I guess Vashti was telling the truth" Vaike said as Flynn began dressing, not bothering to turn away while he did.

"Truth about what?" "I thought she was messing with me, but you really do have a brand on your arse." "Yeah definitely not one of my greatest ideas" Flynn grinned

"Wasn't that the sign of Grimmlocke. What would possess you to get that?" "It's an old pirate tradition" Flynn answered begrudgingly. Knowing Vaike would badger him through the centuries and eventually find out anyway.

"You get a brand resembling your first conquest. Either killing or bedding someone. No criteria on how you go about either. It could be consensual, purchased or taken. Thankfully I killed a man first, earning myself the hooked scythe of Grimmlocke.

If I had my choice again however I would brand my upper arm like most do. The arse hurt more than I expected and I couldn't sit for a week."

"And if you lost your virginity first?" Vaike asked, obviously concerned with how much worse it could get. Well it was originally the hatched egg for Kyarli, Goddess of fertility. But over time pirates replaced it with a phallus."

"You mean?" "Yep if I lost my virginity first, I would have a cock branded on my arse." Flynn walked away as Vaike cracked up laughing.

Stepping back inside Flynn pulled the balcony doors closed. Not wanting Vaike's laughing to wake them. A pointless attempt as the doors clicking shut alerted Vashti's keen hearing, waking her.

"Morning" greeted Flynn. Pressing a finger to her lips Vashti silenced him, pointing to the girl still sleeping beside her. "I have to speak with Garrett" Flynn whispered leaning in to kiss Vashti on the forehead.

Stepping back Flynn glanced down at the back of the young serving girl. Lying face down with one arm wrapped around Vashti. Copper hair spilling across Vashti's own bare chest covering her exposed breasts. Her head nestled against the elven princess's shoulder.

Winking at the pair, Vashti blushed as Flynn crossed to the door, dropping Vashti's clothes on the drawers as he passed them. Like his own they were dry after being hung out overnight. Stopping short of the knob, the sound of sharp knocking against wood halted his opening.

"Who is it?" inquired Flynn. Knowing his wife was still naked and concerned for her dignity. "Please tell me you're not naked." The reply muffled by the thick door's was still discernible as Ailish's.

A barely visible tilt forward of the head from Vashti and Flynn opened the door. "Why are you hoping to see me naked again." Ailish turned pink with embarrassment before turning red with rage. Pushing past Flynn, she barged into the room screaming "you told him?"

The screaming woke the sleeping girl. Surprise, horror then embarrassment, all passing across her features before pulling the sheets over her head. Ailish stood still, mouth agape in stunned silence.

"Well I hate to beg my leave but duty calls" Flynn said pulling the door shut behind him. What was about to transpire could be hilarious or disastrous. Either way he was glad to get out of there.

Flynn passed Baird with guards in tow on his way to the study. Vaike wanted to discuss something with him. After asking on his whereabouts, Flynn headed to the courtyard.

Garrett casually leant against the stone walls of the castle, eyes fixed ahead focusing on the open doors. Calling him over as he exited Garrett pointed out Sterben and another mount. Stable hands rushed around tightening saddle straps and fitting tack while Garrett walked over.

The young lads worked swiftly with both horses ready to ride as they arrived. Garrett swinging into the saddle of a young chestnut mare. Having acquired a new mount since last Flynn saw him. Probably bounty from the siege.

Garrett rode off without a word leaving Flynn to swing his leg up and over Sterben's back and follow.

They rode in silence for five minutes. The only sound heard was the echo of the horse's hooves striking the cobblestone path. Anyone on the road at that time moving aside to let the pair past.

Garrett was the first to speak, breaking the familiar silence. Telling Flynn, he intended to show him instead of just tell him about their military strength.

They inspected several barracks and watched soldiers run through drills. Some veterans and seasoned soldiers flowing effortless through the forms. Practiced thousands of times before.

Divisions of new recruits or mercenaries fumbled through them. Mistakes and errors were regular occurrences amongst the green recruits and undisciplined mercenaries.

Garrett showed him a captured Dragon shot. The weapon used to devastate their forces and the destruction of which brought down the wall. Flynn believed both after a demonstration sent the iron ball hurling a hundred yards striking the earth. The impact of which could be felt from where they stood. He guessed you could hear it also, if your ears weren't ringing from the blast that sent it careening away.

❦

The door clicked shut as Flynn departed the bed chamber. Silence filled the room as Vashti and Ailish stared at each other. Mernda hid below the covers. Only her fingers visible gripping the edge of the sheet.

Sitting up in bed Vashti covered her naked breasts with the same sheet. Shivering slightly as the cool morning greeted her exposed back.

"Get over here." Both women cried simultaneously. Ailish stepping around the bed as Vashti jumped up embracing her friend. Suddenly no longer bothered by her nakedness. Something Ailish had seen regularly before as they would often bathe together when on the road.

Breaking apart Vashti strode to the corner where here robe from the previous night lay. Tossed aside by Flynn when she lost the need for it.

"Mernda this is my good friend Ailish." "I'm aware my lady, I have seen her around the castle." Bashfully pulling the covers down, showing her face, flushed red with embarrassment. "Don't mind her" began Vashti. "She likes girls and finds it hard talking to one let alone two beautiful women." Ailish raised her eyebrow throwing a knowing grin showing it was an obvious fact.

A distraught squeal sounded from the bed as the covers were once again pulled up hiding Mernda from view. "Come now don't be shy. Why don't you go and draw yourself a bath? It will do you good and we have some catching up to do."

"I'm sorry my lady but I must be getting on with my duties I am already late." Whether true or wanting to escape the embarrassment she bolted to the bathroom. Sheets wrapped around her front trailing behind her whilst stooping to pick up her clothes bundled near the bed. Vashti was at least more considerate then Flynn in that regard.

"Sorry about telling Flynn about you being naked next to him." "It's alright I kind of expected it. Besides it doesn't bother me as much as I was expecting." "Having sex will do that to you" Vashti winked with a knowing smile.

As they spoke Mernda left the bathroom fully clothed. "Thank you for your kindness and the evening my lady. I will return later with fresh linen and clothes. My lady." Nodding to Ailish she turned to leave.

"Hold it." Closing the gap in three steps Vashti stopped before the young girl. "I told you call me Vashti." Leaning in closer, lips close enough to nibble her ear lobe like she did last night she whispered. "Now don't be a stranger."

Without a response Mernda turned reaching out for the door handle. Reaching out Vashti pinched the maid's arse as she opened the door. A surprised yelp echoed down the empty hallway. Closing the door, she looked back with disbelief, embarrassment and anger. A glint of enjoyment shone in her eyes as the door closed splitting them up. Vashti understood why Flynn felt the need to pinch her own arse at every opportunity. It was out of appreciation yes, but also to see that look.

Turning back around Ailish stood frozen in disbelief. "So how have you been. I love what you've done with your hair." For it was a completely new hair style. The right side of her head was covered by hair freely flowing and parted in the middle. The left side of her head was shaved back to stubble. Two long scars ran horizontal above her ear.

"No. You don't get of that easy. First were going to talk about that." "About what?" Knowing full well what Ailish referred too. "How long have you been interested in girls. I figured at first it was Flynn's doing I just couldn't figure out how you agreed to it. Somehow this makes less since."

"Well I had never thought about it until last night, and it is not all girls. I'm not even sure if it's just this girl." "They shaved it to treat the wound and I liked it, so I kept it." "What?" "My hair" Ailish said pointing to it with her left hand. 'Either satisfied with her answer or deciding it was all she would get.'

"Well I really like it, it looks fierce. It really says you're not a woman to mess with." "Thanks. It took a while to get used to my reflection, especially at first while the cut healed. By the time it started growing back I preferred it this way."

"So, tell me you and Garrett when did that start?" "Well you know when it started" Ailish giggled like one of the castle maids gathering around for the latest gossip. "We slowly grew closer with each other while we travelled like you and your, Prince charming." Sarcasm hinting at the insult.

"You would be surprised with how much he's changed. He really is my prince charming." "Really. I watched him just yesterday insult, berate and antagonise rulers. Before promptly running away for a quick romp in the hay with you." "Broom cupboard" corrected Vashti.

"Not better" sighed Ailish sitting down on the foot of the bed. "Alright tell me how he's so charming now." "I asked first. When did you and Garrett finally kiss?"

"Alright" Ailish said caving. Still sitting on the bed while Vashti pulled the silk robe off walking to the drawers. Dressing while listening to Ailish tell her about her first kiss.

"Well it goes back to the ambush where he lost his hand saving my life. I felt guilty and wanted to tell him how I felt. The injury made him retreat inwards, I thought I had lost him, lost my chance." Vashti felt a little twang of grief, remembering how she felt when Flynn retreated inwards not so long ago.

"But we had a war to fight so I focused my attention on that. A dragon shot destroyed my tent during the siege. I was away but Garrett freaked out thinking I was hurt or could have been. He commanded the attack to destroy the weapons and was gravely wounded in the raid."

Ailish stopped talking to dab at her wet eyes. The pain of thinking she was going to lose the man she loved still fresh in her mind. Lacing up the waist band on her leather pants Vashti sat beside her friend, placing a comforting arm around her back. Offering her own shoulder to cry on if needed.

The emotional support was enough and Ailish continued on with her story after drying her eyes. "The wall was blown open so the attack began. I had no idea what happened to Garrett but I feared the worst. It wasn't until we had secured the walls that I even got a chance to check on him.

Even that didn't work, in all the chaos he ended up in the wrong tent so I never saw him. It wasn't until the castle fell and we had it secured did we move all the wounded from the camp. We found him in a bad way. Broken bones, head trauma and the healers suspected internal bleeding. They didn't like his chances." Another quick sob before soldiering on.

"I took his hand in mine and told him how I felt. Berating myself for leaving it so late. Wishing I was braver, that I had done it sooner. I wasn't even sure he heard or understood but I swear I felt him squeeze my hand.

I tried to stay by his side as much as possible but other wounded soldiers kept filling the hall. Knowing he wouldn't want me to sit idle while I could help others I worked alongside the healers. Dressing wounds, holding patents down and bringing them water.

When the most severe were treated I went and sat by his side. It was afternoon by this time. Over half a day since the attack began. Apprehensively I knelt beside him. Praying to all the gods he yet lived.

He did and was awake. Smiling when he saw me, I lifted a ladle of water to his lips, holding his head up and helping him to drink. He squeezed my hand again before falling back asleep.

One of the healers saw me kneeling beside him. Noticing for the first time the blood staining the side of my head was my own. I have no idea when I picked up the injury during everything that happened.

A few days later Garrett was on his feet, given the all clear from the healers. Needing a crutch to get around and requiring plenty of bedrest but he was going to survive. Hearing this news, I hugged him tightly. When I felt his right hand on my back, I kissed him before pulling away. He stared back at me blankly before smiling ear to ear.

I panicked a little here and ran away. Finding him later that evening and spending an evening talking and kissing."

"I'm happy it worked out for you. So, tell me, when did you first share a bed?" Vashti asked grinning, gently nudging her in the ribs with her elbow.

"Well if you really must know." "Oh, I must." "It was last night" Ailish blushed hugging her knees against her chest.

"That's big news. Why didn't you tell me straight away? What made you choose yesterday?" Vashti spoke hurriedly, filled with excitement.

"I was going to tell you but I was surprised by Mernda. As for why last night it was you and Flynn." "Us. What do you mean?" Vashti asked confused.

"Well I'm ecstatic to know your together, I knew how you felt about him. But I was even happier to learn he was now immortal. The gods were cruel otherwise making your soul partner mortal.

But then you guys were already married. Having known each other for about as long as Garrett and myself have. With your feelings for Flynn developing after mine for Garretts." "Well other than finding him physically attractive" Vashti added with a grin.

"Yes, but when we first met, he was a self-centred, narcissistic arsehole. Suffering from delusions of grandeur and alcoholism. A serial killer and possible rapist." "No, not a rapist. At least technically" Vashti said defending her husband. "The others are all true, unfortunately."

"But it got me thinking." Ailish continued lightening up the mood. "You are both immortal yet you wasted no time getting married. So why was I waiting, a day to me is like a decade to you so I snuck into Garretts room last night wearing that horrible corset Flynn got me on the rose."

"I bet Garrett loved that" Vashti laughed. "So how was it?" "Well it was quick and it hurt." "The first time does" Vashti frowned remembering how it felt when Flynn entered her for the first time.

"But it gets better from there. You soon won't be able to get enough." "I figured that when you two snuck of yesterday." It was now Ailish's turn to laugh.

"So how big was it?" "How big was what?" "You know" Vashti winked pointing to her crutch. "I'm not telling you that." "Why not?" "Fine then how big is Flynn's?" Ailish said with the finality that the conversation would end there.

Unbothered Vashti held her hands apart, eye brows raised as Ailish looked on in awe, mouth agape. "You've got to be kidding me that's easily double Garrett's. How did that not rip you in half?" "Well Flynn was gentle and he knows what he is doing." "I'm sure he does" Ailish said matter of factly. Vashti wasn't sure if that was a jab at her husband's sordid past.

"How are you surprised by that? You have seen him naked too." "Yes, but I was trying not to look and there was a lot going on. Beside I've only now seen two men naked so I didn't really have a reference point.

Please don't tell Flynn." Ailish added as an afterthought. "I have heard how men boast about the size of their manhood. I'm sure Flynn would love to lord it over Garrett."

"I won't tell him anything but Flynn is well aware how big he is. He isn't aware he is big by elf standards however. I'm trying to keep that from him."

"Okay your turn then. Tell me what Flynn is like now?" So, Vashti did. She told Ailish everything, even the parts she left out when talking to her mother.

She spoke about how she felt when Flynn tore his eye out fighting for her. How he poured his heart out during his Achretic. Their wedding night and their months since.

How losing his sight was making him distant just like Garretts arm. By the time she finished talking her stomach grumbled. Already midday they left the room in search of lunch. Vashti particularly ravenous having missed breakfast.

After eating Ailish said she had something to show her. Talking about their plans for the future the salty tang of the sea greeted her nose. Stopping at the dock to see Baird and her brother already there.

The sun was past its zenith as they completed the rounds of inspection. Garrett leading him to the wharf saying there was one thing he needed Flynn's opinion on. Their navy.

Explaining to Flynn that they captured several of Olaf's ships but they didn't have much idea about it. All the officers were executed when the sailors revolted. Garrett didn't seem to care when Flynn corrected him, saying it was called a mutiny not a revolt.

Everyone stood waiting at the docks for them. Vashti and Ailish side by side, inseparable as sisters. Their fight this morning apparently resolved. Vaike slightly off to the side with Baird beaming with happiness.

Dismounting, following Garretts lead he walked across the uneven timber beams. The scent of fish, salt and sweat filling the air. Flynn smiled, feeling right at home.

Walking down the docks he was shown nine ships, all boasting impressive design and construction. Flynn even recognised the figureheads on two of them.

A copper octopus, greened with age called the abyss and the other called torment. Where the figurehead was a screaming maiden whose hair was made out of tar-soaked rope. During battle the crew would light it on fire, creating a terrifying image. Both pirate ships belonging to feared Captains.

Brigs and Galleons alike made up an impressive armada. Small but impressive none the less. It was missing one crucial thing however. A flagship, a command vessel.

Stating his concerns Baird smiled walking away from the ships to the far end of the wharf. The buildings along the docks hid it from view but two masts jutted above their roofs as they approached.

He didn't need to read the name or see the skeletal horse figurehead. Even painted a different colour Flynn could identify this ship by touch alone. His ship. Nightmare.

"This was Olaf's flagship" Baird said as they passed around the corner of the last building. It was fitted out with Dragon shots that we have since removed. "Aye. A fine flag ship it is" Flynn responded. Struggling to keep his voice under control.

"Yes, I agree. Even with my limited knowledge on the subject. All the sailors and fisherman in port feel the same, even with the limited naval combat experience amongst them." "She'll lead your fleet to much success in the hands of a competent captain" Flynn answered. Needing to leave before his voice betrayed him.

"I'm sure she would. I have however chosen one of the big ships, Galleon I believe you called it, as mine." "What why?" Flynn asked bemused and angry. No longer fighting to keep his voice level angry at being asked his opinion just to be ignored.

"Because its bigger, and bigger is better isn't it?" Baird winked right at Flynn who stood livid. The smile washing of the young Kings face as Flynn took a step towards him.

Hastily Baird spoke trying to quell the storm before it began. "I also intended to give you a late wedding gift, and an even later gift for defeating Olaf. Only one thing seemed sufficient. The best ship in my fleet."

Flynn stood speechless. Completely lost for words as Baird swept his arm up, gesturing towards the ship. Mouth opening and closing as no words came out, so Vashti spoke for him. "You can't be serious this is Flynn's ship?" "Yes, I know, I'm giving it to him."

"No. It is Flynn's ship, Nightmare. The one he Captained, the one he lost." Vashti said, recognising the ship from all the stories Flynn had told her. Flynn strode straight towards Baird, left eye brimming with tears. Gratitude shining brightly in his right.

With his scarred face and eyes with different expressions it looked almost menacing. If his escort was present, they would've probably prevented Flynn approaching the king. The three humans stood stunned, never expecting to see tears cross Flynn's face.

Closing the distance before the others could react Flynn stopped before the King. Hands clamping around his face, forcing him to look into his eyes. Flynn kissed Baird's forehead. The way a child would kiss an uncle or older cousin who brought them a gift.

Turning eye bright with joy and smiling as big as he did when Vashti said yes Flynn gazed at his ship. The new colours were fitting Flynn felt. She needed a rebirth like he did. Never forgetting the things they've done but a new look for a new future.

Turning to Vashti offering his hand Flynn asked one question. "Shall we?" Taking his hand in her own they raced up the gangway onto the ship without a backwards glance.

Five Years Later

Baird woke early. Several hours before dawn, the darkness still encased his castle. To restless to find sleep he climbed out of bed. Gently lifting the dark arm of his wife that was draped across his chest.

Pulling a robe over his bare shoulders Baird walked out onto the balcony. Leaning forward hands gripping the rail he stared out over his kingdom, enjoying the silence.

It was no surprise he struggled to sleep today. It was the anniversary of his coronation. Every anniversary like today he couldn't sleep. Plagued by doubts, worries and concerns. Something he doubted will ever change, despite everything that has transpired since.

The first two years were hard. His first year was spent rebuilding Voldengird and the Blood cliffs fortress. He achieved most of this alone as Garrett and Ailish returned to her home in the mountains to marry. Returning come spring when true to his word King Cordonn marshalled his forces and marched.

With his forces divided they pushed north. After the first sortie from Vaike's forces Cordonn avoided further attacks on the forest. Quickly learning that the elves will not engage unless provoked.

They made it deep into his lands, a week's march from the capitol when the trap was sprung. Troops from Beildronna besieged the blood cliffs where half of Baird's troops were encamped. While maintaining eyes on the rock and Lord Burtons troops, cutting of any reinforcements.

With Jorgenson and Aeedon offering no assistance Cordonn assumed they were all talk. His own hubris. A three-pronged attack fell down on his position whilst marching. From the west came Aeedon's light armoured footmen, wielding various weapons and utilising guerrilla tactics. Jorgenson's berserkers charged from the east brushing them aside. Wrapped in furs to scare their foes wielding massive hammers and axes they crushed skulls and bones.

His own armoured knights charged from the north taking the brunt of the resistance. Squashing them between the three prongs. King Cordonn fell in battle. His head sent home to his young son as a warning to stay in line. The only tactic Baird ever wanted to take from Olaf.

With Ailish marrying Garrett, his own right-hand man, ties with the mountain people were strong. Jorgenson required nothing more than a victory feast with on requirement. Unlimited ale. To secure Aeedon's aid the price was steeper.

The price was Aeedon's younger sister Deeana's hand in marriage. Deeana was fifteen, five years younger than he now was. She was an attractive girl with sun darkened skin and long black hair that glistened in the light.

Knowing it was his duty he happily accepted. Deeana herself performing her duty without complaint. They got along well enough but they never would have picked each other if the choice was their own. Still the last three years have been good and they have grown closer. Supporting each other and working together to rule their kingdom.

It was nothing compared to Ailish and Garretts relationship. Even now Baird envied them, the chance, the choice to marry for love. Even Flynn's devotion was something else. The willingness to tear out his own eye for his love.

Sure, Baird would die for his Queen but to physically harm oneself that was something else entirely.

The sun started breaking above the horizon as he stood staring. Lost in thought, he didn't realise how long he'd been staring. Two delicate hands wrapped themselves around his waist, head resting on his shoulder. "It's still early, come back to bed." "Yes dear."

Turning to leave Baird did a double take. Running inside he quickly raced out with an eyeglass pressed to his face. Laughing he couldn't believe it, he actually followed orders. Vaike gave them five years when they sailed away. Taking nothing with them other than a skeleton crew and Vashti's maid they disappeared over the horizon.

Handing the eyeglass to Deeana he pointed out the sails on the horizon. The ship displaying pirate colours. The skull flag with dual swords behind. Flynn's flag.

"Is it him?" She had heard countless stories about their lunatic companion from him and Garrett. Baird had even established a singles combat tournament in honour of his dual against Olaf.

Eyes brimming with tears Baird nodded. "We had best inform the guards before they fire on him." "Shit your right." Baird winced when he spoke, Deeana disliked swearing. Saying there was plenty of other words to use. 'She is going to love Flynn then' Baird silently laughed.

Dragon shots have been built and positioned to cover the dock since Flynn left, if they don't hurry the guards will sink them. He definitely didn't want to speak with Flynn if that happened.

Pronunciations

Achretic Are-crey-tic
Adair Ah-dare
Aeedon Ai-don
Ailish Ae-lish
Aniteena Ann-teen-ah
Ararait Ah-ree-at
Aurith Ore-ith
Barka Bark-ah
Beildronna Bell-ee-dron-ah
Bortun Bore-tonn
Camilla Cam-mill-are
Cordonn Core-don
Cullnurna Kull-nerr-na
Cruzwigg Kruzz-wig
Dalthenian Dall-then-ee-an
Deeana Deen-ah
Diann Dee-Ann
Duraa Dew-rah
Elisa Ell-eyes-ah
Foden Foe-den
Gism Giss-em
Grimmlocke Grim-lock
Iodem I-oh-dam

Ithiel Ith-ee-ell
Jorra Jaw-rah
Kallen kall-enn
Kantermian Can-terr-mean
Kjorgen Cure-gen
Koyake Co-yake
Kyarli Key-are-lee
Maroxis Marr-ixs
Mordaqi More-de-cai
Nibban Nib-ann
Reyvadin Ray-var-den
Sterben Stir-bin
Sulthard Sool-thard
Thaldesa Thal-dess-ah
Vashti Vash-tee
Veluca Vell-ooh-car
Vlathe Vlay-thh
Voldengird Voll-den-gird
Whyda Whid-ee-ah
Wigni Wig-nee
Yisolde Yiss-uuld
Zardelfan Zard-elf-ann